I Killed
You Once

Maddison, Indiana Thriller
Book 1

Dawn Merriman

ISBN-13: 9798857062098

Dedication

This book is dedicated to my wonderful husband, Kevin and my children. Thanks for all the hours of discussion on this book. Thank you to God for giving me the ability to tell this story.

-Dawn Merriman

Chapter 1

Maribeth

Living can be worse than death. Death requires no struggle. Death only requires giving in.

Life requires battle, a never-ending succession of skirmishes. Each day an agony of combat, each step a hard-won victory.

Today, my steps of victory crunch through melting snow and piles of fallen leaves. My legs burn, regardless of the cold. This daily run grounds me. I've kept the habit from before the police academy, through my detective career, and now here, one of the few things I kept from my previous life.

I push on through my woods. Trees slide past in a blur. My lungs settle into my pace, my chest rising and falling in customary rhythm. Puffs of steam escape my lips into the frigid air. My feet land on the familiar trail, my legs stretching over downed branches without thought. My body has run this path so many times it no longer needs my conscious thoughts to guide it. My mind is free to roam into the darkness. I struggle to keep my thoughts on the path, to skirt the empty abyss that beckons.

My property consists of three-hundred acres of heavily forested woodlands. When I first came here, the woods seemed to stretch forever, an expansive embrace of trees and wildlife. Now I quickly reach my property line and make the turn back towards the cabin, following the remnants of snowy footprints from my last run.

My only companion, my gray and white husky, Indy, knows the path well, too. As we make the turn towards home, he bounds ahead excitedly, kicking up snow and leaves with his fast feet. Indy stops suddenly, several paces ahead on the trail. He raises his nose to the air and catches a scent. The rabbit flashes across the path and Indy gives chase.

He shoots into the brush, his gray fur flashing against the white of the snow. I watch him go, wondering if I should follow, but I run on. Indy can take care of himself in the woods better than I can. He'll come home when he's had his fill of fun.

The music in my earbuds blasts the last of my dark thoughts about death and life away. I match my feet to the beat and plunge forward one step at a time, eager to get home before darkness falls.

A sharp bark intrudes over the music. I slow my pace, turn the volume down, and Indy barks again.

I pull an earbud out. "Indy?" I call into the trees. A

whine and a yelp echo in the stillness.

Panic spurs my feet, and I crush into the brush. One earbud hangs from its wire, bouncing against my chest in a staccato of fear. My breath claws at my chest, hidden branches cling to my feet.

Indy's paw prints lead to a frozen pond and continue onto the thin sheet of snow blowing across the ice. Several yards away, Indy scrapes the edge of an icy hole, desperate to draw himself out of the frigid water.

He yelps in fear, his bright blue eyes pleading for help.

The ice moans beneath my weight as I take cautious steps towards my dog. A crack zigzags in front of me, and the ice gives way. The shallow water bites up to my knees. Gasping against the icy pain, I push on, breaking the ice with clenched fists. The water crawls up to my thighs. Drowned branches and debris pull at my numbing feet.

Indy watches my slow progress with helpless eyes. The water climbs to my crotch, knocking the air from my lungs as it reaches the sensitive skin.

A few feet away from him, I stretch my arms across the ice, strain to reach the thick fur of his neck. It fills my gloved hand, and I pull. Indy yelps and claws at the ice. One paw catches hold, and combined with my pulling, he slides out of the water.

He crouches on the ice, instinctively spreading his weight on his four paws. He scrambles to the bank and shakes off most of the water. Now that he's safe, he paces the bank of the pond, barks anxiously, spurring me on.

Numbness settles into my bones, making my return to

the bank heavy and slow. A submerged branch catches my running boot, tripping me. Icy water clenches around my belly, but I catch myself on the edge of the ice before sinking lower.

Freeing my boot from the branch, I lunge for the bank, pushing hard with my other leg. A hidden scrap of metal slices my foot, the sudden warmth of blood burning against the cold water. Ignoring the pain, I push again for the bank.

I land face down in the dirt and snow, then belly-crawl out of the water. Indy pushes his nose against my face, urging me on with his warm breath. My vision fuzzes, and I shiver in the wind. Using my unhurt foot, I try to stand. My numb leg wobbles, crumples, and I land with a humph. The cold seeps from my soaked legs up to my chest. It slithers under my coat and wraps icy fingers around my lungs.

I will my legs to move, too cold to obey, my muscles only twitch. With my gloved hands, I pull myself through the dirt like an animal. Fallen branches reach out from the snow to scratch my face.

Indy whines and shoves me with his nose, urging. Shadows dance around his broad face, as the sun sinks low in the sky behind him. I manage to drag myself a little farther, then lie panting against the dirt. The cold seeps from my chest into my shoulders.

Indy whines against my cheek. I can barely see his blue eyes in the falling darkness. Behind him, three familiar balls of light appear, and I turn away from their approach.

"I just need to rest," I tell my dog. "Give me a minute."

Music sings softly from my earbuds dragging along beside me. "Dust in the Wind" carries along with the snow on the breeze.

As I have every day for two years, I fight the battle to survive. I don't give in. I don't give up. The cold strikes back, a valiant competitor.

"Maribeth, you have to move," Bryson's voice blocks out the music.

"I can't," I explain to my husband. "Too cold."

"Get up!" he commands. I open my eyes and meet his face.

"You need a haircut," I tell him nonsensically. "You should have gotten one before."

"You say that every time," his warm smile makes a heat flutter in my frozen chest.

"Mom, it's dark," my son, Benny, says from somewhere nearby. "I don't want to be here in the dark."

"I know, baby. Sorry. I stayed out longer than I intended."

"Mom, get up!" My teenage daughter, Lilly, demands. Always headstrong and to the point, she doesn't give in now.

I manage to roll onto my back, and the three of them shimmer above me. The empty branches dance behind them, through them.

"Indy's cold," Bryson says. "You have to get him inside the cabin."

My dog shivers next to me, a crinkling sheet of ice

frozen over his thick fur.

"I can't," I whine to my family. "I'm too tired."

"That's the hypothermia talking. Damn it, Maribeth, move!" In our 17 years of marriage or the last two years, I've never heard Bryson cuss at me. "Get your ass in gear and get up!"

I don't like his tone and anger surges through me. When I try to move my leg, it obeys. "That's it, Mom. Screw this shit and move!" Lilly chimes in.

"Watch your mouth, young lady," I snap automatically. Adrenaline pumps against the cold, and I force myself to my hands and knees.

"It's getting darker," Benny fusses, consumed by his fear. "Get us inside."

Even Indy gangs up on me, pushing against my rear. I pant on my hands and knees, crawl a few steps towards the trail. "Why won't you just leave me alone so I can join you?" I plead. "If you had stayed away, I could be with you now." Tears of frustration burn my frozen cheeks.

"You have things to do yet, Maribeth. Now get going." Bryson urges. "Don't let the kids see you like this."

That works more than the harsh words. I crawl a few more feet, then pull myself up on a tree. My cut foot stings as I step down gingerly. "Pain is good," Lilly says. "Do that again."

As blood pumps through my frozen extremities, the skin tingles and burns. "The sooner you get to the cabin, the sooner the burning will stop," Bryson urges.

I pull myself straight and step away from the support

of the tree. My cut boot flaps in the snow, but I keep moving, each step agony.

"Good girl, keep moving," Bryson says.

Panting and exhausted, I stop to catch my breath once I'm back on the path to the cabin. I want to sink to it, want to curl up and sleep.

Bryson senses my hesitation and tries another tactic. "Chica and Rizo need their dinners."

"My pigs can eat the grass," I point out.

"It's winter, there's no grass left. They need you."

I look up the dark path where the pigs and chickens wait for my return.

"Just give me a minute," I tell my family and lean against a tree. I dig my pack of smokes from the inside pocket of my coat, and fish out a cigarette. It's squished, but miraculously dry. I fumble with the lighter through my gloves until a tiny flame finally appears. The hot smoke warms my tired lungs.

I take a few drags, summon the last of my energy, and march on.

My family follows, cheering me, pissing me off, whatever they can do to keep me going.

The solar light on my porch finally winks through the trees.

Benny runs ahead, "Come on, Mom, we're almost there."

My pace quickens once the cabin comes into view. In my haste, I trip over a fallen log. Bryson moves to catch me as I fall, but I tumble through his outstretched arms.

After all, he's not really here.

Chapter 2

Maribeth

I drag myself up the three steps to the wrap-around covered porch on my cabin. The wood steps creak under my heavy steps. Indy zooms past me, wasting no time going through his dog door and into the warmth of the cabin. Pale firelight pours out of the windows flanking each side of the door. The wind funnels through the porch, stings my chilled cheeks. The sudden blast of cold spurs me to cross the last few agonizing steps.

Leaning heavily on the door, I fumble to turn the handle with my freezing fingers. I finally manage to turn the knob and collapse through the door. I land hard on the polished wood floor and try not to think about the bruises I've collected from my many falls tonight.

The funneled wind from the porch blows through the open door, makes the fire roar to life in the open fireplace, and a few sparks dance up the chimney. Already curled on his bed by the fire, Indy contentedly licks the melting ice and snow from his fur. He looks up with a *you're letting the cold in* expression.

"Come on, babe, almost done. Shut the door," Bryson says.

I stay on the floor but slam the door with my uncut foot. "Happy?" I gripe.

"I'm happy we're finally home," Benny chirps and sits next to Indy.

"You're such a baby," Lilly tells him. "Mom could have died, and you're too busy being afraid of the dark."

"I'm not afraid," Benny replies.

Lilly shrugs and flops on the couch.

"Hot bath for you," Bryson says, looking down at me on the floor.

"You're so bossy tonight. I don't like it," I grumble as I pull off my gloves and hat and toss them across the cabin.

"Whatever it takes," he smiles. The crinkles at the corners of his eyes melt my heart the way they have for years. "As long as you're safe."

I meet his hazel eyes and put all my love into mine. "I'm safe now. Thank you," I say quietly so the kids can't hear.

"Don't do that again." His tender voice holds a steel edge. "Don't ever do that again."

I look away, ashamed of how close I came to losing. If the last two years haven't done me in, how could I let a frozen pond finish me off? I busy myself with climbing off the floor instead of responding.

I call to the kids, "I'm going to take a hot bath."

The water steams invitingly as it fills the tub. Sitting on the toilet lid, I untie my running boots. The sole of the one flops open at the cut, ruined. I toss my favorite boots against the wall in anger, thinking of all the snowy miles it took to break them in. They'll need to be replaced now, and fast.

I peel my soaked socks off and add them to the pile against the wall. The sock is ruined too, cut through and stained with blood. I don't look at my foot, unwilling to see my skin opened by the sharp metal I stepped on.

When the pile includes my soaked pants and my mostly dry sweater, I turn off the water in the tub. The silence in the small bathroom is nearly deafening after the roar of the running water.

Steam obscures the tiny mirror above the sink. I wipe it away with my hand and consider my reflection. My blue eyes, nearly the same color as Indy's, stare wide and frightened. "That was close," I whisper to myself. The mirror is purposely small, only reflecting a small part of me. A lift of my chin reveals the red, angry scar puckered across my throat. I finger it gently with a shaking hand. Lower on my chest, another scar, not visible in the mirror's minuscule reflection beckons. My trembling fingers reach lower, outline the Roman numeral carved there.

"Don't touch it," Bryson suddenly commands.

I pull my hand away, guilty like a child sneaking candy.

I meet his eyes in the tiny reflection. "You and the kids don't have the marks?" I ask.

"We've already told you we don't." His voice so close to my ear, almost touching.

"You did," I whisper.

"We don't now," he soothes. "Don't go down this road, Maribeth," he warns.

I push through him and climb into the tub. The heat of the water like fire against my still-cold skin. I welcome the burn, and slide into the water, tipping my head back on the edge of the tub.

My injured foot stings. I raise it from the water, and fresh blood dribbles down my leg. Just a little blood, nothing serious, but it's enough.

"Don't look at the blood," Bryson tries to help.

My mind betrays me, and the memory slips in.

I pull my SUV into my garage. It's a tight fit next to the shiny new John Deere Gator Side-by-side. Bryson's gift to me at last month's Christmas. "It'll make doing the chores easier," he'd said. "You can haul feed in the back or whatever you need to do."

I shake my head at the Gator. Our tiny farm is really Bryson's baby. The three pigs in the barn and the six chickens were all surprises brought home from an animal swap meet last summer. "Homegrown bacon and farm-fresh eggs," Bryson had said. I'd seen through the ploy for what it was, a reason to keep me home. Most nights, like tonight, he ends up doing the chores alone while I'm gone working on a case.

Sighing heavily, I push open my door. It's late, very late. Quietly, I enter the kitchen. Bryson left a light on for me. It shines warmly on the wooden cabinets of the friendly space designed for family dinners. I turn off the light. I missed dinner again tonight and I don't want the reminder.

Indy whines in his kennel, wanting my attention. I let him out, his thick white and gray fur glows in the moonlight as he dances around me, excited I'm home. I rough up his furry neck in greeting, then let him out the back door to his fenced-in area. "Don't take long," I tell him. "I'm going to bed in a bit." Indy sniffs the frozen grass and ignores me.

I toss my phone on the counter separating the kitchen from the living room and walk in the dark down the hall. I peak in on Benny first. He's sound asleep, curled on his side. A book open on the bed and a flashlight glowing next to him, forgotten as he read himself to sleep. I close the book and sit it on his table, click off the flashlight. His dark bangs have fallen over his eyes, and I brush them away gently. I lean over and kiss his temple, breathing deeply of the little-boy smell in his hair. With a pang, I realize that smell has started to fade, to change as he grows older. He's only eight, but he'll be a young man soon enough.

"Love you, Mom," he murmurs in his sleep. He's used to my late-night kisses.

"Love you, Benny buddy," I whisper near his ear and breathe his scent again.

"Stop smelling me," he mutters and pulls the covers closer around him.

I smile at my son and leave him alone, closing the door

with a gentle click.

No light shines under Lilly's closed door. I want to open it, to go to her. At fifteen, she won't tolerate my intrusion the way Benny does. Placing my hand flat on her closed door, I console myself with a quick, "Night, love."

Flickering lights and low voices filter through the crack in the door to the master bedroom. I push it open and find Bryson asleep on the bed, the TV on. I slip out of my suit jacket and toss it on the chair. I put my badge and gun in the side table drawer, the removal of their weight freeing me to just be. Sitting on the edge of the bed, I kick off my low-heeled boots.

Bryson moans and reaches for me, his hand on my thigh.

"You're home," he mumbles.

I turn towards him and place my hand flat on the plane of his cheek. The beginnings of stubble prickle my palm. "Don't wake up," I whisper. "It's late."

The TV flickers across his face as I drop a light kiss where my hand just was. He blinks rapidly, forcing himself awake. "How'd it go?"

"We had to release him." I stand and unbutton my shirt.

Bryson wakes up fully, pushes himself onto his elbow. "Release him? After what he did to all those women?" His indignation matches my own.

"His alibi's check out." I fume. I don't want to talk about it. I've spent the last few days building a case against Jesse Franklin. Eyewitness accounts linked him to several murders over the past year and a half. My partner, Detective Samuels, and I thought we had enough to bring him in.

"I don't understand," Bryson says.

"Me, either." I pause in unbuttoning my shirt. "He sat across the table from Samuels and me, calm and sure of himself. He has solid video alibis for each of the abductions. He couldn't have done it."

"I'm so sorry, Maribeth. I know you were sure you had this monster."

I sit back on the bed, my shirt flapping open. "That's the thing. I'm still sure. Franklin did those awful things to those women, or is at least involved." The rage I fought down before I even thought of coming home boils again. "Franklin looked me in the eye and said he didn't do it, but his eyes lied. He basically dared me to prove it. I can't explain it, but he knows that I know he's guilty."

Bryson rolls out of bed, comes around to my side, then sits next to me, his body close. "Maybe you're just tired. You've been on this case non-stop for weeks." He's trying to help, but it rankles just the same.

"I am tired. But that doesn't change anything. He killed and marked all those women, and I will figure out a way to prove it."

Bryson puts his arm around my shoulder, and I sink into the safety of his embrace. Staring into the face of a serial killer all night and then watching him walk away free has just about done me in.

"You must be hungry," he says.

I nod against his shoulder and let him take care of me.

"You get a shower, I'll go make you a sandwich." He kisses the top of my head, squeezes me against his side. "Let this go for tonight. Things will look different in the morning."

I revel in the moment, want him to hold me forever, to chase the darkness away. My stomach grumbles loudly, and we both laugh.

"I'll get you that sandwich." He leaves my side and walks towards the door.

"Thanks, love," I call after him. The door clicks behind him.

I take a moment to collect my tired thoughts. The TV murmurs and flickers. Russell Crowe battles other Gladiators in a late-night re-play of Bryson's favorite movie. An especially violent and bloody part sends me scrambling for the remote. I've seen enough violence for today.

The shower pounds on the tile and echoes through the spacious master bath. One entire wall is covered by a mirror stretching above the double vanity sinks. Using the left sink as always, I brush my teeth and wash off the last remnants of my makeup. I pull a brush through my short blonde hair. I toss the rest of my pants suit in the empty laundry hamper, giving silent thanks that Bryson did the laundry today. Familiar guilt stabs me. He's been picking up a lot of my slack lately, and I owe him better.

Naked, I walk into the attached closet full of similar pants suits. I dig in a drawer and find a comfortable nightgown, one with a lower neckline, just a little too much skin showing. Bryson's favorite. I vow to stay awake long enough to show him how much I appreciate all he's been doing for me.

I hang the nightgown on one of the hooks near the shower and climb into the hot water. I lean my hands against the shower wall, holding myself up as water pours over my head and images pour through my mind.

Photos of the seven women I know Franklin killed and mutilated. Each throat cut, each chest carved with the Roman numeral two. Their faces flash through my mind like a horror movie. I push against the images, begging them to stop.

These girls need me to bring them justice. The weight of that responsibility squeezes my chest, leaves me gasping.

My legs buckle under the weight. I slide to the floor of the shower and lean against the expensive tile. Water splashes and dribbles awkwardly down my face, mixing with the tears flowing freely. I cover my mouth with my hands, muffling the sounds. Cleansing sobs wrench my gut and tear my throat. The images of the women slow in my mind, then fade away.

Leaving darkness.

I welcome the emptiness, cling to it. The sobs taper off, leaving me spent and free. Purposely, I replace the horrible images with wonderful ones of my family. Quick flashes of my husband and children give me the strength to stand. Benny's precious smile and Lilly's infectious laugh fill my mind as I wash my hair.

Memories of passionate nights with Bryson warm my blood. I take the time to shave my legs, prepare for making another memory tonight.

When I'm finished, I stand under the water and let the steady stream wash away the last of my dark thoughts. I straighten my back, raise my chin, and physically reclaim myself.

"Come on, kid," I say out loud. "Bryson's waiting."

I suddenly realize he's been gone for a long time. I'd expected him to come into the bathroom, sit with me chatting as I showered, the way he's done so many times before.

A frizzle of fear niggles my neck. I push the residual effect of my long night away and turn off the shower.

Indy barks in the backyard, loud and insistent.

I try to look out the window to see the dog, but steam and the glare from the overhead lights block my view.

My detective mind works overtime. Why's Indy still out?

"Stop being paranoid," I say to my steam-fuzzed reflection.

I towel off and slide the nightgown over my clean skin. It clings to my hips, dips low on my chest. The lace edge of the hem skims my toned legs. Now I just need Bryson to see me in it.

I look into the bedroom, expecting to see him on the bed, back to watching Gladiator while he waits for me.

The weather channel I changed the TV to still plays in the empty room.

Indy still barks out back. The tone of his bark doesn't sound right. Sometimes he just barks at the wind, but now he's barking at something. Maybe the coyotes have gotten close to the barn again. Indy's protective of the pigs and chickens.

Bryson must have gone out to check on them. I try to look out the bathroom window again, but still see nothing but darkness.

I pull on a thick pink robe over my skimpy nightgown and head into the hall.

Halfway down the hall, I freeze.

Benny's door hangs open. I know I shut it earlier.

A few more steps and I see Lilly's door hangs open too.

I should have listened to my instincts.

I should have gone back for my gun tucked safely in its drawer.

I should have run back to my room, called for help.

I should have done anything other than what I did.

I continue down the hall dressed only in the slinky nightgown and robe.

Chapter 3

Maribeth

My cell phone rings, pulling me back to the present. The bathwater has cooled some and no longer burns my cold skin. I'm finally warm after my freezing dip in the pond.

The phone keeps ringing, the tone I've assigned to my sister Nicole. So few people call me, I don't need separate ringtones. If it's not an assigned tone, it's always a sales call.

I'd rather answer a sales call than talk to Nicole right now.

"She'll worry if you let it go to voicemail," Bryson says, leaning against the wall of the tiny bathroom.

I shove up out of the water, the sudden weight on my cut foot throwing a jolt of pain up my leg.

With dripping hands, I hit the answer button on the screen.

"Hey, Nicole," I say by way of answer and shoot

Bryson a withering look. He's no longer with me to see it.

"Hey, sis, how ya doing?" Her voice is overly-bright, overly-cheery. The implied question under the simple words is always the same. *What the hell is wrong with you?*

I assume my role in our familiar play. "I'm good." I grab a towel and dry myself with one hand. "Just taking a bath after my run." I leave out the part where I nearly froze to death, wanted to freeze to death.

"Still running, even when it's cold?" She doesn't know what else to say.

"Every day." I step on my cut foot and wince. "I did cut my boot. I'm going to have to order another pair. Can I have them shipped to you?"

Surprisingly, Nicole hesitates. "When?" Since I've come to this cabin in the woods, I've had everything delivered to her. She then brings it to me. She's the only other living person I've let on my property since the crew finished building the cabin nearly two years ago.

"I don't know when for sure. I was going to order the boots tonight, and they should be here in a day or two. Why does that matter?" I leave the bathroom and enter my bedroom, dig through a dresser drawer for panties, sweats and a hoodie. She waits so long to answer my question, I'm fully dressed before she speaks.

"That's actually why I called. I need to be out of town for the next week. I'm going to a restaurant convention in Indianapolis."

"That's great," I reply automatically. Nicole owns a sandwich shop in Maddison, the closest town to my woods. I haven't eaten there since I came to the woods, but it's a popular place. Only twenty miles from Fort Wayne, the small town of Maddison, felt like a world away from the city and the major crimes unit where I worked. The proximity to Maddison and Nicole was the primary reason I bought this place.

"I hate to be gone, but I think it will be good for me to learn some new things for the restaurant." She's still hedging, and you don't need to be a former detective to sense it.

"You have every right to go to a convention, Nicole. So what's the problem?"

"It's Ella." She's still hedging.

"Did she get into trouble again?" Nicole's daughter, Ella, has been acting out lately. Nothing major, skipping classes a few times. Two months ago, Nicole found a tiny bag of pot in her room. Warning signs for sure, but I've seen way worse in my career and can't help thinking Nicole over-reacts.

"No, she's not in trouble," Nicole says.

"Just come out and tell me what you want, Nicole." I'm tired and cranky and still have chores to do tonight.

"I don't want to leave her home alone, and I don't want to ask Price to take her while I'm gone," she says in a rush. Nicole's soon to be ex-husband, Price, has been a major pain in the ass lately. They've tried to keep things civil for Ella's sake, but Price has made it clear if Nicole doesn't walk his line, he'll go after full custody of their daughter.

"Crap," I mutter, panic swelling in my chest. "Ella

can't stay here," I blurt out before I can phrase it more delicately.

Nicole's anger radiates through the phone, but her voice is smooth. "I wasn't going to ask if she could stay with you." It sounds like she's clenching her teeth. I hear the undercurrent of, *no one should be living out there like you are.*

I backpedal, guilty for my outburst. "I'm sorry, I'm not sure why I said that. What do you need?"

Nicole seems placated. "She's old enough to stay home alone, but could you, I don't know, check on her while I'm gone?"

My mind races with the implication of the simple request. "Like, go to your house?" I never leave the woods. I've set this place up to be mostly self-sufficient. Anything I need, I can order online, and Nicole will bring it to me. I'm not sure my SUV parked under a tree and covered with leaves and snow will even start.

"Jesus, Maribeth! Just forget it. I wouldn't want Ella and me to intrude on your precious private time." She makes the words sound like something disgusting. "I'll just have the neighbor check on her."

"Nicole, I…." I'm not sure how I was going to finish the sentence.

"I knew better than to ask you." She continues, rare anger flashing. "I just thought, maybe you could help me out for a change."

I don't have a response. Nicole has been the only rock I've had to lean on, doing everything for me without complaint. She's been a much better sister to me than I have ever been to her. Panic at leaving the woods battles the guilty knowledge that I owe her.

I open my mouth to say I'll do it, but Nicole has already hung up.

Slumping on my bed, I stare at my phone. With just a few screen touches, I can call her back, make things right. The phone goes to sleep mode, and the screen turns black.

I push the button to wake it up, then open my Amazon app and order replacement boots. With shaking fingers, I change the delivery address to the woods, surprised I even remember it. All my bills are on auto-pay, and what little mail I receive is sent to Nicole's house. She brings it with my monthly grocery delivery.

After placing the order, I bring up Nicole's number. One click and I can call her back. I stare at the screen so long it again goes to sleep mode.

I place the phone on my dresser and head to do the chores.

Indy lifts his head from where he sleeps by the fire. "Don't get up," I tell him. "Just rest."

I pull my chore scrub pants over my sweats to keep the barn dust off them and zip my chore coat over my hoodie. My muck boots sit by the door to the barn, and I step into them gingerly. I probably should do something about the cut on my foot, but ignore the pain for now.

My barn is attached to the cabin by an enclosed porch. One door out of the cabin, then a few steps inside a glassed-in room, and another door to the barn. This is my favorite feature of my tiny farm. I can come and go from the barn without actually going outside. During pleasant weather, I open the glass doors. Icy wind blasts snow against the glass now. In my previous life, I used to tell Bryson I didn't mind doing the chores, I just hated walking to the barn in the cold and wind. We'd tease that if we ever won the lottery, I'd have tunnels built to the barn so I could stay warm. The proceeds from selling our farm combined with Bryson's life insurance wasn't the lottery I wanted to win.

My two pigs, Chica and Rizo, jump from their sleep as I enter the barn. They eagerly push against the fence of their enclosure, dinner has arrived. Their silly antics bring a reluctant smile to my face. I pat Chica on her head.

"You're getting big, girl," I admire her swelling belly. "Not too much longer now until those babies come." I squash a sliver of concern at the upcoming litter. I've never had a pig deliver a litter before, and hadn't planned on it this time.

I bought the pair of pigs off a man on Craigslist. He'd assured me Rizo had been neutered. I didn't know much about pigs at the time. I just knew I wanted something to keep me company, a reason to get up in the morning. And Bryson loved pigs.

The price had been low enough for the pair of KuneKunes, and the man agreed to meet me at the gate at the end of my long driveway. He'd handed the two squalling piglets over, and I handed him the cash. He didn't ask questions, and neither did I.

Looking at Chica's swollen belly, I should have.

Rizo pushes his long nose against my hand, reminding me why I came to the barn. I scoop out their food and toss it in their pen. They push each other and grunt as they dig in.

After checking the heated waterers, another investment well worth it, I feed the chickens in the corner coop. Everyone is fed and tucked in for the night. I turn off the overhead lights and open the door to the enclosed porch, thoughts of my own dinner on my mind.

Something clatters at the far end of the barn.

I freeze and listen. A shuffling sound follows the clatter.

I flip the light back on. The John Deere Gator sits in the far corner of the barn, close to the sliding door for easy access. My orange Kubota tractor sits in front of it. Between the two, something moves.

Chica and Rizo snuffle at their food, oblivious to the intruder.

I take cautious steps towards the equipment, my nerves on high alert.

Automatically, I reach for my hip, although my gun is safely locked up at Nicole's. Still, the habit dies hard.

Crouching low behind the fence's paltry protection, I peer around the corner.

A sudden blur of black springs onto the seat of my Kubota.

"Shit," I exclaim and jump away from the cat with a pounding heart and shaking hands.

The black cat looks at me curiously, hungrily, his yellow eyes intent on my movements, ready to run if necessary. Ashamed of my reaction to the stray cat, I stand straight.

"Better not let Indy see you in here," I tell the cat. Indy has chased strays away several times before. He protects "his" animals, the pigs, the chickens, but draws the line at cats.

The cat jumps from the tractor to the closest fence post and meows in question. "Stay here," I tell him.

I hurry to the fridge in the cabin and grab a container of leftover mashed potatoes. Indy eyes me curiously but lays back down.

In the barn, I sit on the feed bin, light a cigarette, and watch the cat devour the cold potatoes. My heart hurts for him, alone and hungry and scared in the cold. When the food is gone, the cat looks up and takes a cautious step.

I reach to pet him, but he skitters off. "I get it," I tell him. "I don't trust people either."

Lighting another cigarette, I sit in the barn. Rizo and Chica settle down, their bodies pressed together as they sleep. The chickens have long since given in to the dark and sleep on their perches. At the far end of the barn, the cat sits on the hood of the Gator, his belly full.

Even with my new cat friend, my heart feels as empty as the mashed potato bowl.

Chapter 4

Grant

I roll my eyes when I see Mrs. Pickler has required a signature for her package. I'd prefer to leave her delivery on the porch and drive my truck away before she sees me. The lonely widow often pays extra to require a signature, ensuring I will have to speak to her. After years as the UPS guy, I'm familiar with the ploy. For some, my visit is the only highpoint in their day. If Mrs. Pickler wants to pay extra to talk to me for a few moments, I suppose it's all in a day's work.

When the doorbell rings, the two Pomeranians I know are on the other side begin their frantic barking and clawing at the door. They bark so long, I wonder if the older woman isn't home, and reach for the "Sorry we missed you" sticky note for her door.

"Fifi, Bubbles, stop that." Mrs. Pickler commands her dogs. I force a smile to my face as the door opens, and the oddly named dogs pounce on me. "Look, girls, it's

Grant," she tells the tiny terrors nipping at my boots.

"Good morning, I need a signature," I say with the practiced mixture of friendly and professional. Mrs. Pickler stands too close and manages to touch my hand as she takes the electronic pen and board for her to sign on. Her perfume is so strong, I have to turn my face to breathe, but manage not to step away and disgrace my brown uniform with rudeness.

"Looking as handsome as ever, Grant," she says as she hands the electronic board back and takes her package. I pointedly ignore her hungry eyes on me.

"Thank you, Mrs. Pickler," I say and step off the porch. Fifi and Bubbles continue to swirl around my feet, and I avoid them with practiced movements all the way back to my truck. Mrs. Pickler follows her dogs into the snow wearing only slippers.

I bounce up the three steps to the cab of my delivery truck, leaving the dogs behind. Pulling the sliding door shut, I turn to wave good-bye. Mrs. Pickler looks sad and lonely with her package in hand and the snow blowing past. I take pity on her.

I open the door again. "Can you help me with something?"

Her pinched face lights up instantly, and she rushes to the bottom of my steps. Fifi and Bubbles continue yapping until she silences them with a sharp bark of her own. "Stop it." She smiles shyly and looks through her lashes at me. She's at least thirty years older than I am, but she doesn't let that stop her. "What can I do for you?" More coy eyelash fluttering.

Starting to regret my decision, I hurry on. "My next delivery is to an address I don't recognize," I say, checking my board. "I thought I knew all the places out here." I read her the address. "Do you know where that is?"

Her flirting fades away. "Is the name on the package Maribeth Johansen?" she asks seriously.

I check the box and see the name. "Yeah, so?"

Mrs. Pickler looks disturbed, even takes a step away from my truck in her slippered feet. "Detective Maribeth Johansen," she repeats as if I should know what that means.

"It's on this road, right?"

She searches my face, then leans closer. She looks around as if someone will overhear us. "That big gate down the way," she says, motioning down the road. Her attitude unsettles me.

"Great, thanks." I put the truck in gear, suddenly eager to get away from the strange woman.

"You don't want to go there," she says cryptically.

"Why not?" I ask before I think.

"She's bat crap crazy. Everyone knows that." She waits for my response. When I don't give her one, she goes on. "Her family was killed a few years back by some psycho. Any of this ringing a bell?"

I only vaguely remember something on the news about the murder of a detective's family. I'd been too busy dealing with the loss of my own wife at the time to pay much attention to the news.

"Poor woman," I say.

"Nutso, I tell ya. She moved up here and hasn't left the place since. At least, as far as I've ever heard. Total loony, you be careful." Crazy, nutso and loony all offend me deeply, but Mrs. Pickler seems so serious in her concern I let it slide.

"Thanks for the warning," I tell her and shut the sliding door against whatever else she has to say. I pull away absently, hoping Fifi and Bubbles have sense enough to move out of the way of the truck.

I'm familiar with the large metal gate Mrs. Pickler mentioned. It blocks the drive into some prime hunting woods, and I assumed there was nothing more than a few tree stands or even a hunting cabin at the end of the winding drive. More than a few times, I've noticed the woods, even been jealous of whoever owned such an excellent hunting ground.

I had no idea someone actually lived back there, let alone a traumatized reclusive woman.

I pull my truck into the space between the gate and the road. The rear bumper of my delivery truck barely clears the road, and my front bumper almost touches the gate.

Should I leave the box here at the gate or take it to her house?

I look at the box Maribeth Johansen ordered, recognizing the smiling logo on the side that matches half the packages currently in my truck. The black Prime tape seals the box shut. Whatever is inside, she wanted it quickly.

Undecided, I sit in the truck. I'm curious to see what lies down the trail, but if this woman is as disturbed as

Mrs. Pickler says, maybe she won't appreciate the intrusion.

I decide to honor her privacy and leave the package at the base of the gate. I sit the box on the frozen gravel and peer down the lane. I can only see about one hundred feet into the woods before the path turns and disappears into the trees.

Right before the bend, I see a doe on the lane. She stands so still, I wonder if she's actually real or just a very good decoy. One ear flickers nervously, and she steps towards me. Her large eyes lock with mine. I expect her to run away, but instead, she turns slowly and walks down the lane. She takes a few steps, stops, and looks over her shoulder as if to say, *are you coming?*

I push on the gate and it opens with a squeal. The doe still waits.

My decision made, I grab the box off the gravel and bounce back into the truck. The doe has walked past a bend in the lane. When I turn the same curve, she's vanished. I check the surrounding trees for the deer, but can't find her. I drive forward towards the mysterious detective.

My truck rattles and jumps down the uneven lane. Bare branches push in so close they scrape down the sides of my truck like claws. One branch hangs so low, it touches my windshield and slides over the truck with a screech. Snow piles in drifts on the unused lane, and I have to gun the gas to plow through them. The heavy truck slips sideways, and one tire leaves the gravel. I jerk the wheel to get back on the lane, cursing at the folly of my journey.

I'm curious to meet this woman and to see what's hidden back here, but if I get stuck, my supervisor will not be happy. I continue down the drive praying there will be space to turn around once I reach her house.

The trees thin ahead, and a sudden blast of sunshine pours out of the sky. Swirling snowflakes still fall, dancing in the sun. The sound of equipment running seeps into the truck as I make a final slipping turn.

A small house with a wrap-around porch squats in a clearing barely large enough to hold it. The neat cabin is well maintained, the porch cleared of snow and leaves. Some kind of barn or storage area is attached to the cabin. A white fence leads into the woods, and a pair of spotted pigs lope to the fence, curious at my intrusion.

I park the truck in front of the cabin and grab the woman's package. The sound of machinery drones from around back. With hesitant steps, I follow the sound.

I can leave the package on the porch and just leave, but I call "Hello?" instead.

A huge husky dog barrels around the corner of the cabin from the direction of the machinery. I see a lot of dogs on my route, even carry treats in my pocket for them.

This dog makes me jump.

He barks several times, then crouches and bares his teeth. I hold up my hands to show I'm not a threat, then fish a treat out of my pocket. I gingerly offer it to the large animal, my hand only shaking a little.

The dog sniffs at the treat, eyes me warily, then stops growling. He doesn't take the treat, but his posture relaxes out of attack mode.

The machinery continues to drone, mixing with the sound of wood falling. I finally recognize the sound as a log splitter.

"Indy?" a female voice calls from behind the cabin over the machine.

The dog barks in response. "Good boy, Indy," I tell him. He relaxes a little more, but his eyes watch my every move. I take a few more cautious steps around the edge of the cabin.

The bright green and yellow of the John Deer Gator catch my eye first, glowing in contrast to the white and brown of the surrounding woods. A woman dressed in a dark purple Carhartt jacket and dirty jeans loads wood into the Gator. I've found Maribeth Johansen.

She senses me watching her and jumps in surprise, ducks behind the pile of firewood in the Gator's bed.

I hold up my hands to calm her the way I did with the dog. "UPS," I call over the log splitter. She realizes she's crouching for cover and stands tall suddenly. Her tiny pointed chin raises, and her eyes narrow.

She turns her back to me and walks away. I think she's going to run and hide, and her reaction surprises me. Maybe she is as disturbed as Mrs. Pickler says.

She turns off the log splitter, then faces me again. The quiet of the woods descend on us at the loss of the machine's drone. I can almost hear the snow landing around us.

Like a frightened animal, she watches me. Her dog watches me too. I take note of the small splitting ax lying

41

near her, and a frisson of fear snakes in my belly.

The silence stretches awkwardly. I rush to fill the space. "I'm sorry I startled you. I have a package here for you." She makes no move.

Nerves start to tingle down my back, and I regret coming. "Want me to leave it on the porch?"

She still doesn't answer, just watches with her sharp eyes, so blue I can see the color clearly from this distance.

The dog senses the tension and his shoulders hunch, ready to protect her if needed. He steps nervously in place, his paws crinkling on the leaves under the thin snow.

Realizing I still have my hands up, I lower them slowly and take a backward step. "Sorry, I bothered you." My words are loud in the quiet of the woods.

Trusting she won't hurt me, I turn and toss the box on the porch and hurry to my truck.

"Wait!" she cries, the single word echoing through the trees.

Chapter 5

Maribeth

Firewood fills the bed of the Gator. The cabin has central heat, but I like having the fireplace blazing. The flames keep me company, and the satisfaction of cutting wood keeps my body busy.

Indy watches as I pick up the logs as they fall off the splitter. Indy likes the fireplace too. Knowing I can provide the small comfort to him fills me with pride.

I place another log on the splitter, and it falls away in two pieces. My back protests as I haul the half piece onto the splitter again. Once it's in place, I push the handle, and the splitter cracks it in two. I gather those pieces to toss in the back of the Gator.

Indy has left a dog-shaped depression in the snow where he had been.

"Indy?" I call over the sound of the splitter.

A bark in reply comes from the other side of the cabin.

I turn back to my work, split another log into quarters, and gather them to add to the nearly full bed of the Gator.

Out of the corner of my eye, I see the man.

The only man I've seen at my cabin since coming to

the woods. Even Detective Samuels has never been to the cabin. Only Nicole is allowed.

Instinctively, I duck behind the wood piled in the Gator. Shame at my cowardice washes through me. In my previous life, I faced down the worst men the human race created. Now the sight of a friendly UPS delivery guy sends me skittering in fear.

Forcing my back straight with faked confidence, I confront the stranger.

His hands raised in a pose I'm more than familiar with. Snippets of my life as a cop flitter through my mind. The memory of that previous power of my badge spurs my feet into movement. I turn off the splitter so I can hear the man.

"I'm sorry I startled you. I have a package here for you," he says in the sudden silence. His deep voice sounds so out of place in my tiny self-imposed island, I don't know how to respond. Normal human interaction feels beyond my ability.

Indy doesn't seem bothered by the man, and that calms me some. A wild mix of emotions flows through me. Tingles of fear swirl, but excitement and interest and a deep, terrifying longing bubble there as well. I feel like I'm tumbling down a dark tunnel, unable to stop the crash coming at the end.

"Want me to leave it on the porch?" the man asks. A simple question that I'm unable to respond to.

Indy senses my nerves, and so does the man.

The moment stretches. My mind scrambles for words, a response, anything. I know I'm failing this test but don't know what to do.

"Sorry I bothered you." The tall man tosses the box that must contain my new boots on the porch and walks away.

An overwhelming and surprising sense of loss swamps me as he disappears around the corner.

My mind screams *come back, don't leave me here.*

My mouth finally remembers how to work, and I yell, "Wait!"

I hurry around the corner of the cabin, and he stops at the base of the steps to his brown delivery truck. The truck seems enormous and entirely out of place parked in my clearing. The dark shape looms over me as I approach. I focus on the man instead.

Blue-gray eyes meet mine and a sizzle travels down my back. My mouth feels dry and sweat drips under my layers of clothing.

"Sorry if I scared you," the man says again. His deep voice holds a note of gravel and a hint of sugar.

"I'm not used to visitors," I manage to stammer. *Get your shit together.*

Obviously at ease making small talk, he leans with one foot on the bottom step in a relaxed pose. My nerves jump like bugs along my skin, and I pet Indy's head to calm them.

"Nice place you have here," he says, looking around the clearing with appraising eyes.

"Thank you." I look around, too, wondering what it must look like to a stranger, hating that I care what he thinks. "I planned it well," I say stupidly.

"You must get a lot of deer. Is the hunting good?" He smiles fully, and something in me melts a little.

"Tons of deer. I got a huge nine pointer last November. Well, nine if you count the tiny nub of a point," I add.

"If you can hang a ring on it, I count it," he says easily with the hint of a laugh.

"I count it, too." I feel my face break into the smallest smile, and it startles me. "Do you hunt?"

"Whenever I can. I don't have a place like this, though. My uncle has a few acres, and he lets me go there." The soft timbre of his voice fills my ears like precious music I didn't know I missed. I want him to keep talking, to fill the silence of my long day.

"Sounds nice," I offer lamely, scrambling for words.

He saves me, "What do you shoot?" he asks naturally.

"Bow." His eyebrows arch over his lovely eyes in appreciation.

"Bow hunter? That's impressive. Takes real patience and skill to get a buck like that with a bow." That frozen part of me melts a fraction more at the praise.

"I have lots of time, and I practice often." I point to the shooting range at the edge of the woods. Several species of animal targets, made of dense foam, stand at different distances.

"Wow, so many targets. Is that an alligator I see in the snow?" I think he's making fun of me and my range. I've long since mastered paper targets and needed a challenge. Maybe it seems nuts to someone with an actual life.

"I like a variety," I say shyly.

"That's great!" He smiles fully again, not making fun at

all. The strange intimacy of a smile makes me nervous, and I have to look away.

Silence stretches again, but I don't know how to fill it. I'm jumpy and uncomfortable. I want him to stay but also to get the hell away from me.

Even his practiced small talk must not be enough to compensate for my lack of social skills. "I left your package on the porch," he says quietly, shifting his weight to the foot still on the step.

"Thanks for bringing my boots," I say to the ground.

"Hopefully, this weather will finally warm for real, and you won't need them," he says. Even with my lack of skill, I know that talking about the weather is the least intimate of conversations. I make the man nervous. I sense the tension tingling below the surface of his words. The pull of his presence tugs at me as he takes another step into the truck.

"I'm Maribeth." I lift my gaze from the ground and to his intense eyes. I'm not sure why I told him my name. He could have read it off the box he delivered if he wanted to know it.

"Nice to meet you, Maribeth. I'm Grant." He motions to the porch. "Enjoy the boots."

I pull my gaze from his and step back from the truck. "Thank you," I say, hoping he doesn't realize I'm referring to more than the delivery.

"My pleasure," he smiles again, tearing at my heart. "Now that I know you're back here, I can deliver anything you want." The kind words break me, and I turn away slightly, step farther from the truck.

The sliding door clamors shut. Grant puts the truck into gear and executes a perfect 3-point turn. I stand in the snow with Indy and watch him drive away. The large side-view mirrors reflect his face to me. He catches my eye in the glass and waves good-bye.

The brown truck disappears into the woods.

The silence, the emptiness, the loneliness I've grown used to swells huge once he's gone. An empty branch overhead creaks one lonely note over and over.

Chapter 6

Maribeth

My new boots pinch uncomfortably and need broken in. The cut on my foot has mostly healed, but each step of my run pricks my sole.

I push through the pain and wait for the endorphin rush. I've felt edgy and jumpy the last few days. My brush with freezing to death unsettled me more than I want to admit. Bryson says it's normal after a trauma. I almost laughed in his face. I'm more than familiar with trauma and its ability to rock me.

The gray-blue eyes and dark brown uniform of the UPS guy flashes into my mind, followed by a stab of guilt at the tingle of interest that had danced down my spine. I'd convinced myself my reaction to the man was from the shock of another person being in my woods, nothing more. Grant's eyes make me nervous in a way I don't want to analyze.

I need the relief only a hard run can offer and pound the trail in frustration.

My lungs burn from the harsh cold air, not to mention the half-pack of smokes I've already inhaled today. My ears ring with the sound of my breathing, loud in the snow-silent woods. I don't wear earbuds today, my gasping breaths the only music I need.

And Indy's barking.

He's ahead of me on the trail, doing his usual run ahead, then come back act. No matter how hard I drive my feet, I can't keep up with the dog. He comes back to me, his loping gate cheering me on as he has a thousand times.

This time, red stains his muzzle.

I slow my pace at the color, startled.

"What did you get into?" I ask the dog, faking calm. I pat his muzzle, and my glove picks up the red.

Blood.

I stare at the stain on my glove. Fear shivers from my legs to my shoulders. "It's just an animal," I tell myself, feeling foolish. "Probably caught a rabbit or something." My voice sounds tiny in the vast expanse of woods.

Indy sits down and whines, blocking the trail. The fear jolts this time.

I step around the dog, and he moves to block me again. I look down the trail, but it makes a turn over a small rise, and I can only see a few dozen feet.

I push past Indy, but he runs in front of me again, hunches to the ground, and bares his teeth with a low growl.

The fear freezes my blood. Indy has never growled at me, not one time. Whatever's down the path, he's desperate to hide it from me.

Or hide me from it. Indy knows the horror I've seen. He had blood on his muzzle that time, too.

The living room lights shine bright at the end of the dark hall. Indy continues to bark outside, insistent with an edge of panic. I creep to the living room.

Bryson, Lilly, and Benny sit next to each other like movie night on the couch. A tiny flush of relief pours through me. They're watching a movie. It's the middle of the night, and the TV's not on, but my mind tricks me into believing.

I step out of the hall.

The gags tied across their mouths shatter the tiny bubble of hope. Three sets of wild eyes lock on me. Bryson screams against his gag in warning.

A sickening mix of chemical and fruit smell suddenly covers my face. My family fades as the chloroform takes effect.

A sharp slap to the face wakes me. "Wake up, bitch," a male voice hisses. "You don't want to miss this."

I recognize the voice before my eyes open. I'd spend hours interrogating the man earlier today, convinced he killed seven women. The monster invaded my house and stole my family.

I swing at the man, but duct tape pins my hands behind my back. Jesse Franklin laughs at my attempt. "Nice try, Detective."

I try to kick, but he's just out of reach. He's propped me on a chair, the glass coffee table between my family and me.

Bryson and the kids cower on the couch. Benny's eyes wide and desperate above his gag. He leans against his dad for comfort. Lilly's head hangs low, her long dark hair covering her face. Quiet sobs shake her shoulders.

Bryson's eyes burn with anger, primal and deep. He struggles against his ties, wriggles, and grunts, but can't free himself.

"Now that you're awake, we can start the show." Franklin's voice is absurdly calm, like an emcee at a comedy club.

I've seen the bodies left by this butcher. The images from his victims were just playing through my mind a few minutes ago in the shower. Panic and fear rage through me.

And guilt.

I brought this into our home.

Franklin takes a large knife off the glass coffee table and tests the blade with his thumb. "Perfect," he says to the blade.

"Which one first?" he asks me. I can only plead with my eyes, my mouth dry against the rag tied through it.

Franklin looks at my children. He raises Lilly's chin, forcing her to look at him. "I do like young women," he says. Lilly has gone completely pale, her wide brown eyes stark against her skin. Tears of fear slide silently down her cheeks. Still, she shakes the man's hand off her face in defiance.

"I like them feisty," he says. With slow, deliberate movements, he cuts the neckline of her nightshirt, exposing her chest. She doesn't know what's coming, but I do.

I scream against the gag, rock in my chair. Franklin doesn't even flinch at my noise.

"Don't worry, Detective," he says. "You'll get your turn."

With four practiced swipes, he quickly cuts his signature roman numeral two into Lilly's chest. She screams against her gag, the agony piercing my ears. Blood from the cuts seeps down her skin, and Franklin watches the blood, transfixed.

Bryson rocks violently against his ties. Benny whimpers and hides his head.

I can only watch the horror from my seat.

Franklin snaps out of his trance and grabs Benny's hair. "I don't like boys, much, but you're here, so." Franklin cuts Benny's shirt and carves the mark into him with a flash of the blade.

Benny is so shocked he doesn't make a sound.

Franklin looks at me, eager for my reaction to my children's blood. I don't give him the satisfaction. I know the steps in his mutilation, the cutting of the sign is the least of my worries.

"Hmm?" Franklin muses at my lack of response. He turns to Bryson. From my vantage point, I see the uncertainty in Franklin's posture. Young women and a child are one thing, but Bryson is a fully grown, healthy man, muscled from years of construction work. The blade shakes a little as Franklin cuts the mark into my husband. Bryson fights back, and the mark turns out crooked and not very deep. Franklin seems a bit unsettled but covers his uncertainty by hurrying to me.

He doesn't have to cut my shirt away. The slinky nightgown and robe already expose the part of my skin he wants to slice.

"Nice outfit," he goads. I lock eyes with him and refuse to flinch as he cuts my skin. He hurt my family, anger is all I feel.

"Nothing?" he asks. "You really are a cold-hearted bitch, aren't you?"

I glare at him with all the hate and anger raging in me. He flinches and takes a quick step away.

He realizes I made him jump, but quickly recovers and leans in close.

"You should have left us alone," he hisses with hot breath on my ear. "This is your fault."

I shiver involuntarily at his words. He sees the shiver, and a slow smile creeps across his face. "That's better. You should be afraid."

He strides back to my family and admires his work. All three of them look up with pleading eyes and bleeding chests. "Lovely," he says. "I want you to know, this isn't about you," he tells them. "Your mom's too smart for her own good. Can't let her ruin everything we've got going." He looks over his shoulder at me, watching with disturbing intensity.

He walks behind the couch. In a flash, he grabs Lilly's hair and runs the blade across her throat, his eyes never leaving mine.

I scream against the gag, rock in the chair. "Finally, a reaction," he says and grabs Benny and slices him in the same way.

My body revolts at the horror. Bryson screams and kicks, desperate to save his family.

Franklin slices him with a quick flash of the blade.

I squeeze my eyes shut, unable to watch my family die.

Indy barks outside the sliding door, jumping and slamming into the glass. He bounces off and rushes the door again.

"Open your eyes, bitch," Franklin commands. I shake my head and squeeze my eyes tighter.

His hand suddenly grabs my chin, forcing me to look at him. "Open them," he barks.

I squeeze them tighter, still. It's the one thing I can control.

Indy barks and growls, crashes into the glass door again and again. I focus on the sounds of the dog, willing my mind anywhere other than this room of carnage.

"Be a bitch, then," Franklin says. "You're dead anyway."

The blade pricks into my neck, opens my skin.

I listen to Indy bark and accept my death.

Glass shatters into the room, and my eyes fly open. A flash of gray and white fury knocks Franklin away from me as Indy attacks. Franklin screams and falls onto the glass coffee table. The table shatters beneath him, sending large shards of glass flying through the room. Indy pounces on the man, primal and vicious. Franklin swings the bloody knife at the dog, but the knife slips from his hand and skitters across the carpet.

Indy snaps the man's arm in his jaws, and Franklin screams at the sudden pain. He pushes the dog, scrambling backward across the broken glass. Indy sinks his teeth deeper into the man.

Franklin slowly stops fighting back and blood pools below him, seeping from unseen shards of glass in his back. After a final, weak shove against Indy, Franklin lies still.

Indy lets go of his arm and returns to me. I focus all my attention on Indy, refuse to look at my family. Indy pushes his nose against my knee, and whines for my attention.

Blood drips from the cut on my neck. If he'd cut an artery, I'd be dead already. My mind swims, and my vision darkens, but I'm alive.

The quiet of the night settles into the room. Franklin breathes raggedly on the floor. Not a sound comes from the couch.

Indy and I sit together in the carnage. With my hands taped behind the chair, I'm unable to help myself. Cold air pours through the broken glass door. A sudden squeal from the barn breaks the quiet, one of the pigs squabbling with another.

Indy sniffs at our family on the couch. I stare at the carpet. He whines, then lies next to me.

My head grows fuzzier, and my mind fades closer to darkness. I'm too weak to hold my head up, so let it hang, my chin to my chest, sliding in my blood.

"You have to call for help." I hear Bryson's voice so clearly I snap my head up, expecting to see him. He remains crumpled on the couch, obviously dead.

I close my eyes before I see anymore. "Your phone is on the counter." He sounds like he's in the room with me, but I don't open my eyes to look.

"Use Siri, Mom," Lilly chimes in.

I know she's not there, either.

I listen to them anyway.

The gag bites into the corners of my mouth, but I rub my shoulder against it. It takes several tries, each movement causing more blood to pour from my cut throat. Using my tongue and wiggling my jaw against my shoulder, I finally manage to remove the gag.

I swallow hard to wet my dry tongue. With my eyes still squeezed tightly closed, I say loud and clear.

"Hey, Siri."

My phone on the kitchen counter chimes that Siri is listening. "Call 9-1-1," I tell the phone.

"Calling 9-1-1," Siri replies.

Chapter 7

Maribeth

With the memory of my family's murder fresh in my mind, Indy's growl prods me to turn around on the path and run back to the cabin. I came here to hide from evil, to lick my wounds. Whatever he's protecting me from, I trust his instincts.

I retrace my steps and jog a few yards towards home, but my heart isn't in it. "You're being ridiculous," I say out loud and stop on the path. "What could possibly be there?"

I turn once again. These are my woods, and this is my trail, I will go where I want. I created this island to keep me safe and damned if I'm going to let some dead animal Indy found stop me from doing what I want.

I push past Indy and jog over the small hill and around the turn in the trees.

I should have trusted the dog. The body propped against a tree is most certainly dead, but she's not an animal.

Skittering to a stop, I slide down the snowy path and land on my rear.

The young woman sits against the tree, her dark hair, so much like Lilly's hanging over both shoulders. The hair frames the mark carved on her chest.

The Roman numeral two.

For a moment, I think I'm seeing Lilly. Maybe she's just playing a cruel trick on me.

But this young woman is really here, and Lilly never is.

My chest hurts, and I gasp for air. Indy paces next to me, whining, urging me to leave.

I crawl to the young woman instead, taking in details with my long-unused detective's eye.

Long arcs of blood stain the snow where it had pumped from the slit at her throat. She sits on her bottom with legs stretched in front of her and hands taped behind the tree.

The bloody mark on her chest has already frozen into tiny clinging crystals.

Her pink sweater has been cut down the front, opened to showcase the mark. Her jeans are in place, and I can only hope she hasn't been sexually assaulted. Mercifully, Jesse Franklin hadn't raped his victims, but Jesse Franklin has been dead for two years.

Whoever did this hopefully copied Franklin's lack of sexual deviancy, as well.

She wears no shoes, but her socks are soaked and dirty. She'd been forced to walk here through the snow, terrified and freezing. My heart aches for the woman in a rush of emotion that nearly breaks me.

I don't touch her or get too close, preserve the snowy crime scene. Two sets of footprints lead to the tree from the direction of the access road nearby. Only one set of prints lead out. It was too easy for someone to leave the girl on my path.

My path.

The realization sinks like a stone.

Whoever did this knew where he left her. He brought her here for me to find. A killer has been in my woods. A killer who knows just how to torture me.

I'm on my feet and sprinting back towards the cabin before Indy realizes I'd intended to move.

I run like the devil is on my heels.

Because he is.

The flat out sprint leaves me weak and gasping as I pound up the steps of my porch and into the cabin, slamming the door behind me. The safety of the cabin feels smothering and close. I pace my open living room, kitchen, dining area. It only takes ten paces to cover the small space. Agitated, I walk back and forth, gasping and raw.

My heart rushes, and my head spins as the panic attack creeps in. I feel it coming, and struggle to stop it. I slow my breathing and do the four-count in, hold for four and exhale for four.

Indy barrels through the dog door, startling me even

further.

The panic continues to sweep. I hold my breath, knowing the extra oxygen in my blood is causing my dizziness. The panic rises, swirls.

"Bryson!" I scream for help. "Lilly. Benny!"

The afternoon sun shines through the windows. There are still a few hours until darkness will fall and they can come.

I scream their names anyway. Repeating them until my throat grows raw, pace the room until my legs ache. Eventually, the walls press too close. I can't stay in the cabin.

Digging frantically through drawers, I find the keys to the SUV. I push the button on the remote start, and surprisingly, the engine starts. The SUV is covered with snow and last fall's leaves and branches. When I look out the window, the red tail-lights glow through the snow on the bumper, red in the sunlit snow.

I look out the windows and check the woods before I open the front door and walk onto the porch.

The woods are silent. The only sound is the SUV's engine purring under a tree.

Using my whole arm to clear the windshield and my boots to kick the piles away, I dig the SUV out of its hibernation.

Once behind the wheel, I jam the lever and put the vehicle into gear. I gun the gas, and it jumps onto the lane. The SUV feels enormous and unwieldy as I creep down the driveway. I've only driven the Gator of the tractor for the last two years. Indy whines in the passenger seat, sensing my overwrought tension. We slip and slide through the snow piled on the lane, follow the faint remnants of Grant's tracks from his delivery two days ago.

The gate at the end of my lane looms ahead, bright against the afternoon sun on the snow. Shut, but not locked, it blocks my entrance back into the rest of the world. I pull the SUV to a stop and put it in park. I just need to open the gate and drive off the lane onto the road.

And go where?

The sudden thought startles me. I have nowhere to go. Even if I did, I haven't been off my property in so long I'm not sure I can leave.

I try to imagine myself driving through the gate, turning down the road, driving into Maddison, and finding Nicole's house.

The image of me leaving the woods starts the panic attack all over again.

I shiver in the driver's seat and stare at the gate.

"Open the gate, push the gas and just drive away," I whisper.

Something shifts inside me. I know I can't do it. These are my woods, the only place I can survive. If a killer wants to leave me a gruesome gift, I will just have to deal with it. I don't have a choice.

Thinking of the young woman sitting dead and alone on the path, I know I need to call for help. She has family looking for her, and I owe it to them, to her. It's the cornerstone of my entire career, to protect the victims, to give some justice to their families.

I know calling the police will bring unwelcome

attention to my woods. Forensic teams, detectives, the coroner, any number of people will descend on the fragile world I've created.

I'm not sure I can do that.

I don't have a choice.

I postpone the inevitable and call the one person always willing to help me.

I rub Indy's neck while I wait for her to pick up. Nicole doesn't answer until the fourth ring. She's no doubt still angry at me from the other day and debating whether or not to take my call.

She answers with a sigh and says hello guardedly.

"Something bad has happened," I blurt out. I feel her instant panic for her daughter through the phone. "Ella's fine," I rush to add.

"That wasn't nice, Maribeth," she says warily, but relieved. "What's happened?" I can tell by her tone that as long as Ella is okay, nothing else matters. I understand the feeling and the reverse of it.

"Someone left a dead girl on my path," I say directly.

Nicole takes a sharp breath of surprise.

"Jesus, what do you mean?"

"I was running, and there was a young woman tied to a tree on my path. Her throat has been slit," I hesitate, staring at the gate. "She has the same mark on her chest that I do."

I close my eyes and wait for her response.

"That's not possible," she says firmly.

"I saw her with my own eyes."

She doesn't say anything for a long moment. "Did

you?" She says it gently, but the meaning is clear. I once tried to tell her about the visits from Bryson and the kids, and she flipped out. She'd begged me to get professional help, had railed on and on that they weren't really there. After a while, I stopped trying to make her understand. I told her they were short-lived hallucinations.

"I didn't imagine her," I snap. "She's real, and she's dead."

"Are the cops there yet?"

"I haven't called them." The words shame me. Now that the initial panic has faded, my blind attempt at escape seems foolish. I should have called the police right away. I can't explain my actions to Nicole.

"Maribeth, you have to call them." I was prepared for another lecture, but instead, she's soothing, caring. "I can't imagine how this feels, but you need to call for help."

It's her understanding tone that does me in, not the logic of her words.

"Will you come, too?" I hate the pleading in my voice. "I'm scared."

"I've been packing while we've been talking. I'll get checked out of this hotel and hit the road. I'll be back in town as soon as I can."

"Thank you," I sniffle. "I'll call Samuels. At least he won't look at me like a freak."

"You're not a freak," Nicole says. "You just need to heal. This situation isn't helping any."

I huff in agreement, "No, it's definitely not. I'm glad you're coming," I say meekly.

"You're my sister, and I love you," she says simply,

our earlier fight forgotten. I thank her again and hang up. If I only have one person in the world to lean on, I'm thankful it's Nicole.

I stare at the metal gate blocking my woods from the world. Red bars of peeling paint, bright as blood against the sunlit snow. I carefully back up the lane. The red bars of the gate grow smaller, then disappear as I make a turn.

Chapter 8

Samuels

It's way too early in the season to grill, but I can't help myself. There's something primal and satisfying about cooking steaks on an open flame. The aroma of the meat, the smoke from the dripping fat, the satisfaction of cooking it just right, all of it fills me with joy. That first bite melting in my mouth, makes the cold wind blowing down the collar of my jacket all worth it.

I flip the steaks, careful to rotate them just right so they'll end up with a perfect grid of grill marks. Sydney's coming home for the afternoon, and I know she'll tease me if they aren't lined up just right. "You got the hashtags crooked, Dad," she'd say and give me her customary lopsided grin.

I quickly shift the steaks so the grid will be crooked on purpose and secretly hope she'll comment. Now that Sydney's a freshman at college, I'll take any opportunity to connect with her, even if it's just a silly family joke.

Sipping my nearly full beer and lighting another

cigarette, I wait for the steaks to finish cooking and think of another college girl.

Dana Sanders disappeared two days ago. Her mother filed a missing person's report, and we gave her the usual *she's probably just gone off with some friends* line. I want to believe she'll show up, kids that age usually do. But my gut tells me differently.

We found Dana's car in a drug store parking lot. Surveillance tape from the store shows her shopping for a birthday present for her boyfriend. The t-shirt and a card were her only purchases. The cameras followed her to her car, where she opened her door and tossed the gift on the front seat.

Something off camera caught her attention. She walked out of frame and disappeared. The hopeful theory is she saw a friend and was just out having fun, but the friends we've talked to haven't seen her. The boyfriend swears she would never have missed their planned date for his birthday. After two days of searching, there's been no sign of Dana Sanders.

Regardless of what they show on TV, young women rarely disappear from public places the way Dana did. It's been a few years since a woman went missing like this in Fort Wayne, and the man who took those girls is dead.

The Dana Sanders case scratches at the barely scabbed over scars left from those cases. I take a deep drag from my Marlboro and down half the beer in large gulps. With practiced skill, I push thoughts of Jesse Franklin from my mind and focus on the steaks.

Inside the house, our Maltese mix, Esther, barks like a

swat team is crashing through the doors. Could mean the wind blew a leaf past the window or the fridge kicked on. That dog's old lady name matches her personality. Crabby and complaining and easily upset, but also sweet and snuggly. She's technically my wife, Kay's, dog, but I have to admit Esther's good company. When I get home late from work and just want to sit on the couch in the dark, eat chips and watch Sportscenter until the world makes sense again, Esther sits with me. She'll inch her way onto my lap, beg for a few chips and fade to sleep as I absently pat her back. I'd never tell Kay how much I enjoy Esther at those times. Fluffy dogs don't match the image of the seasoned detective. Of course, Kay already knows about Esther's and my nights.

Esther stops barking abruptly. There's only one reason she'd stop so fast, Sydney must be home.

Deciding the steaks have cooked long enough, I flip them on a platter and carry them into the house. The kitchen feels over-warm after standing on the back porch in the winter wind. Or maybe it just seems warm from the welcoming smiles of my wife and daughter.

"Sydney-kitty, you came home. Let me guess, laundry to do?" I tease my daughter. She leans against the counter, Esther in her arms, and rolls her eyes at my use of her childhood nickname.

"Only two bags of laundry this time," she says sheepishly.

I sit the steaks on the counter then take her into my arms. "Our washing machine is always here for you," I tease. Her head only reaches my chest, and she feels tiny and fragile. Hard on the heels of my search for Dana Sanders, I hold on to my own daughter a little too long. I pull her so tight, Esther fusses between us.

Sydney senses my need, has been through this before. She puts Esther down and wraps both her arms around my waist. "I'm fine, Dad," she says against me. "I'm safe and sound right here with you."

She's said these words before, too many times. Growing up the kid of a detective, she's learned that sometimes we need to go home and just hold our own children. She lets me get my fill of her as I meet Kay's eyes over her head. Kay's used to this, too. I hate what I've put my family through with my job, but I can't change it. Detective is not just a title, it's an identity. I'm thankful beyond words they understand that. Too many families are torn apart by it.

God, you're maudlin today, I think. *Get a grip.*

I release Sydney. "You hungry? I did some steaks."

"In the snow?" she asks.

"It's not snowing that hard."

Sydney looks at the platter, and I wait for her response.

She doesn't disappoint, "You messed up the hashtags again," she laughs.

The world snaps back into correct focus, and I settle into my role as family man, my other, more important identity.

We enjoy the rare family meal. Kay and Sydney chat the way mothers and daughters do. I sit quietly at the table and listen to their chatter. The pleasant sounds fill my ears, delighting my tired mind. I offer a response only when asked directly, otherwise letting them enjoy each other and the afternoon. The washing machine churns in the next room, adding to the homey feel of the meal. Sydney sneaks tiny pieces of steak to Esther under the table, and I pretend I don't see.

My belly full of steak followed by another beer, I sit back in my chair and think how blessed I am for these two women.

My cell phone on the counter rings, intruding on our enjoyment.

I snap out of my happy daze. I recognize the ringtone, although I haven't heard it for years. Kay and Sydney remember it too. Back when Maribeth Johansen was my partner, the phone rang like that all the time. I've never changed it. Filled with grief and guilt, I left her number in my contacts. In the first few months, I would find myself with my finger hovering over the call button, wanting to check on her, but too afraid. I never pushed that button. What happened to her family could have happened to mine, and I couldn't bring myself to talk to her about it. I was a coward.

As I listen to the ring tone now, I'm still a coward. The song plays on as Kay and Sydney both watch me matching worried expressions.

"Are you going to answer her?" Kay asks.

The phone rings one last time, then falls silent. The three of us are frozen at the table.

"Is that your old partner?" Sydney asks.

I nod and take another sip of beer. The bottle is empty.

"She must need something for her to call you after all

this time," Kay prods quietly.

I think of Dana Sanders and my earlier thoughts about the similarities to the Franklin case. What are the odds that I'd been thinking of Franklin, and now Maribeth calls after two years of radio silence?

My gut swims with the certainty that something dark is coming. I look at the faces of the two most wonderful women in the world, and a primal need to protect them flows through me. At one time, I felt a similar emotion for Maribeth. As my partner, I would have taken a bullet for her and she for me. We were closer in some ways than to my own family, bound together.

I didn't protect her. She'd taken worse than a bullet, and I'd been home asleep with Kay, Sydney safe in the room down the hall. Maribeth had been alone to face that monster as I'd slept. No amount of department required counseling could lift that guilt from me. After two years of practiced avoidance, I'd gotten to a place where I could ignore the shame and pretend the whole thing never happened.

The phone rings again. The ringtone's the same, but sounds insistent and pleading to my ears.

"You have to answer her," Kay says, meeting my eyes, understanding my battle.

I push away from the table and hold the phone. My finger hovers over the answer button the way it hovered all those other times.

With a burst of courage, I push the button before I change my mind.

"Samuels," I say into the phone and brace for hearing

her voice again.

"It's Maribeth Johansen," she says. Her voice sounds smaller than I remember. It quavers and has a rasp to it like she's been crying. Under that, I recognize the steel I'd always admired.

"Johansen, good to hear from you," I lie because I don't know what else to say.

"I have a..." She pauses, searching for the words. "A problem, I guess."

"What kind of problem?" My words are guarded, and I watch Kay watching me.

"I found a dead girl." The flat words stab and confuse.

"Where?"

"On a path in my woods." Her woods? How was that possible? From what I remember, she lives out in the sticks, hidden.

I fall back on procedure to hide my shaking. "That's not my jurisdiction." I regret the words as soon as they leave my mouth.

"I don't give a damn about your jurisdiction," she snaps, the steel in her voice hardening. "A young woman was murdered on my jogging path. Her throat is slit, and she has the same mark as before."

A dark hole opens beneath me, and I tumble back to the sick months of hunting Jesse Franklin. "The Gemini mark?" I ask, afraid of the answer.

"The same one I have." I flinch at this detail. "She was left for me to find. I'm sure of it."

"Did you call the police there?"

She hesitates, and when she speaks again, she sounds

broken. "I don't want strangers here." She exhales, and I can picture the cigarette she's sucking on. I need one of my own. I'm acutely aware of Kay and Sydney watching this conversation, listening to my end of it. I grab my jacket and step out onto the porch. Johansen waits for me to light my own cigarette and gather my thoughts. We often spent long moments of silence on the phone, both of us thinking. The familiarity of the moment feels surreal.

I think of the missing Dana Sanders. "What does she look like?"

"She looks like Lilly." Quiet painful words. "Young, with long dark hair."

The description matches Dana Sanders. Shit.

I suck on my cigarette like it will give me answers, then watch the smoke blow away in the cold wind. "Where are you?"

"Where do you think I am?" Impossibly angry words that bite. "I'm at the cabin, of course. You're coming, right?"

I take another drag of the cigarette, postponing the inevitable another few moments.

"I'm coming," I say quietly.

"Just you, I don't want strangers crawling all over me."

I can't promise, so I lie. "Just me."

The steel has completely left her voice as she says, "Who the hell did this? A copycat? Some sick bastard who knows who I am and why I'm here?"

The raw pain and fear tears at my heart. "I have no idea. Just sit tight. I'm on my way."

I finish the smoke and drop the butt on the porch. I

squash it with my heel and watch as the biting wind carries it away.

Fresh tire tracks cut through the snow on the far side of the gate, but the snow on this side is untouched. I file the fact away, then swing the large metal gate open and drive through. I follow the tracks through the thick woods and mentally prepare myself for seeing Johansen again. As the lane continues to wind through the trees, the solitude of the woods sinks into my bones. She's been alone out here for years. The sobering fact rolls in my gut.

I should have come before. I'd let her run away and hide, then did my own hiding. She deserved better from me.

The barely buried guilt boils to the surface.

I'm not sure how I expected her cabin to look. I'd purposely not given it any thought. I suppose if pushed, I'd imagined a ramshackle shack with crooked windows and sagging porch. The neat farmstead in the clearing surprises me. The small cabin looks homey and inviting with a wide covered porch wrapped around three sides. Smoke billows from the chimney. Snow trickles from the sky, gently landing on the roof and surrounding trees. Under different circumstances, the image would have been beautiful.

The woman anxiously pacing the porch belies the serenity of the scene.

I park close to the front steps and watch her a moment before turning off the cruiser. She's bundled into a dark purple Carhartt coat, but even through the layers, I can tell she's lost weight. She stops her pacing and stares at my car. She cocks her hips in an unconscious pose of authority, a movement I've seen her make a hundred times. Through the snow falling on my windshield, I can't see the details of her expression, but she lifts her arms in a *what are you waiting for motion.*

"Stop stalling, you coward," I mutter to myself and step out of the cruiser into the silence of the snowy forest.

"Samuels." The simple word of greeting echoes through the quiet. I feel jittery and shy and pull a stocking cap down low on my head to hide my nerves.

"Johansen." I approach the porch, put one boot on the bottom step. She stands over me, and I look up to meet her eyes. We silently take stock of each other.

The corners hold more wrinkles, but her eyes are the same sharp blue I remember. Her hair blows free in the breeze. Once short and blond and always well kept, the blond has long since grown out. Several inches of gray are tipped with her old blond, now faded. She obviously hasn't had a cut or color since she came here. The two-toned hair bothers me. The Johansen I knew wouldn't have been caught dead looking like that. She senses my scrutiny and pulls out a stocking hat from her pocket. She pulls it low over her ears and tucks the blond ends inside self-consciously.

"You look good," I lie for something to say.

"Liar." The thin line of her mouth breaks into a smile, and the woman I used to know looks back at me. "Your mustache has turned gray," she points out with a tiny nervous laugh.

76

I rub my lip and say, "Only a little." My nervous laugh escapes me. "I want to tell you how sor…."

"Stop that," she snaps before I can finish the words. "You're here now. That's what matters."

The reminder of why I've come settles on us both. I fall into professional mode. "Can you show me where she is?"

She nods solemnly then whistles one loud, sharp note. A massive gray and white husky barrels out the dog door.

I recognize the dog, and he remembers me. He wiggles against my legs, wanting attention.

"Indy, how are you, boy?" I ask the dog. "Taking good care of your mom?" Indy puts his paws on my chest, his head nearly even with mine.

Johansen tells him to get down. "I don't mind," I tell her. "Glad he's been here with you."

She pats the dog but doesn't reply, just descends the steps. "Follow me," she commands. She struts sure-footed through the clearing to an opening in the line of trees. Indy bounds along next to her.

I watch her in amazement. I'd expected her to look the way I'd expected the cabin to look, broken and run-down, a ruined shell. She's definitely battered and scarred, but the steel core of her is still there. I know I wouldn't have survived what she went through. I'd be an empty husk of a man, shattered beyond recognition.

Maribeth Johansen strides strong and sure into the woods, looks over her shoulder, and calls to me, "Hurry up, Samuels."

I scramble through the snow and obey.

Chapter 9

Maribeth

Samuels' presence marching next to me feels surreal in my woods. I keep checking out of the corner of my eye to be sure he's truly there, not a figment of my warped imagination. He's solid and real, a physical reminder of who I used to be.

The juxtaposition of my previous life walking through my current life makes my head swim with emotion. I buried the detective in me the day I buried my family. Walking with my partner to another crime scene shakes Detective Johansen awake in her grave. She claws at the dirt surrounding her, but Maribeth the recluse frantically throws handfuls of dirt back on top. I shake my head to clear the disturbing image from my tired mind.

To distract myself, I dig out my nearly empty pack of Marlboros and pull out a white stick. I fumble in my pocket, fishing for a lighter. My pockets are empty.

"Got a light?" I ask Samuels, the familiar exchange uncomfortable on my tongue. I shouldn't need him for anything, should have my lighter and a backup in another pocket. The tiny need stings my pride.

Samuels hands me the lighter and pulls out a smoke for himself without breaking pace. We walk and smoke in silence. My cut foot stings, but I carefully ignore the pain. I will not limp.

As we near the place Indy stopped me earlier, Indy's steps become agitated. I slow to a stop. Samuels looks curious.

"She's just over that rise there. You can't miss her," I tell him.

He looks down the path, his mouth set in a grim line. "You stay here," he says.

I'd had no intention of seeing the young woman again, but I pretend I'm following his directions. I sit on a fallen tree, and Indy shoves himself near my legs.

"Can you leave me the lighter?" I ask, hating myself again for being unprepared.

He hands it to me, his gloved hand brushing my glove in a tiny motion of support and friendship. "Stay with her, Indy," he tells the dog.

Samuels squares his shoulders and starts walking. I watch until he disappears over the hill, then pull Indy closer against my legs. I suddenly feel exposed and alone in the woods, even though Samuels is close enough for me to hear the involuntary "Good God," carry across the quiet snow.

I light another smoke and hang my head, knowing what he's seeing and hating I'm the one who's forcing him.

Three smokes disappear in rapid succession before Samuels appears again on the path. Two spots of red burn his cheeks, bright against the pale pallor of his skin.

We've seen bloody murder victims before, but it never gets easier. I'm secretly glad he still reacts to carnage after his years on the force. Shows he's still human under the thick skin. Proves my partner and friend still has the heart I loved in him before.

"Definitely Dana Sanders," Samuels says.

I stand and start back towards the cabin. "Who's Dana Sanders?" I ask. I don't want to know the poor girl's name but can't help myself.

"A college girl who disappeared from a parking lot a few days ago." He takes a few silent steps, then says "Shit," so loudly it makes me jump. "I'd had a bad feeling from the start of this case, but didn't think it would end like this." He motions towards the dead girl. "What the hell? The abduction and the way she was killed, and of course, the mark carved into her, all look like the work of Jesse Franklin."

"Franklin is dead," I say quietly.

"I know that!" he explodes. I don't take offense to the outburst.

My mind churns the facts against my will. "The second anniversary is coming up. Maybe some sicko fan of Franklin wants to honor him with a copycat murder."

"And torture you further by killing her here and leaving her for you to find?"

The thought that the young woman was brutally murdered for my sake makes my stomach roil. I swallow hard to keep the vomit down and for the millionth time curse the day Jesse Franklin was born.

"What are we going to do?" I ask once I get control of my belly again.

Samuels pulls off his stocking cap and runs his glove over his hair. It's noticeably thinner than when I saw his last. "Shit," he shouts again and pulls the hat back on. "Shit, shit, shit!" He stomps the snowy leaves. I let him vent his frustrations and want to stomp along with him. Detective Johansen would have. In nearly every case, we'd lose it a little at the start. Cuss and stomp and even kick something. We'd never let anyone see us, would school our faces into professional masks when needed. But privately, we'd rail against the evil in humanity together, purge it out of our systems and then focus on the job. It was one of the things that pulled us close and kept us grounded. I'm pleased to see he still does it.

Maribeth the recluse, watches but doesn't join in. I don't have the energy to get mad at humanity. I've seen the darkest man can do. I feel an emptiness so complete it scares me. Earlier, I'd been terrified, my instincts taking over my body and mind. Now I'm just hollow.

Samuels finishes his tirade then stands perfectly still. "You know I have to call this in," he says quietly.

I can't allow myself to have a feeling about that. I climb into the hollowness and wrap it around me like a blanket. "Do what you have to for the girl and her family. Just keep me out of it."

Samuels reaches for his phone. I turn my back on him and continue back to the cabin alone.

I toss a few logs into the fireplace, and Indy settles into his bed by the warmth. I need Bryson and the kids. I'll have to wait until dark to talk to them, but sunset is a long time away.

The small cabin doesn't need cleaning, and I don't have laundry to fold. My stomach rumbles, missing lunch, but I know eating is out of the question. Even at the best of times, food is more of a chore than a treat. The thought of chewing and swallowing right now makes me physically ill.

I check on the pigs and chickens even though it's far from chore time. Chica and Rizo nap in their pen, and the chickens absently pick around the barn, oblivious to the drama surrounding them. I envy their lack of interest beyond their immediate needs. The black cat I named Jingles is nowhere to be seen. I make another mental note that I should order cat food. He's been on a steady diet of leftover ramen noodles. The same menu I survive on. I owe the cat better sustenance.

With nothing that needs doing right now, I'm all loose ends and nerves. I finally decide on target practice and take my compound bow out of its case. I strap the release on my wrist with a satisfying snap. With my bow in one hand and a batch of target-point arrows in the other, I go outside.

Samuels waits by his cruiser. I wonder how long he's been standing out here in the cold. I should offer him some hot coffee or at least a few minutes by the fire.

Instead, I give him a curt nod and stride past him to my

archery range.

"I gave them your address. Is it okay if they come in on your lane?" he calls after me.

"There's an access road that's closer," I say without looking at him. "That's how he got here in the first place."

Without waiting for Samuels' response, I shove earbuds into my ears, running the wire into the neck of my coat and tucking the phone into an inside pocket. I turn the volume up as loud as it will go and let the music block out the world.

Grant had been impressed with my archery range, and looking at it through fresh eyes, I have to admit it's pretty nice. I've placed 3D targets of a variety of animals at different distances from the stand that holds my bow and extra arrows.

I carefully nock an arrow onto the string and snap my release onto the little loop behind the nock. With a smooth motion, I pull the string back and set the knuckle of my trigger finger near the corner of my mouth. I look through the peep and line up the top sight with the closest target, a raccoon on a log. I take in a breath and focus on the raccoon. Just before I let the breath out, I trigger the release, hold the bow in place as the arrow flies.

The thwack of the arrow hitting its mark follows the click of the release. I can't hear the actual sounds over the music blaring in my earbuds, but I've heard it enough times I can practically feel it inside me.

A surge of accomplishment fills me as I lower the bow. I quickly nock another arrow and sight in on the next animal in the staggered line. Click-thwack and the arrow hits the mark exactly.

In quick succession, I shoot the rest of my arrows, the intense focus soothing my nerves. I hang my bow on the stand and walk downrange to collect my arrows. Samuels' cruiser is no longer parked near the cabin. He obviously drove off to meet the local team on the access road like I said.

I shove the thought away and pull my arrows. It takes a few more rounds until the jumpiness fades. My arms begin to ache from all the shooting, but I can't bring myself to stop. The loud music starts to annoy me, and I take my earbuds out. The click-thwack continues. In the distance, I can hear the team at Dana Sanders' crime scene.

I pretend it's just the wind and continue shooting.

Chapter 10

Maribeth

My eyes dart like anxious fish to where the driveway enters my yard, looking for Nicole. She was a few hours away when I called her but should be here at any time. The sun finally sinks into sunset, and I flick my eyes at the drive again.

I pull the string again, my shoulder protesting. In the fading light, I sight in the target. The click-thwack is followed by the sound of tires behind me. I hang the bow on the stand without looking towards the driveway and walk down range to retrieve my arrows. I pull the last one as a car door slams near the cabin.

"Maribeth?" Nicole calls gently. "It's getting dark. Maybe you should pack it up for the day."

I show her the arrows in my hand, "Just pulling the last one."

I gather the other arrows and my bow and join her. I keep my eyes on the ground. Now that she's here, the control it took me round after round of shooting to acquire crumbles in a moment.

She waits at the bottom of the porch steps. Without a word, she takes the bow and arrows from my nearly frozen hands and places them on the porch. I still can't look at her, but I shatter just the same.

My sister pulls me into her arms. I sag against her, wrap around her waist, and let her hold me. The tears I'd kept away all day burn down my cheeks, my breath comes in ragged gasps. My legs give out, and she pulls me down on the steps with her. The hollow inside me floods with grief, and guilt boils over. Sobs choke and tear as I give in to the emotions. Nicole's body shakes around mine, her tears wetting my hat.

We've cried together like this once before. The night we lost our father. We'd sat on a bench outside of the hospital, clung to each other in mutual desperation. Two lonely grown children with only each other to lean on.

I hadn't allowed her to see my grief after losing my family.

That pain had been too deep to share, too consuming to express.

I cry for all the losses now.

"They all died because of me," I sputter into her shoulder.

"None of this is your fault," she sniffles.

I shake my head against her. "Why didn't he just take me? That girl was innocent, my family was innocent. He should have killed me."

Nicole does her best to soothe the consuming guilt and

sorrow. Wraps her arms so tight my face smashes into her zipper. I cling back and let the pain wrap around me like Nicole's arms and drown in the sorrow, not caring if I can swim out of the deluge.

"You can keep swimming," Bryson says behind me.

I stiffen, and Nicole feels it. Her grip on me loosens, and I gather myself up, force my arms to release her.

My throat hurts, and my nose is packed. I wipe my face on the sleeve of my coat.

"Sorry about that," I say to the ground.

"Don't apologize to me," Nicole sniffles. "I can't imagine what all this feels like. I'm just glad you're finally allowing yourself to feel it."

"It's easier to stay empty," I mutter.

"Only in the short term."

Nicole shivers on the step next to me. "You must be freezing." I change the subject noting her thin coat and lack of hat or gloves.

"It's okay," she says, her teeth chattering.

"Come inside. The fire's going." I pull myself off the steps and gather my bow and arrows. The release is still attached to my wrist, and I snap it loose. At the far end of the porch, Bryson and the kids watch us. I touch my finger to my lips in a shh motion. A silly precaution since Nicole can't see or hear them.

"Looks like a lot of activity going on out there," Nicole says, looking towards the woods. Red and blue lights flitter through the trees. The occasional raised voice floats to us across the distance. The lights slam me back to the present situation.

I turn from the lights and from my dead family and let Nicole into the cabin.

Indy raises his head from his bed by the fire, recognizes Nicole, and relaxes again. He keeps his eyes on me, watching, protecting. Nicole pats his head.

"Feels good in here," Nicole says, rubbing her hands by the fire.

The heat of the cabin stifles after my day outside in the snow. I slide my coat off, jam my hat and gloves in the pockets, and hang it on a hook by the door. Sitting on the bench, I untie my new boots and place them gently underneath.

"Those new boots?" Nicole asks.

Like a kid caught stealing candy, I freeze. "Yes," I say cautiously.

"Where did you get them? You never leave the woods, and I didn't bring them." Confusion paints her lovely features.

"I...." Bryson and the kids are now in the kitchen, and I flick a guilty glance in his direction. Why should I feel guilty about having the boots delivered?

"You had UPS deliver out here?" Nicole's voice is a mix of surprise and pride. "You let someone come? Here? That's so great!"

"I needed them, and you were at the conference all week," I apologize.

"Don't sound so guilty. It's just the UPS guy, but it's the first time you let someone on the property, it's a step. I'm proud of you."

The absurdity of her pride over such a simple act

90

makes me uncomfortable.

"Did Grant bring them?" His name on her lips startles me.

"His name was Grant," I hedge, flicking my eyes to the kitchen and my family again. The three of them are listening too intently.

"He's such a sweetheart. He delivers things to the restaurant all the time. Not too hard on the eyes, either," she adds. "Those blue eyes."

I've tried to block the memory of his eyes from my mind. My cheeks burn suddenly, and I guiltily look to Bryson. He seems to be enjoying the situation and chuckles at my discomfort.

Nicole follows my eyes into the kitchen, wondering what I'm staring at. Seeing nothing, she turns her attention back to the delivery man.

"Now that he's been here, you should have more things delivered. It would be a great way to get out there without actually getting out there, you know." She's excited and warming to the idea. "Tiny doses of conversation with a human would be just the thing."

"Nicole, I don't need to bother the UPS guy so I can talk to someone other than you."

Lilly giggles, "Do it, Mom. You could get all kinds of things, maybe some new clothes." Lilly still wears the nightgown she was murdered in. She's often lamented that if she'd known she'd be stuck wearing it forever, she would have put something different on that night. "I could help you pick them out."

Benny seems bored by the strange conversation and

goes to Indy, walking right past Nicole.

Bryson, too, seems amused. "You could use a friend," he says. A tiny part of me stings that my husband isn't bothered by the idea of a cute UPS guy coming to visit.

Nicole's still talking, "You wouldn't be bothering him. It's his job to bring you stuff. Plus, he's nice, genuine. I give you my blessing." Her smile nearly splits her face.

"You make it sound like we're getting married. I've only talked to the guy for a few minutes. This is ridiculous."

"He's single," she prods. "Lost his wife a few years ago. He has two sons. They're in middle school, I think. He even lives in Maddison." Nicole claps her hands suddenly. "This is too perfect."

I can't bring myself to look at Bryson's reaction to Nicole playing matchmaker.

"Good Lord, Nicole. You're about a thousand miles ahead of the actual situation."

"And you're a thousand miles behind. Time to catch up." She paces and plans, the way she did in high school whenever she had her eye set on someone who didn't know she existed. Back then, she usually managed to get her man.

"I'm hungry," I say to change the subject. I push past Bryson and Lilly to get to the fridge. "You want something? I could heat up some soup and make grilled cheese."

Nicole doesn't take the change of subject. "Is there anything you need? Something we could order?"

"Just drop it, Nicole. I'm not interested." I duck my

head into the fridge, pretend to dig deep, looking for sliced cheese.

"Yes you are, you just won't admit it."

I sigh heavily into the fridge and roll my eyes at the carton of milk.

Lilly breaks out in a full-bellied laugh. "She sure is persistent," Lilly says. "Just say yes so she'll leave you alone. Maybe you could order some skinny jeans, dump those ugly mom work jeans you always wear."

"Those aren't ugly, and they're comfortable," I reply.

"What aren't ugly?" Nicole asks.

Lilly really loses it now. "Whoops, sorry," she says through her giggles.

"Leave your mom alone," Bryson chides. "Maribeth, just let her do this for you. What could it hurt?"

I'm tired and hungry and sick of this conversation. "Fine," I slam the fridge shut. "I need cat food. Jingles is tired of eating ramen noodles."

Nicole opens her mouth.

"Don't ask," I interrupt and flash my eyes at her. "Do you want soup and grilled cheese or not?"

Nicole gives up her scheming and helps me make the sandwiches.

We munch our sandwiches and soup in companionable silence. Bryson and the kids are still here. I pretend they're real, pretend this is a normal family having a meal. Benny and Lilly chatter on the couch. Bryson stands by the front door, silently watching out the window.

"Two cars are pulling in," he says.

I send him a *who is it?* look.

93

"Looks like the police," he says.

Indy barks suddenly, and Nicole jumps. Lilly and Benny disappear, along with my imaginary happy family evening.

"Hush, Indy," I command the dog. He gives one last yelp, then stands next to me as I open the door before they knock.

Samuels and a large black man in a sheriff's uniform fill the doorway. "Can we come in?" Samuels asks.

I step away from the door. Indy growls.

"Give me a minute," I say to Samuels and the stranger. With shaking hands, I take Indy's collar and lead him into my bedroom and close the door.

"Detective Samuels, nice to see you again," Nicole says.

"Hey, Nicole," Samuels replies then says to me, "This is Sheriff Kingsley."

The sheriff is built like a linebacker. His broad shoulders strain the seams of his thick coat. His hand engulfs mine when he shakes it, the darkness of his warm skin a stark contrast to my pale cold fingers. "Sorry about all this," he says. The tone is kind, but he can't hide the glint in his eyes. "I have a few questions for you, Mrs. Johansen."

Nicole nervously cleans up our dinner dishes and leaves me alone with the men. The walls of the cabin seem to squeeze with all the extra bodies in it. My heart beats faster, but I manage to remain polite. "Please, have a seat. Would you like some coffee?"

"Love some," Samuels says too cheerily.

The men take off their coats, hanging them on the kitchen chairs as they sit. Nicole starts the coffee maker. Bryson watches from the far corner.

I force my feet to stay still and not run into the night. I'm suddenly too hot, and my chest hurts. There's too much energy in the room, too many people, too many thoughts. I clench my hand, my nails biting into the soft flesh of my palm. The tiny pain focuses me.

"Just sit and relax. They only want to talk to you," Bryson soothes from his corner.

I release my fist and take the chair farthest from the men.

"I understand this is hard for you, given your history and your...," Kingsley sweeps his eyes around my cabin, "Your current situation," he finishes.

"I understand the procedures. Ask whatever you need to," I say as Nicole hands us all coffee then scurries to the couch.

"I'm familiar with the Jesse Franklin case and what brought you out here," he says carefully. "Detective Samuels has filled me in on some of what happened this morning."

I sip my coffee and wait for him to get to the point. I know where he's going, but I won't help him get there.

"I'm also aware of the similarities of the current victim to the ones from before," he takes a sip of his own coffee, and I see the tiny tremble of his large hand. As the sheriff in a town like Maddison, I doubt he's ever seen something as gory as what he found on my path. He may be hugely muscled, but he's just a man. I take pity on him.

"You're wondering why she was killed here. Why in my woods of all places with my connection to the previous murders. You wonder how this new killer knew I'd find her way out there. You're wondering if you have a new serial killer at work in your precious small town. Most of all, you're wondering if I did this." I hold his dark brown gaze and dare him to deny it. He looks down at his coffee for a quick moment, then back to me.

"I am wondering all those things," he concedes.

Nicole shouts from the couch, "Maribeth is a victim here, too. She didn't do any of it!" I appreciate her quick defense.

"He's just doing his job, Nicole," I tell her quietly.

"We don't actually think you have anything to do with it. We know you didn't kill that girl," Samuels says.

Kingsley holds my eyes, searches my face for guilt. I'm filled to the brim with guilt, but not for Dana Sanders' murder.

He finally looks away and takes out a notebook and pen, impossibly small in his massive hand. "Just tell me about earlier when you found her."

I re-tell my discovery, putting in as much detail as possible that might help the investigation. I don't have many details. "Mostly, I was just scared," I finish my story.

"Why didn't you call 9-1-1 right away? Why did you call Detective Samuels first and wait for him to call us?"

I'd expected this question, but I'm not sure I can make him understand. "Sheriff Kingsley, you know what happened to my family, right?"

He nods.

"Then you might understand how witnessing something like that, surviving, when everyone you love dies in front of you, might destroy a person."

Everyone in the room shifts uncomfortably, even Bryson. "It nearly did destroy me. I came here to my woods to escape the pain, to protect myself from the world. I've done pretty well the last two years. I've managed to build an island away from everyone, away from memories. Now, imagine finding Dana Sanders this morning. She looks like my daughter, and she has the same mark carved into her that I have on my own chest. Imagine knowing that the man who destroyed you is back. Imagine the very thing you are hiding from, are protecting yourself from, walks up to you and slaps you in the face. What would you do? Would you immediately call in a bunch more strangers to trample over your safe place?"

"I have no idea what I'd do. Run, maybe," Kingsley says.

"I tried to run. I drove all the way to the end of my lane, but I couldn't leave. I can't leave these woods. I physically can't." Behind me, Nicole sniffles. Samuels stares at his coffee. My face is dry, my chin is high. "So I called my sister, the one person I trust. Then I called Samuels, someone I once trusted. I could have left Dana Sanders there. I could have gotten rid of her body and made this all go away. I did as much as I'm capable of to help her and her family."

"We know you're doing the best you can," Samuels says. "We also know you had nothing to do with Dana

Sanders' abduction and murder." Samuels looks pointedly at Kingsley, who grudgingly nods.

I'm exhausted and ready for them to leave. "Thank you. I wish you all the luck in your investigation, Sheriff. Search my property if you need to, I give you full permission. I would never kill anyone." My words are strong and sure.

A voice deep in my soul says, *liar*.

Chapter 11

Maribeth

My speech to Sheriff Kingsley used more words than I usually say in a whole week. Combined with my earlier sob fest all over Nicole, my throat aches. I sip my coffee to soothe it and wish desperately everyone would leave.

"If there's nothing else you need, Sheriff, I think my sister needs to rest now," Nicole comes to my rescue.

Kingsley pushes his considerable mass away from the table and gathers his coat. "Of course." He pulls it on quickly, eager to get away from me after my impassioned words. "I may need to come back if I have more questions, but I think we're done here tonight."

Samuels pulls his coat on too, but slowly, reluctant to leave me alone. "You shouldn't stay here by yourself," he says.

"I'm not leaving. I thought I already explained that I can't." Desperation makes my voice squeak.

Both officers look at me expectantly as adrenaline pumps through my legs, and I picture myself running into the woods and hiding in one of my tree stands until they leave.

A rap on the door keeps me pinned to my chair. Kingsley takes charge of the situation and lets his deputy into the already crowded cabin.

The dark brown sheriff's department coat flaps against his stick-thin thighs, and his beady eyes dart around the room. Indy barks suddenly from behind my closed bedroom door, scratches at the wood to get out.

"Quiet, Indy!" My harsh command startles everyone. Indy settles down, but whines behind the door, unhappy.

"We're all wrapped up out there," the deputy says, stomping snow off his boots onto my clean floor.

"Thanks, Dallmeyer. We're almost done here too." Kinsley makes introductions. "This is Maribeth Johansen, the woman who found our victim."

"I know who she is," Deputy Dallmeyer mutters rudely, pointedly avoiding looking my way and rubbing his sparse mustache. "Hey, Nicole." he suddenly brightens at the sight of my sister. "What in the world are you doing here?"

"Maribeth is my sister," she says pointedly, not pleased.

Surprise makes Dallmeyer rub his thin mustache again. "I didn't know you had a sister," he says lamely.

"Now you do. Remember it," she warns. I smother a smile. As the older sister, Nicole's always taken the protector role personally.

"Yes, ma'am." Dallmeyer works the edge of his knit hat in his hands. "Is there anything else you need, Sheriff?"

"We were just discussing the safety of Mrs. Johansen staying here on her property," Kinsley narrows his eyes just a fraction to remind Deputy Dallmeyer of his duty. "Since you can't leave, we can put a car out front. Keep an eye on things for you."

The idea of a stranger parked in front of my cabin makes my legs itch to run again. "No, I can't do that," I protest. "I can lock the gate. I usually don't, but it has a keypad."

"A police presence is a good idea, Johansen," Samuels says. "He could sit down the drive where you won't even know he's there."

Panic flutters, but I know Samuels won't give in. "If the car parks at the gate, I suppose that would be okay." My aching throat makes the words creak out.

"We'll still lock the gate," Nicole pipes in. "We can change the code and only give it to the police. Or whoever you want," she adds, and I know she's thinking about the deliveries she forced me into agreeing to.

"That settles it," Kinsley says. "Dallmeyer, you'll take the first shift tonight. Park your cruiser by the gate and keep an eye on things. I'll assign another car to the access road where our perp got in. That should keep you safe."

Two cars parked nearby sounds like overkill, but I agree. Dallmeyer seems less pleased than me. I don't have much confidence he would protect me if needed. Probably just sleep through his late-night shift.

"That's settled." Nicole takes charge, leading the men to the door. "Thank you, gentlemen. It was nice to see you again, Detective Samuels." Nicole's charm is impeccable, but her intentions are clear. The three officers shuffle out the door.

Samuels hesitates on the porch, takes his time pulling his knit hat low on his head. "It really was nice to see you again, Johansen," he says. "I'll keep you up to date on the investigation if you want. Kingsley and I are working it from both ends since she was abducted in my jurisdiction but killed here."

The buried Detective Johansen claws a single hand out of her grave. Maribeth the recluse, allows it this time. "I'd like that," I say to my old partner. "Good night."

I shut the door before I can change my mind and let the recluse win.

"Do you want me to stay with you?" Nicole asks.

I let Indy out of my room, and Bryson waits quietly in the corner. "I have all the protection I need right here. You go home to Ella."

Nicole nods and takes her jacket off the peg by the door.

"Sorry I couldn't visit Ella, check on her. You know I would if I were able."

"I know that now. I shouldn't have pushed you. I just…." Nicole busies herself with buttoning her coat. "This single parent thing is harder than I thought it would be. I need help sometimes. With Mom in Phoenix, I can't rely on her for anything. But you do what you need to get better. Don't worry about Ella and me."

Nicole kisses my cheek and leaves before I can form a response. "I'm a horrible sister," I say to Bryson once I'm alone.

"No, you're not. You just need more time."

"To get better? Is that what I'm doing? Why won't everyone understand this is as good as it will ever get for me? There is no getting better."

I turn my sad gaze to my dead husband. He waited by my side all night, listened patiently.

Now that I can finally talk to him, the corner where he watched over me is empty.

I go through the ritual of evening chores. Chica's belly is swollen, her teats fuller than yesterday. "Not much longer," I tell the pig and pat her on the head. She only grunts and begs for her dinner.

I search the corners of the barn for Jingles, the cat, but he's still nowhere to be found.

Even though it's still early, I tuck myself into bed. I call out for Bryson and the kids, but they don't appear. Feeling betrayed, I curl my body around Indy's furry bulk and lay my head near enough to his back to hear his heartbeat in the darkness.

The two cop cars parked nearby don't offer much comfort. At one time, I would have considered the men my fellow partners in blue, even though their uniforms are county brown. I'd even feel an affiliation with the rude Dallmeyer. Tonight their presence means nothing, and the thought is sobering.

For the first time since coming to the woods, I feel the

need to pray. I don't have the words, not even sure God will hear them from me. I speak the Lord's Prayer into Indy's fur and repeat the words until sleep takes me.

Sleep is not the blissful release I need. Nightmares of blood and slicing swirl through my tired mind as I surface to consciousness, only to wake into the horror that is my current life. I roll over and curl into a tight ball, slip back into slicing terror once again. Dana Sanders' torn and lifeless body flashes alongside memories of the similarly torn bodies of Franklin's other victims. I gasp awake yet again, the scar on my chest stinging. I rub the raised mark and wish desperately that Bryson could be curled next to me. I [pretend he wraps his arms around me, pulls my back to his chest, and soothes the boogeyman away the way he had countless times in our marriage.

Without Bryson, I settle for Indy and reach for his solid bulk.

Indy's not in the bed.

He scratches at my closed bedroom door and releases a sharp yelp.

His distress pushes the sleepy thoughts away, bolting me upright.

"Indy stop that," I whisper, not sure who I'm keeping quiet for. He puts his front paws on the door and barks again.

I slide from the bed and cross the two steps to the door, the wood floor cold on my bare feet.

Indy growls at the door and my blood tingles. Firelight from the living room glows through the gaps between the door and the frame casting a soft glow on the dog's bared teeth.

He growls again, anxious to be released from the room. I put my ear to the crack and listen. Something clatters in the cabin, a small sound like a dish moving on the counter. Indy hits the door with his front feet, his weight shaking the frame.

Trapped in my bedroom, I have no weapon except the dog. I grapple across the dresser, searching for anything heavy. The large glass ashtray that belonged to my dad holds odds and ends, worthless items in a battle. The ashtray is heavy enough to work as a weapon, but the thought of shattering the memento of my father makes me pass it by. An empty coffee mug sits on the corner of the dresser, where I left it before going to bed. I wrap my fingers through the handle and test its weight. It will have to do.

No further sound comes from the other room, but I trust Indy's instincts. Taking his collar and pulling him away from the door, I turn the handle. The moment Indy sees an opening, he barrels out, nearly knocking me over.

A flurry of barking and crashing fills the small space of the cabin, and I bolt out myself, the coffee mug held high to attack the intruder.

Indy scrambles across the wood floor, nails clicking. He's on the hunt, but there's no one there. At least not a person.

He shoves his head under the couch, knocking cushions askew in his excitement. A black blur darts into the kitchen. Indy follows, running under the kitchen table. Chairs fly in all directions, and the table skids across the floor.

The blur pounces onto the counter. Indy jumps but doesn't make it. He bounces off the cabinet doors. The blur jumps to the top of the fridge out of his reach. Indy regains his feet and scratches the fridge, anxious to get to the cat.

With the coffee mug still held over my head, I flip on the kitchen light. Jingles blinks from his perch on the fridge, his twitching tail teasing the dog.

Laughter bubbles out of me in a high nervous flow of tension.

My laughter calms Indy enough to return his four feet to the floor, but he eyes the cat wearily, a low growl in his throat.

"Jingles, what are you doing in here?" I giggle. "Hungry, I suppose."

Jingles meows once in response. Indy growls again, annoyed at yet another intruder in our cabin tonight.

I drag the reluctant dog back to my bedroom and shut him in again. I tell him he's a good dog and scratch behind his ears, but he seems unimpressed.

If I try to pick up the wild cat, I'll only get scratched, so I take the leftover soup from earlier out of the fridge and wave it under Jingles' nose to get him to follow me. Sensing the dog is no longer a threat, he gingerly jumps down off the fridge and follows me through the doors into the barn. I give him the soup and watch as he wolfs it down.

"If you're going to hang around, I'd better order you some actual food," I tell him. He makes a low sound in his throat, a cross between a purr and a growl.

With my arms wrapped around me for warmth and walking on the sides of my bare feet to minimize contact with the cold concrete, I do a quick check on the other animals. The metal roof begins to ting.

I look towards the roof in surprise. "It's raining," I tell the cat.

Jingles only cares about the soup, not the change in the weather.

Chapter 12

Grant

After two straight days of rain, the sudden break in the clouds and streaks of sunshine nearly burns my eyes. I enjoy the change in weather. The relentless drone of rain pounding on the metal roof of my box truck was starting to get to me. I turn off the wipers and go through the bulkhead doors to find the next package for delivery. I shuffle through the boxes and find the correct one. My loader jammed it behind a larger box, and I have to pull hard to release it. The larger box slides off the shelf and hits the floor, crumpling the cardboard corner.

"Crap!" I turn the box over to examine the damage. The solid weight of pet food slides inside the box, and I breathe a sigh of relief. It's hard to hurt pet food, so I won't have to fill out a damage report. I place the larger box back on the shelf to deliver later, then notice the name on the label.

Maribeth Johansen.

A tingle races across my shoulders. The woman with sharp blue eyes has often floated through my mind since I met her a few days ago. Something about the bruised vulnerability of her expression mixed with the strength of a woman who lives alone intrigues me.

The sheriff's cruiser parked at the end of her driveway caught my attention two days ago. I've made it a point to watch the news, even set the DVR to record the morning and afternoon airings. I know all about Maribeth finding the murdered girl. I hurt for the woman who's already suffered so much.

I'd wanted to stop and check on her but couldn't come up with a good reason.

The perfect reason just fell on my floor.

I make a mental calculation of how many stops before hers and make my deliveries a little quicker than usual. Anticipation builds as her stop grows closer. The unfamiliar feeling flows uncomfortably in my blood. When her gate looms ahead, I find myself stretching to shake the adrenaline out of my muscles.

A cruiser guards the closed gate, and my truck barely fits in the space between it and the road. A deputy climbs out of the car and stands at the bottom of my steps. I recognize the man from Maddison, deliveries to his house are a regular part of my route. Deputy Paxton's wife runs a small jewelry company from their home. The number of times I stop there, her business must be booming.

"Hey, Grant," Paxton says up to me, shading his eyes from the over-bright sun. "What you doing out here? I didn't think the Johansen lady got deliveries."

His private information about Maribeth's delivery preferences unduly annoys me. "Guess she does today."

"What'd she order?" Paxton asks. I wonder if it's a piece of information he needs for the investigation or if he's just nosey. I'd put money on nosey.

"A brown box," I say cryptically. It might seem silly, but I never talk about what I deliver. "Is the gate locked?" I change the subject.

"Sure is. You wanna leave the box here, and I can run it up before I leave after my shift?"

After my morning of looking forward to seeing Maribeth again, I don't want to drive away.

"I'd rather go up to the house. Signature required on this one," I lie.

"Suit yourself. The lane's a muddy mess after all this rain, hope you don't get stuck."

"I'll take my chances."

Paxton enters a code on the gate, pushes it open, and lets me through with a wave.

The deputy wasn't kidding about the mud. I slip up the lane, careful to stay on the center of the thin gravel. Without their blanket of white, the woods look dull and dismal. Water drops onto my windshield from the cloying branches, and I turn the wipers on again. They squeak out a depressing rhythm.

The clearing and cabin glow with sunlight sparkling off wet surfaces. A thin curl of smoke rises from the chimney, adding a homey touch to the scene. I park on the highest part of the gravel, careful to keep the truck from sliding into the mud.

I turn off the truck and the quiet envelops the clearing. The splash of water dripping off the porch mixes with the droplets splashing off the nearby tree onto my truck in gentle music. I scan the area for Maribeth, disappointment fizzing in my belly when I don't see her.

Her husky isn't around either.

I gather her box with the crushed corner and carry it to the porch. The wooden steps creak under my boots. I place the box on a rocking chair near the front door, noticing there's only one chair.

The chair rocks lonely with the weight of the box.

"Hello?" I call into the quiet. "Maribeth?"

A dog barks from a short distance in the woods, and then she appears through the trees.

Indy reaches me first, full of friendly wags and rubs against my legs, nothing like the first time we met. I busy myself with scratching the dog to hide the confusing surge of excitement at seeing the woman.

She raises her hand in greeting as she emerges from the trees. I walk across the wet grass, feel a stupid grin on my face. She wears the same dark purple Carhartt coat. Her ponytail is pulled through the opening of a Denver Broncos cap.

The blue eyes I remember are as startling as before. The bruised look a little more prominent. Instinctively, I want to take that look away.

"Denver Broncos?" I fake indignation and disgust, hoping to tease a smile onto her face.

She touches the cap on her head and thankfully goes along with me. "Don't you bash my Broncos," she teases

112

back. A tiny smile slips onto her lips, so I push a little more.

"You do know you're in Colts country, right?" The corners of her mouth lift a little more.

"This," she waves her hand around her property, "Is Broncos country." Full smile now. "You be careful what you say."

A deep satisfaction fills me at the tiny joy I've brought her. "Why the Broncos?" I ask, suddenly curious for real.

"I like their uniforms," she says simply. I'd expected her to say she was from Denver or some other logical reason. She laughs at my surprised expression. The sound sparkles through the air.

"Good a reason as any." I don't know what else to say. Small talk comes easily for me most of the time, but her presence unsettles pleasantly. She doesn't seem to know what to say either.

I'm conscious of my electronic board, calculating exactly how long I've been at this stop. Drivers are kept on a strict schedule, and each stop has only so much time allotted, meticulously tracked down to the second. I know seconds are adding up, but I don't want to leave yet.

The menagerie of archery targets stands like a frozen zoo on the far side of the clearing. "Been shooting lately?" I ask.

A flicker of pain crosses her face, "I shot for a long time the other day."

The shift in her body language tells me exactly which day she means.

"Good way to block everything out when you need to.

Just you and the target and room for nothing else in your mind," I say quietly, hoping she understands.

She'd been toeing the wet leaves, uncomfortable. Now she flips her wide eyes to me. "Exactly," she breathes. "My sister thinks I'm nuts."

I bristle at "nuts" but quickly forgive her. "Maybe you should teach her to shoot. Then she'd get it."

The smallest smile crinkles the corners of her mouth, "I'd like to see that. Nicole isn't much of the outdoor type."

"You sure are. This place is amazing, and you do it all by yourself." The corners of her eyes crinkle along with her mouth. A burst of pride tingles through me. This woman doesn't have much to smile about, and I've brought two smiles to her face today.

"You're sweet." Not a touch of flirting, just a touch of surprise.

"I try to be." My neck flushes at her small praise, and I rub it nervously. On my truck, the board keeps ticking. Reluctantly, I walk back, and she falls naturally into step with me. Out of the corner of my eye, I catch glimpses of her long legs.

"I left your package on the rocker." I don't know what else to say to prolong my visit.

"Oh, good, the cat food."

"You have a cat? What does the dog think of that?" From what I've seen, the huge husky isn't the type to share.

"It's a stray cat, really. And Indy is not a fan." She surprises me with a chuckle. "Jingles came in through the

114

dog door the other night looking for food. Indy nearly trashed the cabin chasing after him."

Hearing his name, Indy raises his head from where he lays on the porch. "Good watchdog, huh?"

A cloud flickers across her features at some painful memory. "He'd do anything to protect me."

"I'm glad you have him, especially now." I don't want to bring up the recent murder, but it seems rude to just ignore it happened.

"Between him and the two cars parked on my property, I'm all set." She doesn't sound all set, she sounds sad and pissed.

I want to offer some form of support, some protection of my own.

She senses it and stops me. "Please don't ask me if I'm going to be okay, or tell me I should leave the woods. I've heard enough of that from my sister. I'll be fine."

She cocks her hips, and I have no doubt she can handle whatever she needs to. "You've got your bow, right?" I tease, hoping for just one more smile out of her.

Her body relaxes, "That I do." Only one corner of her mouth lifts this time, but I call it a victory just the same.

The board keeps ticking. "I've got to keep moving," I say reluctantly, taking slow steps to the truck.

Her feet follow me.

"It was nice seeing you again," I venture as I climb into the driver's seat.

She leans against the door frame, looks up the steps at me. "It was nice."

I feel nervous and awkward and turn the key to cover

it. I can only look at her blue eyes, no words come to mind.

She leans away from the door jamb, takes a step away. "Until next time," I say like an idiot and shut the door.

"Smooth," I mutter sarcastically to myself as I put the truck into gear. Frustrated, I push the gas too hard. My tires throw mud, and the truck slides sideways. "Shit!" I shout in the cabin. I gun the gas, but sink deeper into the soggy ground. I take the electronic board that tracks me and key in the code for a break. I'm not going anywhere at the moment.

Maribeth's laughter bubbles across the clearing as I step out of the truck. She covers her mouth, but the silver notes keep coming.

"Looks like I'm stuck." I survey the damage. My tires have sunk half-way to the rims.

"Little bit," she giggles.

"It's not that funny." My voice is light and easy. Secretly, I'm glad I have a reason to stay. "I'll have to call this in, get another truck to take my packages, then a wrecker to pull me out." Suddenly, the situation loses its humor. "It'll go down as a chargeable accident. Crap, I've got eleven years safe driving in."

She sobers instantly. "Sorry, I shouldn't have laughed," she offers.

"I laughed too." I stare at the stuck truck and feel sick.

"Why would it go down as an accident? You didn't do anything wrong. Not your fault I don't have much gravel."

"Doesn't matter. We're supposed to be more careful

116

than that. Plan for anything." I keep staring at the tires like they'll miraculously float out of the mud on their own.

"Don't call it in. Wait here." Without another word, she strides around the corner of the cabin.

In a few moments, the sound of an engine fills the clearing. An orange Kubota tractor lumbers around the corner of her barn. I stare at Maribeth in the driver's seat, totally in control of the machine. This woman is full of surprises.

She lines the tractor up in front of my truck, climbs down, and takes chains out of the bucket. I hurry to help her chain the truck to the tractor. "You're brilliant," I tell her.

"Let's see if this works before you say that."

She drives the tractor, and I drive the truck. It takes a few pulls and a little rocking, but the mud releases, and the truck drives forward.

I stop on a patch of clear gravel. Maribeth unchains the tractor and pulls it out of the way, then once again leans against my door jamb.

"Now you can call me brilliant," she smiles up. A full smile filled with pride and something else.

"Thank you," I say and come down a step, close enough to touch her. "You have mud on your cheek." I reach a finger to the brown smear, gently wipe it away. I half-expect her to pull back, but she leans involuntarily into my touch. A shiver runs down my arm and into my belly at the touch of her soft skin.

The moment stretches deliciously as her blue eyes

dazzle and my finger lingers on her skin. "Do you mind if I order some more things?" she asks breathlessly.

"I'd love to see you." My voice is low. I drop my hand.

"I can give you the code to the gate." I have codes to other gates and even garages for customers. The code to access this property means more than the simple digits.

"I'd like that." My body wants to step closer to her, but I don't want to spoil the moment.

The moment passes anyway. Maribeth steps back from my door. "You'd better get moving before you sink into the mud again."

I pull my mind back to my job and climb into my seat. This time the truck moves forward when I push the gas. I watch her grow smaller in my side-view mirror with eyes unable to draw away, my fingertip tingling with the memory of her skin.

Chapter 13

Maribeth

The intimacy of Grant's finger on my bare skin still sizzles after he leaves. Hugs from Nicole have been my only physical contact for a long time. Nicole's hugs don't fill me with this odd mixture of excitement, fear, and a cloying sense of longing. I scrub my cheek with my glove until the confusing tingle is only a memory, then busy myself with putting the tractor away in the barn.

After two days of solid rain, I'm anxious to get outside. The walk I took earlier helped offset the jitters, but I need a project to work on. A full stock of firewood fills the lean-to. I cleaned out the barn pens yesterday, a job I could do while staying dry. No stray leaves need to be swept off of the porch. No weeds need to be pulled in the empty garden. I could go for another walk or do my daily run early, but neither option holds any appeal.

The clearing surrounding my cabin drips, and gnarled branches creak overhead. The sun glints on puddles, but does little to dispel the gloomy view from my porch.

I shove the box Grant brought me off my rocker and sink into the seat. Lighting a Marlboro, I stare listlessly at the ruts cut into the drive from Grant's truck. They look like open sores in the ground, mud oozing out like blood. Making a mental note that I'll need to get more gravel this spring, I look away from the reminder of the man's presence.

My cheek tingles again in memory. Frustrated, I jam the heel of my hand against my skin. "There's nothing down that road, kid," I say out loud.

A deep sorrow sinks into me. I feel heavy and listless, my earlier need for an active project vanished. I light another smoke and lean back in the rocker. Fingers of cold creep up my jacket, but I ignore them and rock.

I will my mind into blankness, a skill I've perfected. It refuses the relief now, determined to travel down the one path I don't want to think about.

Dana Sanders butchered on my property.

On our walk this morning, Indy and I checked the place where the killer left the girl. The rain has washed all traces of brutality away. Even the footprints of the forensics team are gone, replaced with wet leaves like the rest of the woods. Without the memory of the dead girl burned into my brain, I could believe it never happened.

But it did happen. Someone murdered Dana to get to me.

A shudder clamors through me, leaving me shaking in my rocker. "Why kill an innocent young woman? Just come for me if I'm your target." I ask the empty clearing.

A squirrel on a branch chatters angrily, annoyed by my

120

sudden outburst. "Do you know who killed her?" I ask the squirrel. "Did you see him?"

The squirrel jumps to another branch and moves onto a quieter part of the woods.

The long-dormant part of my mind stretches awake and looks at the clues against my will. Dana was killed the same way as the seven other women. The same way my family was slaughtered. The same way he tried to kill me.

I wriggle my fingers under my scarf and along the line of raised skin that crosses my throat.

"Jesse Franklin is dead," I repeat like a mantra. "You know he's dead. He didn't do this."

Deep in the recesses of my mind, a small box opens, and the thought I've avoided thinking scurries out. I struggle to control it, to keep it buried. It crawls like a spider. Slithers into the light, insistent on being heard.

Eyewitnesses linked him to the abductions of four of the victims, which was enough to bring him in, but not enough to hold him. Franklin had solid alibis for the murders of the other young women.

Videos of him were obtained from other places the nights of each crime.

He'd sat across from me in the interrogation room, sure we had nothing on him. We didn't have enough. He'd been cleared, released.

Then he broke into my home.

It didn't add up.

Pondering it now changes nothing. My family is still dead. Franklin is still dead.

But now Dana Sanders is dead, too.

"What does it mean?" I shout into the clearing so loudly it makes Indy jump. Not even a squirrel has an answer.

Frustrated, I rock violently, the chair runners grinding into the wood of the porch. I've deftly avoided this line of questions for two years. With a valiant effort of will, I grab the spider in my mind and shove it back into the box. I slam the box closed, bury it once again, and force my mind into the blank state I've perfected.

This time my mind obeys.

The rocker slows, and I light another smoke. I toss butt into the metal can beside me, then fish another out of my pack. I don't light it. The tip of my nose stings, and my rear feels chilled against the wood of the rocker. I replace the cigarette and stomp into the cabin for warmth.

I pull off my Broncos hat and toss it on the kitchen table where I can see it as I add wood to the fireplace. The memory of Grant's words about the hat makes the loneliness of the cabin a little less oppressive.

I don't understand the emptiness that's followed me the last few days. The solace of the cabin that has carried me through countless afternoons now suffocates. I still have a few hours until dark when Bryson and the kids can visit. I hold onto thoughts of sundown and search for something to eat. At least that empty feeling I can do something about.

The fridge is as empty as I feel, and I shut the door again. I check the deep freeze on the enclosed porch between the cabin and the barn. Digging out a frozen pizza, I note the dwindling supply of venison on hand. The meat should carry me through until next season, but I'd feel better with another deer in there.

"You just want to go hunting again," I tell myself.

"Who cares? I can do what I want," I answer.

While the pizza cooks, I wash my hands and face in the tiny bathroom. A flash of this morning's visit from Grant tingles through me. I'm way out of practice with people and especially with men, but I can tell he likes me.

"What in the world does he see in you?" I ask the mini mirror, squinting at my reflection. I take out the ponytail and run my fingers through the limp locks. The inches of salt and pepper, grown in since I came to the woods, contrast with the blonde from my last visit to the beauty salon years ago. The two entirely different colors represent the two parts of my history, a dividing line of before and after.

Neither the gray of age or the blonde of hope are who I am.

Before I can lose my nerve, I dig a pair of scissors out of the drawer. I pull a lock of two-toned hair away from my face and cut it a few inches from the scalp.

I drop the loose hairs into the trash can by the toilet and cut another hunk away.

Indy pads into the bathroom to see what I'm doing. He cocks his head at me in question.

"Don't ask," I tell him and snip another handful of

123

hair.

Stray hairs drift around the bathroom, a large pile of them in the trash. I make a few more snips to shape my bangs and around my ears, the way I watched my stylist do it numerous times. She'd expertly shape my short hair into a feminine style that complimented my face structure. My attempt lacks the finesse of hers, but it's serviceable.

The few inches of hair left have a little volume to them, the general shape of the cut flatters my face. From what I can see in the small mirror, I like what I've done.

"What do you think, Indy?" I call to the dog. "Short and sassy, or just short?"

Turning my head side to side to see better, I'm pleased with the results. "This gray looks like crap, though," I mutter.

I need some groceries anyway, so I call Nicole and ask her to bring me a few things. She's surprised by my request for a bottle of medium brown hair dye from the drug store in addition to milk and bread.

"You want to dye your hair? That's wonderful. I'll be right over." Her voice bubbles with uncharacteristic excitement.

While I wait, I munch on the over-cooked pizza and imagine her surprise when she sees my hair cut. I rarely make Nicole smile, but I'm certain she'll smile today.

Nicole's reaction doesn't disappoint.

"You cut your hair!" she exclaims in greeting. I hurry to help her with the grocery bags before she drops them, a wide grin on my face.

"Does it look bad?" I ask.

124

"It looks great. A little uneven, but we can fix that." She takes me by the shoulders and turns me around so she can get a good look. "Why?" she asks in amazement. "Never mind, the why doesn't matter."

"I just wanted a change, I guess." The simple words make her eyes water. My grin fades. I've done this to her, made any simple act of self-care worthy of tears. We both busy ourselves with putting the groceries away to hide our emotions.

"I brought you some of that caramel corn you love." Nicole pulls a familiar blue box from one of the bags.

"Thank you," I respond, my words loaded.

"I know you like it."

"No, thank you for this." I spread my arms wide to encompass my entire universe. "For the food, for the supplies, for your visits."

She stops, the blue box half-way in the cabinet where she was putting it away.

She doesn't turn around, "You've never said that before." She puts the box in the cabinet and shuts the door gently.

"I should have said it every day."

"What's gotten into you today?" she asks. "You're different."

"I'm not that different." I pull cans of soup from a grocery bag to keep my hands busy. "I'm just thankful for you. Is that a crime?"

She turns away from the counter and searches my face, looking for a clue to my earnestness. "It's not a crime, just unexpected."

Nervous from her scrutiny, I run a hand through my shorn hair.

"That gray's got to go," she says suddenly, breaking the tension. "You look old."

"Well, you're older," I quip. "Always will be."

"Don't remind me. Now, where's the color I brought you?"

An hour later, Nicole snips a few stray hairs, now a pretty brown. "I think we're done." She stands back and survey's her work. "You want to see it?"

The bathroom mirror, the only mirror I own, reflects a stranger. The shape of the nose and the color of the eyes is the same, but the overall effect of the cut and color has transformed me. I look younger, more vibrant. Even the shadows haunting my eyes have faded some. For the first time in years, looking at myself doesn't fill me with revulsion at my very existence.

"Well done," I tell Nicole. "I don't look like myself at all."

"Nope, you don't. And that's the point of a make-over, isn't it?" Nicole checks the time on her phone. I don't have a clock in the cabin. Tracking time never seems to matter. "I'd better get back to the restaurant before the dinner rush."

Not for the first time, I realize how very different our lives are. She's constantly surrounded by people. Ella, employees, customers, friends. Nicole's life is full of people and places to be, things that need to be done.

Just the thought of all that emotional energy makes me dizzy.

"I see a new box by the trash," she says slyly. "Did a handsome delivery guy possibly bring it?"

"You are so nosy," I tease. "Yes, Grant brought it this morning." My cheeks suddenly feel warm.

Nicole pointedly looks at the box then at my hair. "Makes sense now."

"Don't go there," I warn. "He just brought the box. It's his job. Then he got stuck in the mud, and I pulled him out with the tractor."

"Tractor? How romantic," she teases.

"It wasn't romantic." I realize I'm touching the place on my cheek where Grant wiped the mud away. I drop my hand quickly.

"It could be if you let it." Nicole gives me a quick, half-hug then hurries out the door.

I wait for dark by lying on the couch and watching silly comedies on TV. The canned laughter and ridiculous situations carry me away from the cabin, offering a glimpse of what life could be without serial killers and bloody dead girls. I envy the characters, they don't have armed guards on their property keeping the bad guys away.

Shadows fill the cabin followed by my family.

Lilly squeals as soon as she sees me. "OMG, your hair! I love it."

I run my hand over the short brown tresses. "You do?"

"You look pretty, Mom," Benny says quietly. "Different, but pretty."

I look to Bryson for his reaction, "Beautiful." He

127

reaches to touch me, remembers he can't. "It was time for a change."

I glow under the acceptance. "I missed you," I say. "The days are growing longer now. I hate it."

"We're here now," Lilly says and flops down on the couch near me. "We should do something fun tonight."

In life, Lilly had reached the age where hanging out with her family was the last thing she wanted to do. We're her only option now.

"Like play a game?" Benny asks hopefully.

"Maybe. What do you want to play?" I ask.

"Minecraft," he says quickly.

Lilly shoots that down just as quickly. "That's a computer game. You can't do that."

"Mom could play, and I could watch," he pouts.

"I don't have a computer here," I point out gently. "I don't have any games, actually." I look to Bryson for help. He shrugs, out of ideas.

It feels like old times, us trying to entertain the kids and keep them from squabbling. "Remember that trip to Lake Michigan?" Bryson asks suddenly. "Where it rained for three days, and we were stuck inside in our rental cabin?"

I catch onto the story, "And the kids fought the whole time?" I smile at the memory.

"That trip sucked," Lilly adds. "You made us play Monopoly and Scrabble, ugh."

"I like Monopoly. Do you have that?" Benny asks.

"Sorry, Benny Buddy, I don't."

"We danced that last night," Bryson continues. "Acted

128

like idiots."

"I won the dance contest, and you lost," Benny says to Lilly.

"Bet I can beat you tonight," Lilly joins in.

Using my phone, I play music for us. The kids take turns trying to outdo each other. Bryson and I even join in, acting especially silly to make the kids laugh. Even Indy gets into the fun, and I dance with his paws in my hands. The dance contest is called a four-way tie. When Benny protests, we give him the award for most creative moves. The same way he won the last time.

Without too much effort, I can imagine we're back in that rental cabin on Lake Michigan. My family is really here with me. We're really laughing and talking and enjoying ourselves.

Without too much effort, I can imagine we are all still alive. Not four ghosts, with me just as dead as they are.

A slow song Bryson and I love starts to play. Our eyes meet, and the laughter stops. A delicious tension burns between us as he comes to me across the floor. We sway to the music, our bodies so close we almost touch, almost. I yearn to put my arms around his neck, to feel his hands on my hips. I need to press my cheek to his chest, to hear his heartbeat. I need the solid heat of his body against mine.

We sway near each other, cold air between us.

"I miss you," I say so only he can hear me. "I don't know how much longer I can do this without you."

"You'll never be without me," he whispers back. "Even when I'm truly gone, I'll always be with you."

A shot of fear stabs my core. "What do you mean truly gone?"

He skirts the question. "You can't go on like this forever, Maribeth. You can't stay in this limbo for the rest of your life."

"My life ended when yours did," I say miserably.

"Did it?"

I pull away from him as if he'd slapped me. "How can you ask me that?"

"God spared you for a reason. At some point, you will have to face the truth and do what He needs you to do."

I step farther away from my husband. "I don't want to," I plead, panicked. "I want to stay here with you and the kids.".

"Wherever you go, we'll be with you." He takes a step to follow my retreat, the kids suddenly next to him.

"I want you here, in this place, with me." My voice breaks, and the fun of the evening fades like it never happened.

"We are all here, Mom," Lilly says. "Even when you don't see us."

"I don't understand," I cry.

"You will," Bryson says gently. "Not tonight, but you're getting there."

I reach my arms to my family, desperate to touch them one more time.

The music on my phone is suddenly replaced with the general ringtone of a stranger.

My eyes flit to the phone then back to my family.

They've disappeared.

Only Indy keeps me company.

"Come back!" I scream into the emptiness. "It's still dark, you can stay!"

The phone continues ringing in response to my screams.

I stab a finger at the screen to answer, "What?" I bark.

"Mrs. Johansen, this is Sheriff Kingsley. We've got Dana Sanders' killer in custody," the deep voice says. He fills me in on the basic details, then quickly ends the call.

I want to shout in excitement, to share the news with someone. Indy is sound asleep, and I don't wake him. "They found him," I whisper to the fire. The crackling of the flames fills the room. I imagine the sparks are miniature fireworks of celebration.

Chapter 14

Sheriff Kingsley

Cold water splashes on my pants and dribbles into my boot. The rain has finally stopped, but puddles of icy water lay in wait all across the parking lot of the Sheriff's station. My pant leg is the first casualty of the puddles' vendetta.

A large sedan fills a visitor's parking spot. Two Pomeranians jump at the closed window, yapping furiously as I walk by. Even with the sun shining, it's still cold. I hope Mrs. Pickler's dogs don't freeze to death in the car. It's not their fault their owner is a piece of work. At least she didn't bring them into the station the way she did yesterday.

Mrs. Pickler waits on the bench inside and pounces before I can shut the door behind me.

"Did you catch him yet?" she demands.

"Good morning, Mrs. Pickler," I say through gritted teeth. Most residents of Maddison are friendly and easy-going, content to live their small-town lives, and leave me to do my job. The murder of Dana Sanders has understandably upset the town. Mrs. Pickler has appointed herself as the town's representative, though I doubt many residents agree with her opinions.

"Sheriff, I demand you tell me what you've found out," she pouts.

I take a sip of my to-go coffee before responding. "I'm sure you do."

She huffs. "That woman lives practically next door to me," she whines. "She's a menace to the safety of this town."

"You told me that yesterday," I say and keep walking to my office.

The tenacious woman follows. "Nothing like this ever happened here before she came. She should be in jail. Either she killed that poor girl, or she knows who did and won't say. Why are you protecting her?" Venom drips from her words. The lack of sympathy and quick judgment of the human race should surprise me. The depths of evil in man stopped surprising me long ago, but this unfounded hate bothers me.

"Mrs. Johansen has done nothing to warrant being in jail. She's a victim in this situation." I place the coffee cup on the desk to keep myself from throwing it at the woman.

"Victim?" she huffs. "She's a lunatic. A psychotic. And you're wasting resources on protecting her. I've seen the cars parked at her gate."

"Mrs. Pickler," I warn. "She's a member of this town and deserves our protection."

She huffs again. "I don't have a car guarding my house."

"When a killer decides to leave a dead woman on your property, then you can have a car," I say sarcastically.

Her face flushes a bright red. "I'll be back tomorrow to see if you've managed to accomplish anything," she says and turns with another huff. "There's an election next year. Don't forget that, Sheriff Kingsley."

"How could I forget? You keep reminding me." I mutter to myself after she leaves.

I busy myself with the reports from last night's shift. Luckily, there's not much to go through, just a disorderly call at the local pub and a domestic at an address I, unfortunately, recognize from a similar call last week. A knock on my open door draws my attention from the reports.

"Sheriff?" Deputy Dallmeyer nervously rubs his thin mustache. I understand he's only been with me for a few months, but his continual unease grates nerves.

"Yes?" I turn my full attention on the thin man. He lingers in the doorway, looks down the hall.

"Can I come in?"

Good Lord, just get to it already. I motion him in.

"What can I do for you?" I make my voice friendly to put him at ease, something my other deputies don't require.

"I had a thought on the Sanders case," he starts.

135

He has my full attention now. "I'm all ears."

"As you may or may not know, there are groups on the internet for just about anything."

I nod, wondering where he's going with this.

"There are even groups where people can discuss crimes that have affected them personally." He gauges my reaction.

I nod again to keep him talking.

"Crimes like the Franklin murders." He looks away, and I realize the cause of his hesitation. Kelly Klondike was the second victim of Jesse Franklin. The woman was also Dallmeyer's cousin. Her murder five years ago was the impetus to Dallmeyer going to academy and becoming a police officer.

I choose my words carefully. "Have you seen something on the group that might help with this case?"

Dallmeyer's shoulders drop some of their tension. "There's been a lot of buzz about the Sanders case, due to the connection with the Johansen woman and Franklin's victims," he hedges.

"I imagine," I'm losing patience with his stalling. "Is there something, in particular, you are trying to tell me, Deputy?"

"Most of the posts are pretty vile, how Johansen deserved what she got because she let Franklin go on killing so long." He rubs his mustache again and hurries on. "Standard sicko stuff, you know."

"Unfortunately, I do know."

"This one guy, he goes by Broncoboy84, he used to be pretty vocal about his hatred of Johansen and her partner.

A few posts started hinting at how smart Franklin was and how he should have killed Johansen when he had the chance. He got a lot of flak for that one, so he stopped those kinds of comments." He swallows, then goes on. "In a recent post, he mentioned Sanders being marked. 'she was marked by this devil,' were his exact words."

I sit back slowly in my chair, the hinges creaking under my weight. "We didn't release that the killer marked her."

"Exactly. Maybe it doesn't mean anything, but...." Dallmeyer looks towards the open door, then leans closer across the desk. "I know who Broncoboy84 is. We kinda met a few months back." His eyes slide to the side, "He lives in Maddison."

My entire body tingles, but I school my face to remain calm. "Who is he?"

"Freddy Munson. He lives out in the trailer park north of town. He has a record, mostly disorderly stuff and an old DUI. His ex-wife took out a protective order against him last year after he showed up at her new place and threatened her."

I fight the excitement racing through me. This is the first decent lead we've gotten in this case, but I don't want to jump to conclusions. Anonymous posts and threatening your ex are one thing. Slicing a young woman's throat is another.

Dallmeyer seems unsettled by my calm. "Do you want to go pick him up?"

"On what? We've got nothing to bring him in on."

Dallmeyer's eyes light up like a magician revealing his final trick, "He has a bench warrant from a missed court

137

date."

"Grab your coat."

We found Freddy Munson at home. When he opened the door and saw Dallmeyer and me, he made a half-hearted move to run. "Don't even try it," I growled. He came into the station without further fight.

The man sits across from me in the interrogation room, his arms crossed, resting atop his ample gut. Greasy hair hangs to the collar of his flannel shirt, the top of his head glistens with sweat, easily visible through his bald patch.

"Why am I here?" His tone an equal mix of indignation and fear. "I didn't do anything."

"We picked you up for your warrant," I explain again. "But we'd like to ask you a few questions while we have you. I'm just waiting on my deputy."

Munson shrugs, pretending nonchalance his body language belies.

Dallmeyer enters the room, and Munson goes stiff. His eyes dart from the deputy to me, wide and panicky.

"Why's he here?" Munson asks. "Bad enough he hauled me in."

I look to my deputy, curious about Munson's reaction to him. Dallmeyer just shrugs.

I ignore Munson's question. "Let's get started, shall we?" I switch on the tape recorder on the small table. A video camera in the corner by the ceiling is already running, but I like to have a backup. I remind Munson that he isn't under arrest and is just being questioned at this time.

After a few warm-up questions, to get him talking, I get to the real reason he's here. "Do you know who Maribeth Johansen is?"

Munson pales at the sudden change of subject. His eyes flicker to Dallmeyer, then to the tabletop. "I know who she is."

"How about Dana Sanders? Do you know who she is?"

Munson's head jerks up from its contemplation of the table. "I didn't kill her," he blurts out.

"I only asked if you knew who she was."

"I'm not stupid. You're looking for someone to pin her murder on. I didn't do it."

"Calm down, Mr. Munson. We're just talking here," I say easily.

"Are you familiar with Broncoboy84?" Dallmeyer asks.

"You know I am," Munson replies, meeting the deputy's eyes.

"The same Broncoboy84 who recently posted about the mark carved into Dana Sanders," Dallmeyer continues.

"I never said that."

"It's right here." Dallmeyer slides a print out of the screen from the group discussion. "That is your post, right?"

Munson nods. "That's my post, but I didn't know that girl had a mark carved on her. Do you mean a mark like Franklin's other victims?"

"Don't play dumb, Munson," I say.

Dallmeyer slides another paper across the table. "Are

these posts from you, too?"

Munson reads the page, and his face drains of color. "I was drunk when I posted that. Of course, I don't think Franklin was brilliant or that the detective should have been killed." His eyes plead with me to understand. "I was just talking tough, you know. Running my mouth."

"Sure, I get it. Easy to say whatever you want in a group like that. Hiding behind a keyboard and making threatening statements."

"I never threatened anyone," Munson exclaims.

"Except your ex-wife," Dallmeyer points out.

"That was different. Really, you've got me all wrong. I didn't do anything."

"Your neighbors say you were out of town the days Dana Sanders was missing. Where were you?" I ask.

"In Fort Wayne," Munson says lamely.

"Doing what?"

He looks at the floor, "I'd rather not say."

"Kidnapping Dana Sanders and keeping her somewhere, by chance?" Dallmeyer asks.

"Of course not," Munson looks around the room for inspiration. "I went to see this girl I know. But we got in a fight, and she wouldn't let me stay at her place."

"Go on," I prompt.

"I got real messed up that night and slept in my truck. The next night I met some new people, and we kept drinking and partying, you know."

"Sounds fun," Dallmeyer says sarcastically. "So you got high and drunk for a few days. That's your alibi?"

"That's what I did," Munson says. "I don't need an

alibi, I didn't go near that girl or the detective."

"These 'friends' you made, can any of them vouch for you?" Dallmeyer asks, leaning across the table.

"They're not that kind of friends," Munson says miserably.

"Uh-huh." Dallmeyer says, leaning back in his chair.

"You got fired from your job at the sandwich shop a few weeks ago, didn't you?" I ask, changing tactics.

"Yeah, so?"

"You were a dishwasher at Subs and Such, right?" I push. "Showed up drunk to work for the third time, and were let go?"

"Getting fired isn't a crime," Munson protests.

"You do realize that Maribeth Johansen is Nicole Rogers, your ex-boss's, sister?"

Munson makes the connection. "I didn't know that," he says quietly.

"Sure, you didn't," I say. "Let me put this together for you. You go online, spouting off about how Franklin was great and should have killed Johansen. In a group meant for surviving family and friends of the victims, I might add. That's horrible right there. You publicly wish harm to Johansen. Then you get fired by her sister. So you snap. Your life sucks, so why not make yourself famous. You find yourself a young woman that looks like Johansen's murdered daughter, and you kill her just like Franklin would do. You mark the Gemini sign on her chest and slit her throat and leave her for Johansen to find. Does all this sound about right?" My voice is a quiet storm.

Munson slumps in his chair and refuses to answer.

141

"Maybe you thought you could frame her for the murder somehow? Was that the plan?" I push.

Still no answer.

"Even if we didn't think she was guilty, even if you got caught, you'd still win, wouldn't you?" I go on.

"I don't understand," Munson finally says.

"You're the copycat of the famous Jesse Franklin. Your name will be all over the news, in the papers. Heck, they might even start a group discussing you. You'd like that, wouldn't you? To be famous. Sure beats being a low life drunk who can't keep a wife or a job as a dishwasher."

"I don't want to be famous," Munson whispers, unconvincingly.

"Oh, but you're famous now," I hiss. "Frederick Munson, you are under arrest for the kidnap and murder of Dana Sanders."

<u>Chapter 15</u>

Maribeth

The day feels brighter and lighter knowing the man who would kill an innocent girl just to torture me sits in a jail cell. With the threat locked up, sheriff cars no longer guard my driveway. The lack of strangers on my property fills me with a sense of hope and freedom.

I didn't ask for details from Sheriff Kingsley about the man in custody. A small part of me wants to rush down to the station, face the man and demand answers. The larger part of me wants to forget about this newest installment of the horror movie my life has become.

I fill my morning with cutting back the overhanging branches that shroud the lane to the cabin. Since I rarely use the driveway, I hadn't realized how overgrown it had become. Frankly, I didn't care. My wild flight down the lane in my SUV left a scratch down one side of the truck.

I pretend that's the reason I'm cutting branches.

Nicole's car easily fits below them, but a large box

truck would struggle.

The powerful vibration of the chainsaw in my hands fills me with a sense of control. The sweet sound of the machine sings through the trees. The physical labor clears the spider webs from my mind and the jitters from my body.

Working my way towards the gate, I form piles of branches to burn later. As I cut the final limb near the gate and drag it to a pile, I'm surprised to feel a smile on my face. I place the chainsaw carefully in the bed of the Gator and take a sip from the water bottle I keep there.

My eyes keep sliding to the gate.

It calls to me.

And look at the gate.

I empty the water bottle and wipe a dribble off my chin.

I toss the empty bottle into the Gator, and my feet take me to the metal bars. I run a gloved hand along the steel, pick at a chip of peeling paint. I stare through the gaps to the road beyond.

The hours of wielding the chainsaw have filled me with unfamiliar courage.

I punch the new code into the lockbox.

Tentatively, I push against the gate. It swings away with the slightest metallic squeal. The lane stretches only a couple yards to the open road.

I step through the gate and wait. My pulse quickens, but nothing terrible happens.

I take another step towards the road. A flutter fills my

belly, and I wish I'd brought Indy with me this morning.

"Do it," I tell myself out loud.

I break into a sprint and cover the few feet to the road. With eyes squeezed nearly closed, I turn right and run.

My feet pound the hard pavement. My blood pounds in my ears.

I run with abandon as fast as my legs can take me. The edge of my woods is on my right, but soon I've passed my property line. Open fields stretch on both sides of the road. The lack of surrounding trees and the immensity of the sky finally overcome my burst of courage.

I stop at the road's edge, stand in the tall grass. I spin slowly, taking in the vast expanse of land and air. I feel exposed and raw and exhilarated. I twirl under the vast openness until my head spins.

Raising my arms wide, I tip my head back in thanks and open myself to the beauty of the moment. I soak in the victory, as small as it is.

A car zooms past, intruding on my private moment. I drop my arms. The buffet of air blows against my body, then the car continues on its way.

I suddenly feel ridiculous. My woods are clearly visible just a short way down the road. I haven't really gone anywhere. The driver of that car has a destination far from here, can arrive there without a thought or care. The farmhouses in the distance hold families going about their lives without the open sky threatening to crush them.

My earlier exhilaration plummets to dread. The beauty of the open fields now feels menacing and oppressive. The blue of the sky smothers.

Desperate to return to the trees, I sprint back to the gate.

It snaps closed with a satisfying clank that echoes through the still woods.

I double-check the lock, then climb into the Gator and drive up my newly cleared lane. Even with the low branches removed, the surrounding trees comfort like a familiar blanket.

The late afternoon breeze sways the tall branches reaching above my head and flutters the leaves twenty feet below my tree stand. I shift uncomfortably on the narrow seat, careful not to move too quickly. Dressed head to toe in camo and with a sheet of camo draped around the frame of my stand, I should be well hidden. But deer have keen sight, and a sudden movement might scare away my prey.

I lean against the tree trunk. A knot in the wood pushes uncomfortably into my back. I shift again to find a better position and make a mental note to move my stand later.

The serenity of the woods lulls my tired mind. Memories of previous hunts with my family bubble to the surface.

"You sure she's not too young?" I'd asked one morning several years ago.

"She wants to go," Bryson had responded. "Don't you, Lilly?"

Lilly's blue eyes, so like mine, peeked out from under the blaze orange hat that nearly swallowed her head. "You said I could go," she pleaded. "I'm all dressed and everything." She raised her arms wide to show off her new camo outfit, also like mine. "I look like a hunter, don't I?"

"You look perfect," Bryson told her.

"You'll have to sit very still and be quiet," I pointed out gently. Regardless of my concerns, I wanted Lilly to come with us, wanted to share the beauty of the woods with my daughter.

"I can be quiet, I promise." I couldn't deny her, and we'd set off into the woods behind our house.

True to her word, Lilly kept her lips pressed together, and didn't wiggle between Bryson and me in a two-man stand. The morning slipped from darkness to a blaze of pink and orange. Her tiny body next to mine filled me with wonder. High in a tree with my family, enjoying the sunrise was a precious moment captured from the chaos that was our lives. The baby in my belly kicked, Lilly snuggled close against me, Bryson snuggled her other side.

Perfection. Pure perfection.

"Look, Mom." Lilly's mouth was so close to my ear, I felt the heat of her breath. She didn't raise her arm, just pointed with her chin at a doe stepping carefully over a nearby hill. The sunrise blazed, her body a dark silhouette against the glory. The deer stopped, sniffed the ground. "She's so pretty," Lilly whispered in awe.

Bryson moved to raise his gun.

"Don't," I whispered. Bryson lowered the gun, drawn into the spell.

The three of us watched the doe until she wandered

away back down the far side of hill.

"Wow," Lilly said, her young voice full of awe.

Bryson looked at her, then met my eyes. "Wow," he echoed and slipped his arm behind our shoulders, pulling us even closer in the tight space.

I had been complete that morning. Full to the brim with love and acceptance. One precious moment in time of absolute perfection.

Perfection like that can't last, can only be remembered.

This afternoon, open air reaches around me, stretches to the ground far below. I feel exposed, alone in this stand.

My toes tingle with cold. The heavy socks I wear inside my boots made my feet sweat on the trek out. The sweat chills me now. I wiggle my toes to warm them.

A crack of a broken branch draws my attention away from my damp feet. Off to the left, something moves in the woods.

I peer through the bare trees, watching for movement, listening for another crinkling step.

A few moments later, I see the buck. He takes expert steps through the brush, nearly silent. His brown fur blends into the brush and high grasses. Only the whites of his inner ears and the dark black spot of his nose visible from my vantage point.

With bated breath, I wait for him to get closer. My hand grips the bow resting on my knees, an arrow already nocked and waiting. The four points of the broad-head tip glimmer in the fading light.

The deer takes a few tentative steps in my direction,

his nose testing the air. I focus my attention on him, willing him to come my way. I'm good with a bow, but he's still out of range.

I hear Bryson in my mind, "Patience, Maribeth. Don't spook him. Let him come to you."

I follow the memory of his advice and wait with twitching fingers. The deer takes a few more steps, skirts the range of my bow.

Wait. Just wait.

The deer turns away from me. Adrenaline pumps through my muscles, and the urge to raise my bow and take the shot pounds through me.

No yet.

The deer looks over his shoulder at something far in the distance. He sniffs the air again, his body tense with indecision.

This way, come this way.

Behind me, a squirrel scampers up a branch. Both the deer and I ignore the sound.

He lowers his head again and takes several steps in my direction.

That's it. Keep coming.

With my bow still on my lap and hidden behind the camo drape, I silently click my release onto the string, place my hands correctly to draw. The deer steps behind a stand of trees and disappears for a few tense moments.

My blood sings with adrenaline, and my fingers shake as I wait for him to reappear.

His black nose and white ears peak out of the stand of trees. His broad side follows.

He's in range and walking closer. He pauses and looks over his shoulder again, into the woods. His ears move, rotate to focus on the sound behind him, oblivious to my presence in the tree.

Painfully slowly, I raise my bow. I line my sight just behind his shoulder. I pull back on the string, position myself for a smooth shot.

Suddenly, he kicks and bolts straight towards my tree. A blur of brown fills my sights. I adjust my aim as quickly as possible as the range grows shorter.

He closes in, panicked. I don't have a good shot, he's coming at me too fast.

Don't take it.

I click the release.

The thwack follows.

The deer kicks in surprise, then barrels under my tree. I watch helplessly as he crashes past. The bright pink fletching of my arrow bounces along with him, hanging from low in his belly.

Gut shot. Shit.

I stifle a scream of frustration, shoving my gloved hand against my mouth to keep quiet. My whole body shakes with excitement and disappointment.

He could run for miles, far from my property, far from where I can find him. If I can't find him, he might die an agonizing death.

The thought makes me sick, every hunter's fear. "You shouldn't have taken the shot. Shit," I mumble. "You know better than to take a bad shot." I shove my head hard against the tree trunk, push my feet against the

150

grated floor of the stand. Shame washes over me.

For once, I'm glad Bryson isn't with me. He taught me better.

Chapter 16

Maribeth

I wait in the gathering dusk, hoping the deer will go down. Hoping I can find him in the dark. I can't chase after him yet. He'll most likely lay down once the initial rush of adrenaline wears off. With luck, he'll bleed out then. If he hears me, he'll run again.

The longer I wait, the better.

The sun drops behind the trees with barely a glimmer of color. No spectacular art show tonight peeking through the gaps, just the inescapable slide into darkness.

The shame fades along with the sun. Replaced by resolve.

The seat next to me fills with Bryson's presence. "It happens to all of us, Maribeth," he soothes.

"I know," I whisper miserably. "But, I knew better than to take the shot."

"Everyone does things they know better than to do. It's part of being human."

"Being human sucks," I whine.

"Beats the alternative." He raises his hands, referring to his present form. A different kind of shame fills me, and I sit forward and hold my head in my hands.

"I'm so sorry, Bryson." My voice barely audible. "I never thought he'd come for you and the kids."

"He made his choice. You had nothing to do with it."

I shove my hands hard on either side of my face, to hold back the words, years unspoken. "It was completely my fault. He was after me." My nose runs from the cold, drips onto my boots in grotesque splatters.

"Is that why you're here?" Words both gentle and angry.

I sniffle and nod miserably.

"Punishing yourself won't bring us back."

"But it keeps you close."

"Does it?" In life, Bryson's constant support was often mixed with hard questions. He'd made me look at things differently, made me stretch my understanding. In life, I'd enjoyed the challenge of his questions, welcomed his perspective.

Now, his challenge rankles. I don't want to stretch, I don't want to understand. I don't deserve to know.

"You're here with me now," I point out. "This is better than nothing."

Even Bryson's analytical mind can't argue.

Or so I thought. "But it's not better than what you could have."

I don't want to hear it. I wipe my running nose with my gloved hand, remove my release from my wrist. "I have a deer to track." I change the subject abruptly.

I expect Bryson to protest, or at least to offer to help.

The seat next to me is empty.

"You always disappear when I need you," I mutter miserably. "Don't worry, I can find him by myself." I say to the dark.

Since I'd had a clear view of where the deer crashed into the woods, his blood trail is easy to spot. Using the flashlight on my phone, I follow the drops of blood. Stopping at each new drop, I fan out until I find the next. Occasionally, I lose the trail and have to backtrack.

Often, I stop and listen, ears straining for the distinctive sound of a struggling animal. Mostly I hear coyotes howling in the distance and the low hum of traffic even farther away.

Slowly, methodically, I follow the trail. Sometimes I follow fresh hoof prints in the mud or overturned leaves. A few times, I find a large amount of blood and disturbed leaves. These are the places the deer laid down. Coming across his third resting place, I get nervous. It's rare for a deer to keep getting up. I waited a long time until I started tracking him, I'm not the thing he's running from.

My neck begins to tingle with the feeling of someone watching me.

I pull my eyes from the bloody ground and scan the

155

woods. I'd been so focused on the trail, I hadn't paid proper attention to my location. With 300 acres surrounding my cabin, there are plenty of places to get lost in the dark. I do a quick check of the moon, and mentally retrace the direction I went from my stand. I'm near the far northeast corner, by my calculations. A few hundred yards more, and I'll reach my property line.

A low shuffle of leaves catches my attention, and I hurry in the direction of the sound.

The deer lays half-hidden in a pile of bloody leaves. He tries to jump and run as I approach, struggles to get his legs under him again.

He only manages a half crawl in his exhaustion. A sickening wave of shame pours over me. No hunter wants his prey to suffer.

This deer is suffering.

I know what needs to be done and move quickly before I lose my nerve. My knife flashes in the moonlight as I grab his head and expose his throat.

He tries to kick, to escape, but I hang on to his fur.

"I'm so sorry," I choke and slice as deeply as I can. The sharp blade cuts clean, and the remaining life of the deer spurts onto the ground.

Only moments pass until he lies still, at peace. My mouth waters, and my belly threatens to heave. I don't allow myself the release of vomiting. I deserve the nausea. Taking that shot was impulsive and reckless, and the deer paid the price. Another brick of guilt adds to the already tall wall.

I kneel next to the deer and say the prayer of thanks

Bryson taught me. "Thank you for your sacrifice. You have died so I may eat. I am truly grateful."

The prayer feels inadequate this time.

The distant coyotes yap again, closer this time. I feel exposed and vulnerable. The cabin is far behind me, my bow waits at the tree stand. My field dressing knife and the bent arrow protruding from the deer's belly are my only weapons.

I'm alone surrounded by fresh blood.

I set to work gutting the deer. The tingle of being watched urges me to hurry. I make a clean slice from his throat to his belly, careful not to hit the gut sac and spill his digestive contents and its foul smell. The internal organs slide out of the slit, steaming against the cold night air. I reach inside and pull and cut until the carcass is empty.

My task accomplished, I sit back on my heels to catch my breath. There's surprisingly little blood. When done correctly, the organs come out intact and attached to each other. I eye them with interest, curious. A few I recognize easily, the others are mysterious packages. I touch an organ with the tip of my knife, wonder if it's the spleen or pancreas or what.

"Should have paid more attention in biology," I mutter out loud.

A branch cracks several yards behind me.

I freeze and listen, my knife gripped in my hand. The following silence screams with menace. An animal wouldn't try to be quiet, would continue walking, shuffling through leaves.

"Hello?" I call, my voice loud.

No response.

My scalp tingles and my fingers ache from gripping the knife so tightly.

"Stop being paranoid," I chastise. I think of Benny and his irrational fear of the dark. Maybe he's not so irrational after all.

I grab the deer by his front legs and drag him towards the path. Even field dressed, he's heavy. Panting and huffing, I struggle through patches of thick brush, brambles catching my coat. I have to stop several times to disentangle.

The undeniable feeling of being watched follows my slow progress. The singing of the coyotes has grown closer. Adrenaline and fear push me faster as I drag the deer clumsily.

A patch of downed tree trunks blocks my progress. I stand on one of the logs, pull him by his front feet. He snags on a hidden branch, and I can't lift him over the log. I set my feet and adjust my grip. Then pull with all the strength I can muster.

The snag lets loose suddenly, and I lose my balance. I fall backward off the log, the deer falling with me. He lands sticky and wet, his open chest on top of my heaving one. The deer's head lies next to mine, rests on my shoulder in an embrace.

The smell of his fur, of his blood, of his insides chokes my nose. His weight crushes me into the ground.

I squeal in fear, scramble, and push away from his body. My boot catches in the open cavern of his belly, hooks on his pelvis. I push hard, flexing my thigh. He slides away. I crab crawl away from him, then pant on the ground until my ears stop ringing.

Above my head, two branches scrape against each other, playing an eerie song to the night.

To my right, another branch cracks, the step of some large animal, or worse.

I spring to my feet and run in the direction of the cabin. This deer is too heavy to drag home alone.

I tell myself I'm running to get the Gator, not running from fear. I find the path and just run.

I crash into the barn, throwing the sliding door sideways with more force than necessary. The pigs jump from their sleep and grunt their indignation at being startled.

"Sorry, kids," I tell them. "Momma's in a hurry."

I jump into the Gator and back it out of the barn at reckless speed. The headlights fill the path, and I feel better for their light. It only takes a minute or two to find where I left the deer. I jump out of the Gator before it comes to a complete stop.

I scan the woods for lurking shadows, shady figures. "Stop being ridiculous," I tell myself. "It's only in your head."

It takes several attempts to get the deer loaded into the back of the Gator, but I manage to get him into the bed.

Loading the heavy deer into the Gator leaves me gasping and leaning against the machine. I suck in deep breaths until my heart slows.

The branches still creak against each other above my

head, but the oppressing feeling of strange eyes on me is gone. "Silly girl," I mutter and climb into the Gator. I resist the urge to look over my shoulder to analyze every shadow as I drive home. I have enough shadows to deal with, I don't need to imagine new ones.

Chapter 17

Grant

All Saturdays should dawn bright and sunny. The oppressive gray sky this morning feels like an insult to weekends. I'd hoped to take Charlie and Kyle to the batting cages today, but there's a bite in the air, sharper than the last few days. I sip my coffee and scan the sky beyond my kitchen window. Maybe it will shape up to be a decent day later, but the morning looms sadly over me.

If other weekends are any indication, the boys will sleep until nearly noon. At fourteen and twelve, they've reached the age where sleep comes easily and abundantly.

I haven't slept well for years. The bed feels too big, too empty, too cold. Waking does nothing to dispel the emptiness. During the week, I can keep busy at work, keep my mind away from thoughts of Sarah Jane.

This morning, thoughts of my dead wife feel too close. The kitchen cloys without her presence. The picture of her and the boys taped to the fridge usually comforts. Her smile is bright and genuine. That was one of her good days, fleeting times near the end where the darkness hid. I'd fooled myself into believing the darkness was actually gone.

Was it always there? Did she hide it from me, protect me from the gruesome reality that would soon consume her? Even in this picture, did she know the darkness would win?

I stroke her photographed face. "Why did you leave us?" I ask for the thousandth time.

The photograph doesn't have the answers. The doctors tried to explain, but they didn't have answers either.

Sarah Jane had battled, but in the end, she lost to herself.

Like a fool, I'd thought my love for her could pull her out of the suicidal spiral. I'd thought I could save her.

The claws of darkness had sunk so deep none of us could remove them.

Not even Sarah Jane.

"Get busy," I say out loud, pulling my eyes from her picture. I rinse out my coffee cup and put it in the dishwasher. I wipe down the counter until not a crumb or minuscule stain remains.

The cleanliness mocks, highlighting the empty hours until the boys wake up and fill the house again.

I can't sit in this empty kitchen.

I jot a note to Charlie and Kyle that I'm going to pick up donuts. I scan the sky as I climb into my pick up. Maybe the weather will be better this afternoon. A day outside at the batting cages could still happen. I hold onto that hope, as tiny as it is.

Downtown Maddison isn't exactly bustling, but there are a few cars parked in front of Subs and Such. The sandwich shop serves breakfast sandwiches and donuts on the weekends. Small towns like Maddison struggle to survive, and the restaurant needs to milk every dollar it can to stay alive. The Mexican restaurant down the block does a pretty good business in the evenings. The Ramble Inn tavern across the street will fill up after dark. This early in the morning, Subs and Such beckons between a realty office and an antiques and gift shop. The realty office is closed at the moment, and the antique store hasn't changed its front window display since I was here two weeks ago. I never understand the compulsion for people to open antique shops in floundering small towns. The rent is cheap, I'm sure, but I doubt many in Maddison care about antiques. The few that do drive to the antique mall out on the interstate. I admire the owners' enthusiasm but doubt the feasibility of their endeavor.

Subs and Such has managed to mix the brick walls and battered floor with metal counters and exposed ductwork into a thoroughly pleasing space. Booths line one wall, each mismatched one sourced from different failed establishments. Even the chairs and tables clustered near the middle don't match each other. A massive chalkboard behind the counter painstakingly spells out the menu.

One empty booth and two empty tables invite me to sit and enjoy myself for a while. I pass the open tables and take the only vacant seat at the counter.

I know the owner, Nicole, from my frequent deliveries.

She approaches now with a genuine smile. A few strands of blond hair have escaped her messy bun and frame her blue eyes. The shade of blue triggers a glimmer of memory I can't place.

"Good morning, Grant," Nicole says cheerily. "No boys today?"

"They're still sleeping."

"Lucky kids. Ella probably won't roll out of bed for a few hours, either. Those were the days, weren't they?"

Her purposefully over-wistful question makes me smile, just as she intended.

"Coffee, two sugars, two creams, please," I order.

She turns to get my coffee, and I take the moment to scan the room. A family I know from Charlie's baseball team fills the corner booth. The husband lifts his chin in greeting.

I nod back.

I recognize a few others from my delivery route. One draw-back of working in the town I live in is I get to know a lot of the people. Sometimes it's a curse. In my current mood, the room full of half-acquaintances comforts.

Nicole returns with my coffee, and I take a tentative sip. As with most things in this place, it's perfect. "That's good," I tell her.

"Hope so. Just coffee today?"

"For now. I'll probably get some donuts for the boys when I leave."

"You're a good man, Grant. How about one now to start you off with?"

I can't resist. Nicole places a plain glazed on a small plate. My favorite, even though she didn't ask.

I munch my donut in silence, letting the various conversations of the room flow, snippets catching my attention, then fading away like smoke. The energy from all the people soothes my unsettled mood from earlier. The day suddenly doesn't feel so unbearable.

A blast of cold air blows through the front door as Deputy Dallmeyer enters the restaurant. Even off duty and out of uniform, he manages to exude an air of overblown self-importance.

Dallmeyer leans between the man sitting on the next stool and me. "Nicole, coffee, please," he calls into the kitchen. He said please, but his attitude doesn't match his words. Nicole gives him a strained smile. "Hey, Buckley, what's shaking?" Dallmeyer says to the man in the next stool.

"Heard you got the son of a gun who killed that girl in custody?" Dallmeyer's companion says. My ears perk up. I'd heard the news, but I'm curious for more information.

"Sure did. I figured it out, too," Dallmeyer boasts.

"So no more late-night guard duty?" Buckley chuckles.

Dallmeyer waits until Nicole sets his coffee on the counter and walks back out of earshot. He leans closer to his companion, his thin hips jutting into my side. "Three nights I wasted on that crazy bitch when I could have been at the Ramble Inn." The words are low, meant for his friend's ears only.

I stiffen. He didn't say her name, but I know exactly who he means.

"What a psycho," his friend replies so quietly even I can barely hear. "Living out there alone like that."

Pretending to reach for a packet of sugar on the counter, I push my arm against Dallmeyer harder than necessary.

He turns in surprise at the passive-aggressive shove. "You got a problem?" he snaps, no longer trying to be quiet.

"Just with men who call traumatized women crazy bitches and psychos." My voice is firm and steady. I won't give him the satisfaction of showing my anger.

Dallmeyer's face reddens at being overheard. "Maybe you shouldn't be eavesdropping on conversations that are none of your business."

"Maybe," I concede. "But Maribeth is my business." I take a slow sip of coffee and sit the cup back down on the counter. The donut sits heavy in my gut and blood pounds in my ears, but I'm pleased to see my hand isn't shaking.

The other conversations in the room dwindle as the customers are drawn to our interaction.

Dallmeyer takes a step away from the counter, so he's no longer shoved against my leg. "How's that? You sleeping with her?" The companion asks, leaning his wide head into the space.

Nicole tries to intervene. "Buckley, don't start anything. No one's sleeping with my sister." She emphasizes the word sister, clearly stating her side in this skirmish.

My eyes flash to the blond. I had no idea Nicole was Maribeth's sister. Now the familiar blue of her eyes

166

makes sense. The rest of the room doesn't seem surprised. I must be the only one in town that knows almost nothing about Maribeth.

Buckley and Dallmeyer scan the room of staring faces. The man I know in the back booth stands up and takes a few steps towards us. Gives me an *I got your back* look.

"Deputy Dallmeyer," Nicole emphasized the word deputy, "Would you two like to-go cups for your coffees?" She flashes him a brilliant, if hard, smile.

Dallmeyer turns on his friend, "Don't start trouble, Buckley, or I'll have to haul you in for disorderly." Dallmeyer pulls a few bills out of his wallet and tosses them on the counter. Rubbing his thin mustache, he looks at me, obviously wanting me to make a move so he can fight back.

"Have a nice day," I say sweetly, my smile every bit as hard as Nicole's.

After the men leave, the room erupts into hushed twitters as each table discusses the almost-altercation. The man from the back booth pats my shoulder and returns to his family. I can't even remember his name. I didn't know Nicole was Maribeth's sister. I really need to pay more attention to the people around me, get more involved with my town.

"Dallmeyer's a prick," Nicole says so only I can hear. "You should have seen how he treated Maribeth the night of the murder."

My mind spins. My few encounters with Maribeth almost feel like a dream. It's strange to sit here talking to her sister.

"He's got little man syndrome," I say. She raises her eyebrows in question. "You know, when little skinny guys like that act tough to make themselves feel bigger?"

"Men are weird." She shakes her head and laughs. The tension leaves my body at the sound.

"I didn't know you were Maribeth's sister. I delivered out there a few times recently." I test the waters.

"She's making progress. Normally I take her everything she needs." She considers me, then goes on. "You're the first person besides me that's been allowed onto her property since…." She doesn't need to finish the sentence. "Well, until all the police the other day."

"She looked pretty good to me. I think your sister can take care of herself."

"Do you?" Loaded question.

"I mean it as a compliment." I think about the way she pulled my truck out of the mud with easy confidence. "She runs that whole place alone. She seems pretty tough."

Nicole chooses her words carefully. "Maribeth is like a raw egg. Her shell seems hard, able to withstand anything. But crack it, and she's a gooey mess inside."

I take another sip of coffee, "Aren't we all like that?"

She laughs out loud. "Fair point. I suppose we all can crack."

I reach for my wallet and change the subject. "Can I get a dozen plain glazed to go?"

"Of course." I drain the last of my coffee as Nicole boxes up the donuts. She comes back with one large box and one smaller one.

"Sometimes I take Maribeth donuts if there are any left at the end of the day on the weekends. I'm super swamped today."

She places the two boxes next to each other on the counter, scans my face, testing me.

The smaller box holds cream-filled long johns. "Does she like long johns?" I ask.

"Her favorite." She slides the smaller box towards me a fraction of an inch.

I gladly take the bait.

"The boys won't be up for hours," I say and place the smaller box on top of the larger one. "Good day for a drive in the country."

"Looks like there's a change in the weather coming." Nicole's smile is a mix of victory and hope.

Chapter 18

Maribeth

The faintest glow of gray shifts beyond my bedroom curtain. Without looking outside, I know the rising sun hides behind a bank of clouds. I've gotten good at judging the weather by the first glows of sunrise. Morning after morning, I've laid in bed and watched the light shift from the darkness of night to the glow of day.

Another day alone.

No longer a comforting thought.

I roll over and stare at the curtains, mentally calculate how many hours until the darkness falls again, and my family can return.

They didn't return last night. After my conversation with Bryson in the tree stand, he didn't come back. The kids didn't visit at all.

I try not to resent them for that, know they can't control it.

It still stings.

I don't need the darkness to remember them. Saturday

mornings, when I wasn't buried in a case, I could spend time with my family. Bryson would wrap his arms around me, snuggle his sleep-hot body against my back. One thick arm would slide under my neck, his other wrapped around my waist. A cocoon of safety, I'd think to myself. With him wrapped around me, nothing could get to me.

When the kids were really little, they'd join us in the bed. Their small bodies would squish between us. Benny's little boy angles would shove against my belly and chest as he'd wriggle to get closer. Lilly would pretend to fuss at him, but wear a satisfied smile just the same. Bryson would wrap his strong arms around us all, his fingertips just brushing my hip with the kids between us.

Perfection.

Our bubble of contentment felt like it would last forever.

Indy shoves his nose into my back, wanting to go out.

The perfection crackles away as the present crashes in.

The light behind my bedroom curtain shifts into a brighter shade, but it's still gray.

The wood floor chills my bare feet. In the living room, the fire has burned to ashes in the night. I normally wake at some point and re-stock it. After struggling to get the deer to the cabin and hung in the lean-to, I'd slept soundly.

I stir the ashes, look for a lingering coal. Deep in the pile, a faint red glow glimmers. The fire lives. I feed the coal tiny scraps of wood. The toothpick sized pieces catch the glow and a minuscule flame licks onto the next. Carefully, I add larger sticks until the fire spreads. Finger-sized sticks catch hold and the tongue of flame swells. I rub my arms against the cloying chill of the cabin, anxious to make the fire bigger. I force myself to be patient. If I throw a log on now, the baby fire will smother. Too much too soon will swamp it.

A few more finger-sized pieces, then a wider piece. The flame strengthens. Each stick consumed by the flame turns to coal, adding to the base of heat hidden in the pile of ash, feeding the next piece of tinder.

Painfully slow, the fire grows. Step by step, it expands. Soon the pile of burning sticks swells with flame. I push a small log near the pile, hair thin slivers of wood reach from the split core of the log towards the pile of flames. The flames catch the slivers and they glow bright, then darken, curl into oblivion. I shove the piece closer and more slivers catch. The flame embraces the log, pulls the larger piece into its heat.

I add another log and watch the same dance of flames overtaking the wood. Soon the fire roars with a life of its own, doesn't need my constant painstaking care.

I hold my cold hands to the heat, let it sink into my bones. I lean nearer, the heat penetrates the skin of my face, dances behind my closed eyes. The flame I grew from a remnant of a coal fills my empty heart.

I pull on my coat and hat while I wait for the coffee to brew. My body's anxious for a morning cigarette, a dull need. Since I live alone, I could smoke inside instead of braving the cold. Bryson hated that I smoked. He also realized that as a detective, I needed the coping mechanism. I rarely ever drank, don't even have alcohol in the cabin now. I know myself well enough. The oblivion I could find from alcohol would be too hard to ignore. My obsessive personality would lose to the siren's song.

So I smoked. Always in the garage or outside and never in front of the kids. I'd allowed myself the vice, needed the outlet.

The coffee steams in the cold of the morning. A cigarette hangs from my lips. I click the lighter, and the flame dances instantly. I hold the flame to the cigarette, and it crackles to life. I drag heavily. The exhaled smoke mixes with the steam from my breath. I walk the porch, looking over the clearing the way I do every morning.

The muted colors of the woods swim together in the growing light. A watercolor from some artist's gray period. I fight the melancholy thought and turn the corner of the porch.

A different kind of painting meets me.

Strewn across the white boards of the porch lay packets of color and strings of colon.

The guts from last night's deer are spread along the boards.

I freeze in shock at the gore. My hand holds the cigarette a few inches from my mouth, stalled.

Indy has part of a liver in his mouth, munches greedily on the treat.

"Drop it!" I shout at the dog.

Confused, he cocks his head. In a rare moment of disobedience, he takes the liver and runs towards the trees with his find.

Revulsion coils in my belly. Questions swirl in my mind.

Did coyotes drag this here?

Unlikely. If the pack I heard last night found the guts, they would have eaten them the same way Indy can't help himself. I'd left them in the woods for that very reason. So they could feed the animals.

If the coyotes or some other wild animal didn't drag them here, who did?

I don't want to think about the answer. I can't think about the answer. There's only one animal that would do this, and he's in jail right now.

I lock the thought away in the buried box of my mind. I force my mind to empty of rationale. Refuse the trickle of fear.

I turn my back on the guts and sip my coffee. I walk back around the corner of the porch where the gore is out of sight. I sit in the rocking chair and enjoy the rest of my cigarette, and then another.

I rock until my coffee cup is empty, and the watercolor of the woods clarifies into crisp edges. I stub out my cigarette butt in the metal can by the rocker, then go to the barn.

On auto-pilot, I do the morning chores. Chica's teats are swollen, her time growing closer. I rub her belly, push my hand firmly into the mound of life inside her. A tiny foot pushes back insistently.

"Soon, Chica," I tell the pig. "You'll be a momma soon."

She snuffles her food and ignores me. Soon the babies

175

will be here, but not this morning.

Jingles the black cat slinks into the barn, making a rare appearance. The cat's still wild and untrusting. I understand the distrust and give him his space and his breakfast.

The chickens make soft noises in the morning, completing my small menagerie. I watch my animals as I smoke another cigarette, avoiding the next chore.

I can only avoid the mess so long.

The tractor roars into life when I turn the key. I back out of the barn and drive around the cabin. A flat shovel lays in the front bucket, ready for its dirty business. Pulling the tractor close to the porch, I line the dump bucket up with the edge of the planks.

A few quick shovel-fulls and the guts fill the tractor bucket.

I don't think about what I'm doing. My body completes the task efficiently without me thinking.

I drive the tractor to my burn pile and lift the bucket with the hand controls. Once high enough, I turn the controls to dump. The organs and entrails slide out of the bucket, splash onto the remnants of trash I've burned here.

Another trip to the barn, and the bucket is full of feed bags and other things waiting to burn, as well as a can of gas. I toss in a few logs from the lean-to. I need this fire to burn hot.

I stuff the feed bags around the guts, load the logs on top, then douse the whole thing in gasoline.

With myself and the tractor a safe distance away, I

light a small piece of bag wrapped around a stick. Tossing the small flaming packet onto the pile, it catches the fumes and whooshes. The blowback heats my cheeks, but I don't flinch.

The gas soaked bags catch easily, and the fire spreads fast and wild. I watch only long enough to be sure the pile will burn away, then climb back on the tractor.

Tires crunching on gravel rises over the spray of the hose as I clean the last remnants of this morning's defiling of my porch. A red truck I don't recognize pulls out of the woods and into my clearing. Indy bounds out from where he'd hidden with his spoils earlier, rushes the truck.

My neck prickles as I turn off the hose. Only a handful of people know the gate code, and I'm sure I locked it yesterday after my short run down the road.

"Hey, Indy," the man calls to the dog. Indy lets him rub his ears, dances in excitement.

The voice is familiar, the clothing is not. A different kind of tingle runs up my neck as I realize the brown uniform has been traded for jeans and a dark green coat.

I toss the hose aside, and scan my clean-up. A small unidentifiable piece of something hovers near the edge of the porch. I slide it off with the toe of my boot.

Grant waves a hand in greeting, holds a box up for me to see. "Hope I'm not intruding. Your sister sent you donuts."

Leave it to Nicole to set this up.

I plaster what I hope is a pleasant expression on my face and step around the porch to meet him.

"Nicole makes the best donuts," I say. "Thank you."

"Hope it's okay I just showed up and let myself in the gate." His searching look breaks my hard shell. A genuine smile fills my face.

"I gave you the code," I point out, taking the box of donuts.

"Doing some burning?" he motions towards the smoking burn pile.

"Just cleaning up a little." I turn my back on the smoking ruins. "Want some coffee with these?"

"Love some."

Grant fills my small cabin. His presence more potent than the several people that were here the other night. He looks around the small space, drinks in the few details of my home.

"This fireplace is amazing," he says earnestly. "Where did you get all the stone? Or did someone build it for you?"

"The stones were collected from the property. Most of them I picked up when they were putting in the foundation and driveway. It's amazing how many things are buried just below the surface once you actually look."

"I bet."

"I collected the stones, then had a mason build the fireplace."

Grant runs his hands across the lumpy surface in obvious appreciation. I've stared at the stones so long I no longer see their beauty. "It's gorgeous. This one looks like there's words carved in it. Think it might be an old headstone? What does it say?"

"Elr-something, I guess," I reply lamely, turn to get his

178

coffee. "How do you take it?"

"Two sugars, two creams, if you have it." He hangs his coat on a kitchen chair and settles at the table.

I make his coffee and another for me, then join him. I'm jittery and nervous and take a donut to give my hands something to do.

"I'm not intruding, am I?" he asks again, sensing my agitation.

"No. I'm glad you came. I just don't have many visitors," I tell him honestly and take a bite of donut. The cream squishes out, and I feel it land on my chin.

"Crap," I say, grabbing for a napkin. "Guess I'm not used to eating with people either."

Grant laughs, deep lovely notes dance around the kitchen, and pulls a nervous laugh from me too. The tension of this morning melts.

"You look different in regular clothes. I didn't recognize you."

"I get that a lot. People often just see a uniform and not the person behind it, you know?"

"I do know. It was the same when I was in uniform, before I became a detective and graduated to pants suits. Even that was a kind of uniform." My words surprise me. I hadn't meant to talk about my work before.

Grant hesitates, "How long were you an officer?" he finally asks.

I don't think, just answer. "Eight years before I moved up to Major Crimes back in Fort Wayne. Three years as a detective."

"That's impressive." I search his face for insincerity but

find none.

"I suppose. I don't think about it much." I take another bite of donut, don't make a mess this time.

"Do you miss the force?" The off-hand question startles me. The donut suddenly feels thick and choking. I sip my coffee then swallow hard. "I'm sorry. I shouldn't have asked that," he adds.

I meet his eyes and tell him truthfully, "You can ask me anything you want. Nicole treats me like a child, and my mother rarely asks questions. It's just, no one's ever asked me if I missed it."

"So, do you?"

I consider the question. "I miss the puzzles, the mentally putting clues together to get to the truth of a case." Even this tiny truth shakes me.

"Do you think you'll ever go back, after...?" he motions around the cabin.

I don't have to consider this answer. "There is no after for me."

It's his turn to look startled. My words sit heavy between us, our earlier ease tarnished. Grant mentally steps away, and a new kind of pain fills the void I created between us.

"Would you like to see my pigs?" I change the subject abruptly, wanting him to stay.

"I love pigs," he answers with relief. I get the distinct impression he's not ready to leave, awkward as I am.

Chapter 19

Maribeth

I show Grant my little farm, feel my face beaming with pride as he rubs Rizo behind his white and black ears.

"I've never been this close to pigs before," he says. "I see them on other farms, but I've never actually petted one. Well, at the 4-H fair, I guess."

"They're pretty amazing once you get to know them. They make good friends."

Once Chica realizes I'm not going to feed her again, she flops down on her side, her massive belly heaving. "She's due any time now." I say.

"How can you tell?"

"See that line just above her teats? That's called a milk line. Means the babies will be here soon." Grant's blue eyes question. I hold up my phone, "Internet. I've been reading up on it."

"You can learn anything online," he muses.

I climb over the fence into the pen. "Want to feel the

babies?"

He quickly joins me. Rizo shoves his nose against his leg. Grant jumps. "I don't think he likes me."

"He's just testing you. Pigs have a hierarchy, he's wondering where you fit in." I stand up. "Just walk into him, like this." I walk into Rizo, push him gently with my knees. Rizo steps away, conceding to my status. "He moved his feet first, so he lost. Now you do it."

Grant steps gingerly into the pig. Rizo pushes back.

"You have to mean it," I say. "Don't let him win."

Grant steps again, shoves a little with his knees. Rizo huffs, but steps aside. "Wow," Grant says. "Did you learn that on the internet too?"

"Actually, Bryson taught me that trick. He loved raising pigs." Talking about Bryson to this man jolts me.

"Smart man," is all Grant says. "Why isn't she testing me?" he squats next to Chica, still laying in the straw.

"She would if she was feeling better. Rizo is above her, so I guess she's content to let him do the work. Plus, these are KuneKunes, so they're extra friendly. Normally boars can be very dangerous, so don't go jumping into strange pens now."

Grant smiles, "I won't."

I coo to Chica and rub her belly. She grunts in response. "Here, push gently." I take Grant's hand and hold it in the right place. "Feel that?" His eyes meet mine as our bare skin touches. I'd meant did he feel the piglets, his eyes answer a different question.

Chica's belly rolls under our palms. "Was that a piglet?" Grant exclaims.

I nod, pleased by his excitement. Chica shifts and grunts again, growing agitated by our intrusion.

"We should probably let her rest," I say. I stand and look around the pen she shares with Rizo. I've been meaning to divide the pen so Rizo can go outside, but is kept away from Chica during her farrowing. The extra fence panels are in the rafters of the barn. I should have gotten one down long ago, but they're heavy and not easy to manage by myself.

I have a sudden thought. "Can you help me with something while you're here?"

"Of course. What do you need?"

I explain about the fence panels and needing to block Chica in. Grant readily agrees. A few minutes later, I'm in the rafters, sliding a panel down to his waiting hands. Looking down at him, his open expression and eagerness to help catches me off guard. I'd forgotten what it felt like to have a partner in any sense of the word.

Grant helps me place the divider in the pen, each of us holding an end as we lift it over the fence. He cuts wire off a spool as I twist the pieces to hold the panel in place. In a matter of minutes, the job is done. A job that would have taken me half the afternoon alone.

"Well, that was easy," I say once Chica is resettled with fresh straw.

"Glad to help," he responds. "It can't be easy doing everything here by yourself. Not that you haven't done an amazing job."

He's leaning on his elbows against the fence watching Chica. His body is so close, if I move just a fraction, I can touch him with my hip. He shuffles his feet, and his hip touches mine. I pretend not to notice his movement. Sure he did it on purpose.

I should move away, put space between us.

I lean ever so slightly towards him. The air between us disappears.

Grant looks sideways at me out of the corner of his eye. I do the same. Our faces are so close, I can smell his cologne. The earthy spice tantalizes, draws me into its spell.

His lips close in, his eyes locked with mine. I want to run, I want to scream.

I want his kiss.

He sees the confusion in my eyes, turns his mouth away at the last possible moment. His cheek brushes mine, smooth from his morning shave.

The skin on skin contact sizzles, intimate and precious. I close my eyes, revel in the moment. Grant slides his cheek along mine one more time, then pulls away.

The cold in the barn chases his heat from my skin.

Neither of us speak. I'm too scared to even breathe. I want this. I want more than this.

I can't have it.

I take half a step away. I moved my feet first, in the pig world, I lost.

"Thanks for your help," I say before I drown in his nearness.

"My pleasure," he says low and smooth.

I take another half step away, keep my eyes on the pen.

"Can I come to see the babies once they are born?" he

asks.

"I'd like that." My voice sounds strange, husky and full. "They might come tonight."

"Maybe I'll stop by tomorrow to see." He doesn't look at me, directs the words to Chica.

I swallow hard and nod. "They might not come until later, or the next day."

"I'll still stop by, if that's okay." His hand moves a few inches closer to mine on the fence. I don't reach for him, but don't move away either.

"Tomorrow, then," I say, my little finger rubbing the side of his palm.

"I've got to get home. My boys will wake up soon. I left a note that I was getting donuts. They'll be disappointed if there are no donuts when they wake up."

A stab of jealousy pierces the tender moment. "You're boys, of course," I nearly choke. He has children. I'd forgotten that detail. Live children are waiting for him to come home. "You'd better get back to them."

"Charlie and Kyle. Fourteen and twelve. They're old enough to stay home alone, but you know how it is with kids."

I stiffen. I remember how it was, but I don't know how it is.

Grant realizes his mistake and hurries to save himself. "God, Maribeth, I'm sorry. That was shitty of me to say."

I swallow hard and turn to face him straight on. "You have nothing to apologize for," I say directly. "Your boys are part of you and your life. I don't begrudge you that." I swallow again, find the courage I need to be honest. "I

185

like you, Grant. It scares me to death, and I don't know what to do with it, but I like you. If you care about me at all, you'll be open with me, honest with your words. I can't take anymore kid-glove handling. I get enough of that from Nicole."

He blinks several times before he responds. "I like you, too, Maribeth, but I don't want to hurt you by saying something stupid."

"There's nothing you can say that will hurt more than what I've been through." The back of my throat stings, and my eyes prickle. One tear slides down my cheek, but I don't wipe it away. I just focus on the unbelievable blue of his eyes, lose myself in their clarity. "I'm not a pity case."

He wipes the tear off my cheek, "I don't pity you. I admire you. You're the strongest person I've ever met."

"It's easy to be strong when you have no other choice."

The clear blue of his eyes suddenly clouds over. "There's always a choice," he chokes. "You're too strong to make the wrong one." There's something indefinable under his words, a deep hurt I don't understand.

I suddenly feel the need to comfort him and step into his arms. He doesn't try to kiss me, just presses my ear to his chest. The top of my head brushes the bottom of his chin, a perfect fit. I listen to his heartbeat and cling to the back of his coat. I wordlessly give comfort and receive it. A basic human need that requires no explanation.

I could hold him like this all day, but his boys are waiting. I'll not take him away from them for even a moment more than necessary. "You should get home," I say against his coat.

Grant squeezes me gently, then lets me go. "Can I still come by tomorrow?"

"You should be with your boys."

"They're going to the movies with some friends."

An unexpected relief washes over me. "In that case, I'd love to see you."

Grant releases me, then squeezes my hand. "I'll be back tomorrow," he says.

"I'll be here," I reply, stupidly. Where else would I be?

Chapter 20

Maribeth

I watch Grant drive away, a strangled feeling in my chest. "Not for you, not for you," I repeat as the woods swallow his truck. The words feel heavy on my lips. A tiny shoot of hope wriggles to life in my heart. "Why not?" I ask the sky. "If I can't have him, why did you bring him here?"

The sky doesn't answer.

I need to run, to burn off the energy Grant's presence kicked up. My feet itch for a new path, my eyes yearn for something other than trees, my soul aches for something to fill it.

After a quick switch into running boots and cranking music in my earbuds, I take off into the section of woods opposite where I killed the deer last night. The path leading to where I found Dana Sanders is also off-limits. This section of woods has more hills and a generally rougher terrain to cover. I welcome the challenge.

Indy stays close as I run, senses my agitation. Memories of Grant's cheek against mine, of his heartbeat in my ears crash through the music I use to distract my mind. I turn the song up louder, push my legs harder. "Not for you," I chant to the beat of the music. If I say it enough times, maybe I'll believe it.

The path turns near the place where Indy nearly drowned, and I almost froze to death. With everything else that's happened since, I haven't thought about that night. "If you'd just let me go, I wouldn't be going through this now," I say to Bryson and the kids, although they won't appear for another few hours.

The thought sobers and I slow to a walk and turn into the woods towards the small pond. It's no longer frozen, just a dark hole of water in the brown of the woods. There's no trace of where I'd lain, washed away by the rain and the wind.

I don't need to see marks on the ground, the details are burned into my memory.

If I had died here, no one would have found me. It would have taken days until Nicole realized I wasn't answering her calls, maybe a few more days until she came looking. This part of the woods is remote, the pond's not on the path. I might not have been found for weeks, if at all. Wild animals would have torn me to pieces, my bones scattered across the property.

The guilt would have destroyed Nicole. Even my mom would have suffered.

Guilt.

I know it intimately. At least I spared them that.

I drop to my knees on the spot and bow my head. "Thank you for saving me," I pray sincerely, no longer angry. I don't know what else to say, just open my mind and hope God reads my meaning.

I climb to my feet and jog home, away from my almost grave.

The afternoon passes with alternating sessions of watching comedy reruns and checking on Chica. While I was running, she'd pulled all the fresh straw into a nest in one corner of her newly divided pen. She scratches at the fences, paws at the ground, paces the smaller space. From my internet research, all signs of impending delivery.

The reruns offer little distraction from my worry about Chica. I want to sit with her, to watch her. My presence in the barn seems to annoy her, so I give her space. I watch TV with Indy and peek into the barn occasionally like the nervous Grandma I'll never be.

On one of my peeks into the barn, I see Chica has settled down, now lies on her side panting.

"They're coming!" I squeal to Indy. "The piglets are really coming."

Everything I've read says to leave her alone, let nature do its thing. I can barely contain myself. I pace the ten steps of the cabin, try to leave her be.

My excitement gets the better of me. I lock Indy in my bedroom to keep him away, then sneak silently into the barn. Chica doesn't seem to notice, so I move closer, sit outside the fence and watch.

I don't have long to wait. Chica pulls her back legs up,

then kicks and stretches. The first unbelievably small piglet slides out onto the straw. It blinks his large eyes and flops around. Amazingly, it gets on its feet after just a few uncoordinated moments and instinctively bumbles around Chica's body, looking for a teat. The piglet is precious and perfect and painfully cute.

A few minutes later, another piglet slides out, quickly followed by another that lands on the first. I stare in amazement at the miracle happening before my eyes. Before long, three more babies tumble around and over each other. Six precious snouts and tails.

Each spotted body carries its own pattern, a jumble of black splotches on white fur. Peeking under their tails I count five boys and one girl. The lone female is nearly white with three black spots in a line down her spine.

After snapping a few pictures of the babies, I text them to Nicole.

"They finally came!"

"So beautiful. Congratulations!"

I watch the babies until my legs ache from sitting on the concrete. Pins and needles stab my foot as I get up to leave. The pain is a small sacrifice for the wonder I just witnessed.

"You did great, Chica," I whisper from the door. "Your family is beautiful." I shut the door on the wondrous scene of new life snuggled in straw.

The birth of the babies had been a nice distraction, but the deer needs skinned and quartered today. Tomorrow I'll do the laborious process of deboning, grinding and wrapping it for the freezer.

The deer swings on the rope around his neck attached to a rafter of the lean-to. The afternoon has gotten away from me, and shadows begin to fill woods outside the open door of the lean-to, so I hurry to accomplish the job. With my freshly sharpened skinning knife, I cut a line through the fur and skin of the neck, careful not to cut too deeply into the meat. Once the skin is cut, I grab it by the edges and pull downward. It peels down a few inches, folded over like removing a sock. I run the tip of my skinning knife in the crease between the body and the skin, releasing the connective tissue. I pull the skin down a few more inches and repeat the process. Once I get enough skin loose, I stab holes large enough to catch with my hand, one on each side. I slide my hand into the holes and pull. The skin peels further down the body.

The left shoulder doesn't want to peel away. I pull again, and most of the skin comes down, but patches of fur remain. "What the…?"

Someone has cut into the deer's shoulder. I tear away the fur patches, pull frantically at the skin. The muscle has been marked.

The roman numeral two, the sign of the Gemini.

My eyes refuse the symbol. It can't be real.

I reach inside my shirt, feel the matching scar on my chest.

Running the tip of my knife in the slice marks, my mind dances with disbelief. "Did I do this?" I whisper. I touch the mark on the deer with my finger, trace the angry lines.

Thinking back to last night, the details feel blurry. I'd been tired and upset, did I cut this? Is it possible I just don't remember? Maybe I'm the one who put the guts on my porch. Maybe I've actually lost it?

The mark mesmerizes. It holds my eyes so long, shadows fill the small space of the lean-to and darkness falls. I can't make the existence of the symbol mesh with reality.

A movement out of the corner of my eye draws my attention to the nearby trees. A shadowy figure stands under a tree. The shape of a man.

A shape I recognize.

The shape of Jesse Franklin.

I drop my knife in surprise, and it clunks against a stray log on the ground. I jump away from the vision and bump into the half-skinned body of the deer. Cold flesh pushes against my cheek as the marked shoulder rubs against it.

Panicked, I shove the deer away, take my eyes from the shadow in the trees.

I snatch the knife off the ground, ready to attack.

The space under the tree is empty.

I take a few steps out of the lean-to, the knife held tight in my hand. I wish I'd let Indy out of my room. I trust his senses, but can no longer trust my own.

"Franklin?" I scream into the woods.

The breeze in bare branches is the only response.

"Maribeth?" Bryson's voice behind me.

I spin, the knife still ready to stab. "It's just us," Bryson calms, his hands up.

"Did you see him?" I ask desperately.

"Who?" Lilly chimes in. "There's no one out there, Mom."

I look into the woods, confusion fuzzing my brain.

"I saw Jesse Franklin. He was standing under that tree right there."

"The man who killed us?" Benny's voice shakes with fear.

"Put the knife down, Maribeth. Franklin's not out there," Bryson sounds so sure. I look at the knife I'm holding against my family, so does Bryson, "You're scaring the kids."

I lower the knife instantly. "Sorry, kids." I look again into the empty woods. "I thought I saw something."

Bryson reaches towards me, encouraging me to put the knife back in its case. I find the case where I left it on a log in the lean-to, and snap it closed with a satisfying click.

"It's too dark to finish the deer now," Bryson soothes. "You can finish tomorrow."

"Someone carved the mark into it," I whisper so only he can hear.

Bryson inspects the deer, then looks into the woods. "I don't think all this time alone out here is good for you," he says.

"You think I did this, don't you?" I snap.

"I think you're exhausted. Maybe you saw what you thought you wanted to see."

I look at the faces of my children, faces I want to see. "Are you three really here?" My voice strangled. "Are

195

you even real?"

"I'm real, Mommy," Benny's sweet voice pipes in immediately. "Can we go in now?"

Lilly takes Benny by the hand and leads him away. An instant shot of jealousy pumps through me. She can touch him, but I can't. I'll never touch my son again.

"Wait," I say. The kids stop and look back. "Chica had her babies today. Do you want to see them?"

"Piglets?" Lilly bounces with excitement, looking more like the little girl she was than the young woman she'd almost grown into.

"Come on, I'll show them to you."

I push thoughts of carved deer and shadowy hallucinations out of my mind. If I don't try to touch them, I can pretend my family's actually here with me. I can show my new piggy family to them. We can enjoy a moment of normalcy.

Not that I remember what normal is.

Chapter 21

Samuels

Esther begs for another chip, her large brown eyes pleading. I give in to the small dog, and she snaps the chip from my hand, grazing my fingers with her teeth.

"Careful, Esther. Jeez," I complain as she gobbles the chip down, and I ruffle the fur between her ears.

Sleep eludes my overactive mind. Even my usual routine of checking on the college basketball scores and sharing a bag of chips with Esther can't stop the thoughts pounding through my brain.

With the apprehension of Freddy Munson for Dana Sanders' murder, my days have been busy. My partner, Danny Alexander, and I had squeezed in a visit to the Maddison jail. We'd questioned Munson directly for his abduction of the girl. The interview didn't sit well with me. Munson seemed genuinely confused by our questions. I've interrogated enough monsters to know they're skilled liars. Munson didn't come across as skilled, he was scared. It takes a special kind of evil to kidnap Dana, hold her for two days, then kill her at Johansen's. Munson was no angel, but I didn't get the right vibe from him for this brand of brutality.

Franklin had been careful, precise. He'd kept us chasing him for nearly three years. Every time we'd get close, he'd have a rock-solid alibi for the times the girls disappeared. Video alibis that showed his face clearly. He'd killed the women, then dumped their bodies in a different location. We never found DNA from him on the women. It wasn't until after Franklin was killed attacking Johansen's family that we figured out the whole story. He'd capture the women and take them to his home. Few people in the dilapidated warehouse district cared what their neighbors were up to. Even fewer people would report it if they saw anything. The details of what he did to the women there were known only to Franklin. Thankfully for the women, sexual assault wasn't his taste. Lord knows what psychological torture he put them through. Their bodies were always clean, except for their own blood. We assumed he made them shower before he sliced them. They were all found wearing the clothes they disappeared in. The clothes were clean, any evidence freshly laundered away.

Even the choice of victims had been precise. Jesse Franklin had a type. Each woman had brown eyes and curly dark-blonde hair. The chosen victims represented something to him. A psychologist would say the women were stand-ins for the mother who abandoned him. Cindy Baxter never married Jesse's father, Paul, and she was killed in a car crash when Franklin was too young to remember her. Paul and his son moved to Fort Wayne soon after. Some memory of his mother and a deep hatred for her absence must have simmered in Franklin's subconscious.

Dana Sanders was different. She was younger, her long dark hair chosen for her resemblance to Lilly Johansen. Dana had been showered and wore laundered clothing too. We hadn't released that info to the public during the Franklin case. Those similarities, combined with the Gemini mark on all their chests, keeps niggling at me.

From my talk with Munson, it was obvious he was incapable of carrying out such a careful, detailed plan. He could have grabbed the girl, then killed her and similarly marked her, but he had no way of knowing about the cleaning up beforehand.

Only Franklin knew that part. And the team on the investigation.

That detail bothers me more than any other. Did the info get leaked after Franklin died? Did Munson find out the actual steps Franklin used and followed them as a tribute to the monster?

Munson didn't have a clear alibi for the time Dana was missing. But where would he keep her? A search of his trailer turned up nothing.

Did he follow Franklin so carefully, he even used the same place to keep the girl?

Franklin's house was thoroughly processed after he died. As far as I knew, it was still vacant. It wasn't an easy rental in the first place due to the neighborhood.

Afterward, no one wanted to rent a home where seven women were held captive and then murdered.

"Did Munson use his house?" I ask Esther as I give her another chip. She snaps the chip out of my fingers, more carefully this time. I make a mental note to call the landlord and see if I can take a look around the house again. I don't have a warrant or a solid reason to look, but I do have the key in a file somewhere. All I need is permission.

With something concrete to work on tomorrow, my body finally relaxes enough for me to sleep. I turn off the TV even though I didn't pay attention to any of the scores.

Esther follows me eagerly down the hall to where Kay sleeps. She bounds onto the bed and curls up against my wife. I slide in on Kay's other side. She moans softly in her sleep. I put my arm over her hip and hold her close. Her warm body soothes my tired one. The scent of her shampoo fills my nose.

Perfection.

Any concerns I'd had about the landlord allowing me to visit Franklin's kill house evaporate a few sentences into our conversation.

"Of course, I don't mind if you see the house again," he'd said. "Heck, you can buy it from me if you want."

"I don't want to buy it, I just want to take another look around," I reply.

"Make you one hell of a deal. I can't bring myself to even go there. Haven't touched it since I gave you the keys the first time. Had it winterized, and the utilities turned off, but that's all."

"It's exactly as it was?" I ask. "No one's been in it?" I can't believe my luck. I'm not sure what I hope to find at the house, but if all Jesse Franklin's things are still there, I might get lucky.

"I don't want to see where he did those girls that way," he says soberly. "Bad enough I know I cashed checks from a serial killer. As far as I'm concerned, that house needs to burn to the ground and turned into insurance money." He stops talking, remembering he's on the phone with a police officer. "Not that I'd do that, mind you. I'm not a criminal," he says quickly.

"Don't worry. I'm not afraid you're going to go the arson route."

"Is there any particular reason you want to see it now? Does it have to do with that copycat killer up in Maddison?"

"I'm sorry, I can't give details about an investigation."

"I understand. Bad enough there was one Jesse Franklin in the world. Now it seems there's another. People are sick."

"You have no idea." I end the call and look at the key I dug out of the original files. The piece of metal glints in the morning sun with a tiny light of hope.

The small two-story squats on a block filled with similar run-down houses and open lots. Only a few appear to be inhabited. The neighborhood is quiet, even for a Sunday afternoon. Sagging porches hold old couches or metal folding chairs. A string of Christmas lights dangles from a porch two doors down. I imagine they leave them up all year since Christmas was two months ago. The tiny nod to festivity tucked between two boarded-up houses makes the neighborhood feel even more sad.

Tall grass and weeds choke Franklin's postage stamp sized yard, and the covered stoop is flanked on either side by overgrown bushes. The evergreen branches nearly touch the second story windows and cover the first.

I do a preliminary walk around the house, searching for footprints or broken weeds, some indication anyone has been here in the last two years. Everything appears untouched, but the strip of cracked concrete running from the house to the alley could allow someone to come and go without leaving footprints in the high grass. A chain-link fence runs along the alley. An open expanse of broken asphalt beyond the fence separates the houses from an abandoned warehouse. Even the warehouse is the same. Maybe a few more broken windows since the last time I was here, but otherwise nothing has changed. We'd checked out the warehouse the first time and found no hint that Franklin used the empty space for his awful deeds. The row of windows high on the wall only served as watching eyes, blind to the horrors inside.

Those eyes silently watch me climb the sagging back porch. I carefully choose my steps on the rotting boards, placing each foot over a support joist. Chips of deep red paint have peeled from the wood of the back door, exposing white paint underneath. I put a fingertip under a loose section of paint, and a chip falls to the porch, a blood-red spot of color against the brown of the wood.

The square of glass in the door is too filthy to see through. I cup my hands around my face and strain to see inside. The gloomy outline of a stove and refrigerator are the only shapes I can make out.

I step away from the door, finger the key in my pocket. "You're stalling," I say out loud.

I've been in this house before. I've faced the home of the monster who butchered seven women and my friend's family. I did it before because I had no choice.

"You don't have a choice now, either," I tell myself. "Just open the damn door."

I jam the key into the lock, half-hoping it won't turn. It turns easily. With cold fingers, I turn the knob and enter the kitchen.

The silence of the house rings in my ears. It looks the way I remembered from when the techs processed it. Dirty dishes from Franklin's last meal still sit in the sink. Untouched for years, they're covered in black slime and dust. Faded takeout menus still hang on the fridge, their edges curled with age. Half a pot of coffee waits in the coffee maker, now congealed to a solid black mass. A stack of mail on the kitchen table sits next to an overflowing ashtray full of dried husks of cigarette butts. The room looks like what it is, a snapshot of the last day of Jesse Franklin's life. He obviously expected to return home after his butcher fest.

He never came home again.

I listen to the silence of the house and continue my exploration. If Munson had used this house for his own version of insanity, he obviously didn't eat in the kitchen. The front room appears unused, as well. The sagging couch and battered coffee table wear a thick coating of dust. Even the TV is still in place. Thieves and squatters have steered clear of the horrors that happened here.

The steps of the narrow staircase leading to two bedrooms creak under my feet, the worn carpet slick. One bedroom holds a bed Franklin didn't make on his last morning alive. A dresser with mismatched knobs and several half-open drawers sits in the corner. The entire room is covered in dust, untouched. I click the door shut on the room and look into the other one across the landing.

This room is empty except for a few boxes piled in a corner. Even a demented man collects. I don't remember from the reports whether these boxes were searched or not. With Franklin dead already, the search of his house was more to confirm he'd taken and killed the women, than a search for clues. We'd found plenty of evidence against him in the basement. These boxes were most likely ignored.

Curious, I lift the flap on the top box. A face smiles up at me.

I jump back, startled, my hand going to my hip. Stealing my nerve, I peak in again. The plastic Santa face looks back.

"Shit, Samuels. It's just a decoration for God's sake," I mutter. Disgusted with myself, I dig through the rest of the box and find more Christmas items. I try to imagine a man like Jesse Franklin hanging holiday decorations, but can't wrap my mind around it.

The second box holds baseball and football trophies, the small plaques on each etched with the name Paul Franklin. Jesse's father. A loose pile of newspaper clippings from Paul's early life as a high school stand-out athlete is mixed with various ribbons and medals. The fresh-faced young man in the photos bears only a passing resemblance to the gaunt man Paul became. After high school stardom, the disappointment of real-life drove Paul to alcohol and later to drugs. His bright future ultimately ended at the sharp end of a broken bottle in a bar fight just a few months before Jesse Franklin snatched and killed his first victim.

I sit back on my heels and think. These boxes must contain the last of Paul's estate. A life boiled down to three boxes stashed in his son's spare bedroom. Jesse had been only twenty-two when his father was killed. Did the shock of that loss, compounded by boxes of his father's previous stardom, break something in Jesse? Was Jesse searching for his own stardom?

The thought makes my stomach roil. Does it even matter now? The man has been dead for a long time, his infamy well established. If that was his demented plan, he succeeded.

Half-heartedly, I slide the last box closer across the dirty carpet. Sealed shut with yellowed and cracking tape, one sharp tug pops it open.

The box is full of photo albums, long ago packed away and forgotten. One album holds copies of Paul's newspaper clippings I've already seen, so I toss that one aside. Two other scrapbooks are filled with Paul's life. Handwritten notes are added to some of the pages, listing places, dates, and names of the people in the photos. The cursive writing has a decidedly feminine flourish. I imagine Paul's mother carefully notating the albums, lovingly chronicling her only child's life. Luckily the mother who cared for her son so well didn't live long enough to see what her grandson became.

I close the album on the bittersweet notations and take out the last book. The words "My Child's First Years" are embossed in blue on the cover. I flip it open, expecting to see Paul Franklin's early life lovingly recorded.

The baby pictures inside are not of Paul Franklin.

A photo of identical dark-haired boys together in a hospital crib is taped to the first page.

"Jesse and Jacob" carefully printed in bold block letters below the picture along with a date I recognize as Jesse's birthdate.

"Shit!" I exclaim, my words echoing through the empty room.

I quickly flip pages. More pictures of identical twins fill the book, each milestone written in with the same block letters as the boys grew older.

My mind struggles to make the connections.

Jesse Franklin has an identical twin.

Chapter 22

Maribeth

Millions of people go to church on Sunday mornings.
Even Bryson and I used to take the kids as often as my
schedule allowed. The ritual of brushing and braiding
Lilly's hair and tying pink bows at the ends was a weekly
balm to my jangled nerves. I'd dress Benny in a dress shirt
and sweater vest, a mini copy of his father. Those
mornings with my family clean and pressed and lovely
gave me the strength to get through the following week.
We'd sit together in a pew, Bryson's strong hand holding
mine. The word of God would flow through us.

I turned my back on God the last time I sat in a church
pew. My family was dressed in their Sunday best. Lilly's
hair was not braided. Benny's sweater vest didn't match
Bryson's.

Nicole held my hand instead of Bryson.

The word of God meant nothing to me.

Today may be Sunday, but the only church I know is

the woods. The only world I know is the woods.

The woods feel like a cage. A cage I built to keep out the world. Now the cage keeps me in.

To fight my melancholy mood, I focus on doing chores. Search for a scrap of happiness while watching the baby pigs.

Happiness alludes.

I take my daily run early, eager to escape the walls of the cabin and the barn. I think about Grant and his promised visit later today.

Even his blue eyes can't chase the gray from my soul.

One thought consumes me.

Did I carve that mark into the deer? Have I crossed the fragile line of sanity?

I cut my run short and sprint as hard as I can back to the cabin and the lean-to where the deer still hangs.

With my hands on my knees, bent over gasping from my hard run, I hesitate outside the lean-to.

Maybe the mark was just a hallucination. Maybe this life is a hallucination.

Maybe I died that night bleeding in my living room.

Indy noses my leg. I brush him away and step into the lean-to.

The half-skinned deer hangs from the rope tied around his neck, the roman numeral two carved into his shoulder clearly visible in the daylight.

The mark mocks me, taunts me.

"Shut up!" I scream at the mark.

Frantically, I open the knife case I left here last night. Knives of all sizes tumble onto the leaf-littered ground.

Grasping the largest one, I hack at the mark with frenzied strokes. Indy barks in confusion, fuelling my mania. I swipe again and again, matching my blade swings to Indy's barking rhythm. My vision tunnels, all I see is the cuts from my knife obliterating the mark, mutilating the deer's shoulder.

Exhausted, I drop to my knees beneath the deer. My hand aches from my rabid attack. I force my fingers to release the knife, and it falls from my hand, stained with blood.

Indy sniffs the knife, then licks my face and whines.

His need pulls me from the abyss of darkness in my mind. I get to my feet and take a mental step away from the edge.

The poor deer's neck stretches beneath the rope, his skin pulled half-way down his body, his shoulder a mangled mass of gashes. This deer was supposed to be food for Indy and me next winter. His death was supposed to provide us life.

I'll never eat this deer.

With determined steps, I lead Indy inside the cabin and lock him in my bedroom.

I go through the double doors to the barn, sparing a quick glance at the baby pigs.

The sliding door at the far end of the barn crashes along its track as I slam it open. The Gator roars into life, and I back out dangerously fast.

I back the Gator's bed under the deer and pick up another knife. With one slice, I cut the rope hanging the deer from the rafter. His weight crashes into the bed of the

Gator, nearly pinning me under him the way he did in the woods. Only one boot is caught this time, and I remove myself easily.

The knife bounces on the passenger seat as I speed into the woods. I drive blindly, taking turns on the path at a breakneck speed. A bump in the path jolts the Gator, and I fly out of my seat for a breathless second. The deer bounces too, topples on the edge of the Gator, then settles back into the bed.

Only when I feel I'm as far from the cabin as possible, do I slow my wild flight. I back into the woods a few feet, slam the Gator into park and tuck the knife into my boot.

Panting and huffing, I pull the deer off the Gator. It lands in an awkward pile of long legs and loose skin.

"Wasted," I mutter to myself. "You wasted him."

"The coyotes can still eat him. He didn't die for nothing," I answer.

I drag him as far as my tired legs will allow then collapse next to his cold body. I press my cheek into the ground. The pungent scent of earth and leaves fill my nostrils. Hidden stones and sharp sticks scratch into my skin. My harsh breath blows the dirt near my mouth. Each gasp kicks up a tiny swirl of dirt and leaf fragments.

Cold air slithers up the back of my jacket, cools the hot sweat that clings to my shirt.

I don't move for a long time. Indulge in the pain of the shivering cold, the biting of the ground into my cheek. A stick pokes uncomfortably into my side.

I push against the stick to increase the discomfort.

The physical pain is real, tangible. My emotional pain

is a swirling cacophony of dark mist.

I focus on the physical pain until the swirl in my mind settles.

The knife in my boot pricks my leg.

Spent and empty, I push myself to my knees and pull the knife from my boot. The glittering metal dances through the air as I move it slowly before my eyes.

The church of trees around me grows silent.

The voice in my mind is clear and sweet.

"You can't stay here with them," it says.

"I can't leave," I reply, my eyes fixed on the blade.

"You can't stay here with them," the voice repeats in my mind.

Three coffins flash in my memory. I mentally walk to the smallest one. My son seems to sleep. I brush his long bangs off his forehead, the way I often did as he slept. The way I did the last time I saw him alive. In my mind, I kiss his cheek, the way I'd been incapable of doing at his actual funeral.

"Good-bye, Benny Buddy," I whisper. With a slow hand, I grasp the lid of his coffin, the glossy wood and smooth satin so real against my fingers. Gently, I close the lid on my son.

I approach Lilly next. In my mind, I run her silky hair through my fingers. Separating it into three pieces, I make a small braid. My dry lips touch her cheek. "Good-bye, my precious girl," I whisper near her ear. My hand shakes as I close the lid on my daughter.

Even in my imagination, I struggle to force my feet to Bryson. Dragging steps bring me to his side. The strong planes of his face appear to sleep, the way I watched him sleep next to me countless times. I place my hand on his chest, will him to breathe again. He lies still.

"I'm so sorry I couldn't protect them," I tell my husband. "I never meant this to happen to you. All I wanted was to love you," I choke out. The pain of loss tears my heart as I creak out, "I have to let you go now."

Bryson's lips are cool and smooth beneath mine. I linger there, my lips on his. My hand clings to his sweater, wraps the fabric around them. "I can't. I can't," I pant against his lips. "How do I let you go?" I beg. "Help me let you go."

The voice in my mind repeats, "You can't stay here with them."

I untangle my fingers from Bryson's shirt, pull my face away from his.

"Good-bye, my love."

In one fast movement, I shut his coffin.

Kneeling in my church of the woods, I watch as the three coffins fade from my mind. The knife still clenched in my fist, I know what I must do.

I climb shakily to my feet and lean against a tree for support. I raise the knife and look to the sky. "Good-bye, my loves!" I shout.

With lightning-fast motions, I carve into the tree. Three small crosses stand out against the darkness of the bark.

I know their bodies lie in a cemetery far from here. These crosses are for me.

A sudden shaft of sunlight breaks through the overhead

branches, and my shadow stretches before me. A trick of light and branches form a shadow cross above my head. I hold my arms out to the side, the shadow of my body creating a matching cross to the branch shadows.

The knife tumbles from my hand and lands next to the deer.

The deer I no longer need.

Chapter 23

Samuels

I flip through the pages of the baby book again, force my mind to make sense of what I'm seeing. In all the background work we did on Jesse Franklin, we'd never heard about a twin. As far as the public records are concerned, he was the only child of Paul Franklin and Cindy Baxter who never married. The death certificate of Cindy Baxter said she died in a car crash at the age of 29. Friends of Franklin, even his school records, corroborated that information. Jesse was an only child raised by his father Paul, after his mother died.

What happened to Jacob?

Stuck to the back cover of the baby book, I find two birth certificates.

Jacob and Jesse, born to Paul Franklin and Victoria Wilson.

"Who the hell is Victoria Wilson?" I ask the empty room.

I shove the birth certificates back into the book, then

jam the whole book inside my coat. A quick look through the box of albums offers no more clues. Anxious to get the book back to my office and track down Victoria Wilson, I make my way down the narrow stairs and through the dusty front room.

My hand turns the knob on the kitchen door when a noise from the basement stops me in my tracks. I turn to face the basement door directly behind me. A whirring sound seeps through the closed door.

I know what's down those steps. The bizarre scene has plagued my nightmares. The weight of my pistol in my hand grounds me. I suddenly wish I had called my partner Danny Alexander. It's our day off, and I didn't want to bother Alexander with my wild goose chase of visiting this house.

The whirring continues behind the scratched wooden door. The utilities to the house are disconnected, nothing should be running down there. I'd come here to see if Munson had used the house. The book will have to wait.

I push the door, and it opens on a shadowed staircase. I light up the stairs with my flashlight in one hand and my pistol in the other. The book I'd shoved into my waistband cuts into the flesh of my side.

The door at the bottom of the steps is closed. The thin beam of my flashlight glints off the metal of a new padlock. The hasp securely closed.

I carefully descend the stairs. The third step creaks loudly. Beyond the locked door, I hear a shuffling sound. My blood runs cold.

"Hello?" I shout. Something or someone moves in the

basement.

Balancing on the rickety steps, I kick the door. The wood splinters, but the door holds. I've seen the scratch marks on the other side of this door, feeble attempts of the women to open it. If it could have been kicked down easily, they would have escaped.

I take careful aim at the new lock and blow it to pieces with one shot.

My ears ring from the gunshot, a faint squeal of fear from someone inside mixes with the sound.

The door pushes open easily without the lock. With my gun and my flashlight drawn, I step over the splinters of wood and enter the black basement.

The narrow beam of my flashlight swings around the open room. The furnishings are the same. A set of twin beds with matching Star Wars bedspreads are pushed against the far wall, neatly made, and covered in dust. A kitchenette fills one corner of the room, a dining table and four chairs set for a formal dinner.

Near the kitchenette, I find the source of the mechanical whirring I'd heard upstairs. A generator has been attached to the breaker box. I find a light switch and try it. The basement floods with light, and I blink against the brightness.

If I didn't know better, I could imagine I'm looking at an apartment. A TV and couch fill another corner. A gaming console plugged into the TV, the controllers laid carefully on top. A throw blanket hangs over the back of the couch. It could be a happy home.

It's the home where Jesse Franklin kept his victims

prisoner in a fantasy of the perfect family. Forced to play his mother, they made him dinner, tucked him into bed at night, pretended to take care of him.

Until he broke them. Once they couldn't play, he marked them, killed them, then discarded them. Then he'd find another woman to play mom.

There's not many places to hide in the apartment. Whoever squealed when I shot the lock has to be here.

"Police," I shout into the empty room. "I know you're down here. Show me your hands."

I hear movement from the couch and train my gun on the sound. With nerves wire tight, I take careful steps across the concrete. My shoes scratch on the bare floor, and my heart pounds in my ears.

"I know you're there. Show me your hands, and you won't get hurt."

From beneath the blanket on the couch, two hands slide out.

Small hands.

A child's hands.

I flip the blanket back, my gun drawn and ready.

The terrified face of a young boy blinks up at me.

"Please don't hurt me," he cries pitifully.

For a moment, I'm sure I'm looking at Benny Johansen. The dark hair and long bangs are a near match to the style Benny wore. His age is the same, maybe eight or nine. Even his large brown eyes are similar.

I stare in shocked silence at the boy, not sure if he's real or a ghost of the child I once knew. Fat tears of terror roll down his cheeks.

The tears bring me back to the present, and I lower my gun.

"You're safe now," I tell him. "Is there anyone else here?" I scan the room again.

The boy shakes his head, his lips quivering.

I search the room quickly, even looking under the beds, but there's nowhere to hide.

"Let's get you out of here." I reach my hand for the boy, and he places his entirely too small palm in mine. "Let's get you back to your family, okay?"

Even on the cramped stairs, the boy won't let go of my hand. The steps are too narrow to climb side by side, so I holster my gun and shove my flashlight into my coat pocket. I pick the boy up and settle him on my hip. He buries his wet face into the crook of my neck and shakes in my arms as I carry him upstairs and outside.

The wind slaps against us. The boy's only wearing pants and a shirt, no coat, so I wrap my own coat around him. He shivers against me as I carry him to my car.

I manage to unclasp his arms from my neck and place him gently in the front seat. I start the car and turn up the heat. "There you go," I tell him. "We'll get you warm in no time."

He turns his dark eyes to mine. "I want my momma," he says pitifully.

"I'm going to call her, I promise. What's her name?"

"Monica Pepple," he says. "I'm Teddy Pepple."

"Nice to meet you, Teddy Pepple. I'm Detective Samuels." I shake the boy's hand. "You are very brave. Can you be brave just a little longer?"

219

Teddy nods so hard his bangs shake across his forehead, the resemblance to Benny still startling. "I can be brave."

"Good. I need to make some calls. Can you stay here in the car? I'll be just outside, you can see me through the windshield. Okay?"

"You're not leaving, are you?" terror floods his eyes.

"I'm not leaving. I'll be right here."

He nods, and I shut the car door behind me. I turn up the collar of my coat against the wind, then call my unit. After giving the pertinent details, I return to the warm car. The baby book jabs into my hip, momentarily forgotten. I pull it out of my waistband and toss the book in the back seat.

Teddy doesn't look at the book. His eyes locked on my every move as I settle into the driver's seat.

I curse the man who'd hurt an innocent child.

"Did you get a good look at the man who did this?"

Teddy's eyes swim with tears again, but he shakes his head no. "He put a bag over my head."

"How long have you been here?" I've technically been off work the last few days, but it seems like I would have heard something about a missing eight-year-old.

"Just since this morning," he whispers. "I was playing in my front yard. Then he took me…." his voice trails into more tears.

I thank God he hadn't spent much time in that basement, but his answer poses more questions. If he was abducted this morning, then Freddy Munson couldn't have been his kidnapper. The boy's resemblance to Benny

Johansen can't be a coincidence any more than Dana Sanders' resemblance to Lilly.

Teddy slides his hand into mine, his skin still chilled in the blasting heat from the car. Questions swirl in my mind, and I desperately need a cigarette. I'm anxious to get back into the house and search for something to tell me who did this to the boy.

But I won't leave Teddy alone.

I place my other hand on top of his, rub it gently to warm him. The boy leans across the center console, his dark head pressing against my shoulder.

"You're safe now, Teddy. Your mom's on her way," I whisper into his hair.

Teddy pushes closer into my shoulder, and we wait.

Who the hell took this boy, and what is his connection to Jesse Franklin?

Chapter 24

Maribeth

My cell phone rings, waking me from dozing on the couch. I check the screen, the displayed name shakes the lingering grog from my head.

"Hi, Grant," I answer. The cheer in my voice surprises me. After my emotional morning, I wasn't sure I could feel anything but pain.

"Is it still okay if I come over today?" His shy nervousness makes me smile.

"I was counting on it." I push Indy out of the way so I can sit up. "The baby pigs came yesterday. Wait until you see them."

"I'm going to drop the boys off at the movies, then I'll be right there."

The normalcy of the conversation feels strange after the drama with the deer. "Sounds good."

After ending the call, I run a hand across my face. Remnants of dirt from my time laying on the ground still cling to my cheek. The pain from this morning threatens to crush my mood. I refuse to let it.

My symbolic good-bye, combined with crying myself to sleep wrapped around Indy and a few hours of rest, have left me with an unfamiliar feeling in my chest.

With a shock, I realize the feeling is hope.

I didn't know hope was something I was still capable of.

The hot water of the shower thrums against my short hair. I run my fingers through the strands, releasing bits of leaves stuck there. The leaves fall to the floor of the shower, swirl in the water. I toe them towards the drain. The pieces of broken leaves wash away.

The pieces of my broken self go with them.

I feel good. Not super amazing, everything's okay good, but the heaviness I'd grown accustomed to has subsided. Barely bearable has shifted to a weight I can carry.

Inspired, I dress carefully for Grant. Using my fingers and the blow dryer, I style my hair into a flattering arrangement. I have to dig through the bathroom drawers, but I find an old eye-liner and highlight my eyes. The woman looking back from the miniature mirror looks almost like the me I remember.

Except for the scar across my neck and the other scar on my chest.

I rescue a turtle neck sweater Nicole bought for me from the oblivion of clothes forgotten at the bottom of my closet. The blue color makes my eyes sparkle, and the high neck covers my scars.

With growing excitement, I pull on the nicest pair of jeans I own, ones without stains or tears from hard work. They zip a little too easily, but still cling to the few curves I have left.

Passing by my usual boots, I choose a pair of black sneakers. They're not the most fashionable shoes, but they'll work for what I have planned.

"How do I look, Indy?" I walk around the cabin in the unfamiliar feeling clothes. "Will Grant recognize me?"

Indy watches me with his unbelievably bright blue eyes, unimpressed with my fashion choices.

I'm feeling brave and bold, but terrified. "You can do this," I repeat to myself as I pace the cabin. "You can do this."

My nerves get the better of me. I need Nicole.

She picks up almost instantly. "Everything okay?" she says instead of hello.

Her instant concern rankles my already taut nerves. "Why wouldn't I be okay?" I bark. The absurdity of the question hits me as soon as it leaves my mouth. Yesterday I dumped guts on my own porch, carved an evil mark into an innocent deer, and then saw the ghost of a killer. Maybe Nicole has reason to be worried.

But she doesn't know how close my mind came to finally snapping.

I rush to fill her hurt silence, "Sorry, I didn't mean to be rude. I'm just nervous."

Nicole takes my apology with her usual ease. It's

amazing what she lets me get away with sometimes. "What are you nervous about?"

"I have a date. Well, I guess you could call it a date."

Silence again, but shocked excitement this time. "I knew it!" she finally says. "With Grant, right? The donuts worked."

I smile into the phone. "Yes, your donuts worked. We had a nice morning yesterday, and he's coming over any minute."

She squeals like a teenage girl, "Ahh, I'm so excited. I knew he was a good match for you."

"Don't get ahead of yourself. It's not really a date or anything."

"What are you wearing? Do you have your work clothes and boots on?"

I finger the soft fabric of the turtle neck sweater. "The turtle neck sweater you bought me."

"Did you put on makeup?"

"Just a little."

"Hate to tell you, Sis, but you're on a date."

That word sobers me. "Am I ready for a date?" This time I sound like the teenager, a shy, confused child stepping out into the world of grown-ups.

"Only you know what you're ready for. But you did get dressed up before you called me, so that says something."

I run my hand down my sweater. "Something's better than nothing," I mumble.

"You can do this, Maribeth. Just take one step at a time. You don't have to run off and get married or anything. Just be honest and open with him. He's been through stuff, too. He gets it."

I don't have time to ponder her comments. "He's pulling in now. Wish me luck."

"Have fun and call me later. I want all the details." Her obvious excitement fans the flames of my courage.

"I will. Promise." I end the call and watch Grant exit his truck, notice he's wearing nice clothes too. I didn't tell Nicole about the full scope of my plans for this afternoon. I didn't want to get her hopes up in case I chickened out.

I take my cleanest coat from the hooks by the front door and look at Indy. "Wanna go for a ride?" I ask him.

This gets his full attention. He jumps to his feet, scratches across the wood floor, and jumps at the door. "Didn't know if you'd even remember what that meant," I laugh at the dog. "Guess you do."

I zip my coat against the cold and meet Grant on the porch.

"Wow," he says when he sees me. The single word melts my apprehension. The woman in me glows at the instinctual appreciation in his eyes.

"You don't look so bad yourself." The easy banter flows off my tongue. "I know you were expecting to see baby pigs, but I wondered if you could do me a favor instead."

"Anything." He places one foot on the bottom step, rubs Indy's excited head.

"Can you take me for a drive?" Indy jumps again at the words, runs towards Grant's truck in anticipation.

Grant searches my face for a moment, understands the

227

immensity of the simple request. "I can do that if you want," he says cautiously.

"Let's go before I chicken out." I step bravely down the steps. One step at a time, I reach the truck.

My heart flutters, and my fingers turn cold as I reach for the door handle.

Chapter 25

Samuels

I don't let go of Teddy Pepple's hand until the EMTs come to check him out. Even then, his tiny fingers cling to mine, his big brown eyes pleading.

"It's okay, Teddy. They just want to make sure you're not hurt."

He doesn't let go of my hand. "Will you come with me?"

I pull the boy across the center console and wrap my arms around him. Cradling him against my chest, I climb out of the car and carry him to the back of the ambulance. "I'm right here," I soothe as I set him in the open ambulance door. "I'll stay until your mom comes. Will that be okay?"

Teddy nods and allows the medics to do their tests. His eyes continually dart to me, making sure I don't wander away.

"Teddy!" A woman's voice calls over the din of police

activity in the street. Teddy jumps to his feet and sprints to the woman's waiting arms.

Wanda Pepple cradles her son, both bodies shaking with relief.

I approach them slowly, giving her time to enjoy Teddy's safe return. She meets my eyes over Teddy's head, mouths the words, "Thank you."

The boy looks so much like Benny, but Benny's mother will never hold him again. A sharp ache stabs my chest, knocking the wind out of me.

I saved this boy, but I slept while Benny was slaughtered.

I have to look away. I have to walk away.

I give the woman a grim nod and motion for another officer to take over. I turn my back on her relief.

With a practiced force of will, I shove my emotions aside and focus on the job.

Lighting the cigarette I desperately need now, I walk down the street and back to my car. I open the back door and lean in to find the baby book I threw there earlier. An engine nearby roars into life. The book has fallen to the floorboard, and I bend to dig it out.

The engine growls closer, followed by the screech of tires braking.

The closeness of the sound startles me. I slam my head on the door frame as I swing towards the sound.

Several feet behind my car, yellow crime tape blocks the street, dances across my vision along with the stars from hitting my head.

A small white pick-up has rushed the tape, stopped

with its bumper inches from the yellow barrier. The driver throws the truck in reverse, and smoke rises from his tires as he slams the gas. I try to see his face, but my vision is still shaky, the driver's head turned away from me.

The truck speeds away in reverse, then makes a desperate three-point turn. Out of habit, I check the plate, but it's covered in mud and unreadable. The little bit I can make out doesn't look like an Indiana plate. Illinois maybe? The truck careens through the first corner and disappears.

"What the hell was that?" my partner, Danny Alexander, says behind me.

I rub my sore head, "Who knows." I hand him the baby book.

"What's this?" he asks.

"Jesse Franklin's baby book. I found it in a box upstairs." Alexander shoots me a quizzical look. "Open it."

Alexander flips to the first page. I watch his face as he makes the connection. "Jesse Franklin has a twin?"

"An identical twin."

"Holy, F-ing shit!" My partner exclaims colorfully.

It doesn't take long to process the house again. The thick coat of dust on most of it is untouched, leaving the techs little that needs to be gone over. Whoever's been using this house to continue the legend of Jesse Franklin is as careful as he was. We'd hoped to get something off the generator, a new addition to the property since the utilities were disconnected. The shiny body of the machine has prints all over it, but even a cursory look by the fingerprint team tells them the prints are from different people.

"He most likely bought it off the floor," a tech explains to me. "Lots of customers touched it before our guy bought it. We'll work on it, but I don't think we'll find anything useful."

"Let me know," I tell the tech with a sinking feeling.

"This guy is good," the tech mumbles under his breath as he turns back to his job.

He didn't mean for me to hear his endorsement, but I do. "Just find me something," I snap to his retreating back.

Social services sends over a specialist to interview Teddy Pepple. I don't expect much from the boy. He didn't see his abductor and from what Teddy said earlier, he'd been taken, then left in the basement alone. I don't have long to wait for the social worker's preliminary report.

"Sorry, Detective," the woman in a too-tight pants suit says to me. "Teddy didn't see who took him."

"I knew that already," I grumble. "Did the guy say anything to him? Any detail?"

The woman shifts her shoulders at my gruff tone. "He's just a boy, Detective. I can't push him too hard. I'll meet with him again tomorrow in my office. Maybe he'll remember more by then or feel safe enough to share it."

I blow air in disgust and push harder, "Nothing at all?"

"Teddy says he just kept using a bad word."

"Just one?"

"Well, one more than the rest. The guy kept talking about 'the bitch'." She checks her notes. "The bitch will pay."

The information isn't new. We already know who 'the bitch' is.

My partner saves me from having to comment to the social worker. "Samuels," he calls to get my attention. I thank the social worker and hurry to Alexander and his laptop. "Think I found Victoria Wilson."

Finally, something I can use. "Show me."

Alexander holds the laptop in his hands and shows me a Facebook page for a business in Chicago, Astrology by Victoria. I tingle with excitement. "Astrology, of course," I muse.

Alexander clicks on the pictures. "Look familiar?" A woman with long dark-blond curls smiles out of the photos. Now that I see the actual woman Franklin was basing his victims on, the resemblances are uncanny.

"Jesus, they really do look like her," I say over my suddenly dry tongue. "Is there a number listed?"

"Right here." Alexander clicks on the number with a Chicago prefix.

My fingers shake as I dial, but I don't hit the green button to connect it. The middle of a crime scene is not the place to carry on this conversation. Alexander follows me to my car. Once inside, my notebook and pen ready, I hit the green icon to start the call.

Adrenaline swims in my gut as the phone rings. I can feel Alexander's tension across the center console.

The phone keeps ringing.

I look at Alexander and raise my shoulders in a what now expression.

"Hello?" the woman's cautious greeting floods my ear. "Astrology by Victoria." She makes the statement sound like a question. The woman is already on alert.

I push the speakerphone icon so Alexander can hear. "Is this Victoria Wilson?" I force my voice to sound casual and curious.

My tone works and the woman's, "Yes it is. Are you interested in a reading?" sounds less wary, more professional.

I plaster a fake smile on my face, knowing it will change my tone even if she can't see me. "Ms. Wilson, this is Detective Samuels from Fort Wayne, I was wondering if you could help me with something?"

She hesitates, I can almost hear her thoughts, "A detective from Fort Wayne?!"

I hurry on, "No need to worry, Ms. Wilson. I got your name from a friend, and there's something you can help me with if I could bother you for just a few minutes."

I'm counting on the woman's hope for a paying client to override her caution.

"I suppose so," she hedges. "I always appreciate a referral. Who was this friend who gave you my number?"

"Not a friend exactly, but I think we both know them."

Victoria's not falling for my ruse, "And who is this person?" she asks pointedly.

"Jesse Franklin." I hold my breath, hoping the name shocks her enough to continue the conversation, but not enough to hang up on me.

She takes the bait without missing a beat. "Jesse Franklin is dead."

"That's true." I let the words sit, sink in, put her off guard. "His twin brother isn't."

Alexander and I watch the phone, waiting for the call to end and the screen to go blank.

The line remains open, so I push on. "Ms. Wilson, you can either talk to me now about the boys, or I can have a unit there in Chicago pick you up. We can talk in an interrogation room."

More silence, but she doesn't hang up.

"The choice is yours. But we have a situation here. Another young woman has already been killed, and today an eight-year-old boy was kidnapped." I give her time to process the gravity of the situation. "You can help us, Ms. Wilson." I push a little harder, taking a gamble. "You can stop him from hurting someone else."

The sound of her lighting a cigarette and blowing smoke near the phone fills the car. "Call me Victoria," she says finally. "What do you want to know?"

Chapter 26

Maribeth

Grant opens the passenger door for me before I can grasp the handle. I climb into the offered seat. "Can Indy come, too?" Nerves flutter in my belly, both from the adventure and the faint whiff of Grant's cologne.

"Wouldn't go without him." Grant opens the back door of the truck, and Indy bounds inside.

I take slow breaths and watch Grant walk around to his door.

Grant takes the turns of my lane expertly. "I see you cut back the branches on the lane," he says.

"I still need to burn the piles," I say to hide my growing fear. The fluttering in my belly blossoms as the gate comes into view. Grant stops the truck.

"You sure you want to do this?" he asks. "We can hang out at the cabin if you'd rather."

I look him full in the face. "I need to do this. I need to make steps. Does that make sense?"

"It makes perfect sense. I just don't want to force you to do something if you're not ready."

"I might not ever be truly ready, but I've made a lot of progress today. I want to keep moving forward."

I open the door and climb out, saying, "I'll get the gate."

Taking deliberate steps, I approach the keypad. "You did this once before," I tell myself. "Just punch in the code and open the gate."

The gate unlocks with a click. I put both hands on the top bar and walk with my eyes squeezed tight. When I open them again, I'm on the other side, the road stretching in both directions from me.

Grant pulls through and waits for me to close the gate and climb back into the truck.

Indy licks my face as I buckle in. "Where do you want to go?" Grant asks.

"Just drive."

It only takes a moment by truck to reach the open expanse of fields that I visited the other day. The place zooms past, even though he's driving slowly for my benefit.

"I ran down here a few days ago," I tell him. He seems surprised.

"Really? That's great." I can tell he's trying to be kind, trying to sound impressed by the minuscule victory. "You're an amazing woman, Maribeth," he adds.

Maybe he's impressed, not pretending. "I don't know about that," I say and watch his face, instead of the world whipping past the window.

"You're a lot stronger than you give yourself credit for. Most people would have lost it after going through what you've gone through."

I almost lost it this morning. I want to say the words out loud, but it feels like too much, too soon. I sneak a peek out the window. Unfamiliar homes slide past. My stomach flutters wildly, and I fear I might vomit all over his truck.

"Can…." I swallow hard. "Can we stop somewhere? I feel a little sick."

Grant slows the truck and pulls over near a bridge. "We could walk down to this creek and sit for a while."

Bless this man.

The creek splits through open fields, but trees line the banks. I climb out of the truck, the immensity of the sky making me dizzy. Vast and impossibly open, yet smothering at the same time. My heart thuds in my ears, and the fluttering in my belly makes my mouth water. I run for the cover of the trees by the creek.

These aren't my trees, but they soothe me just the same. I gulp air and swallow hard to keep from vomiting.

Indy darts past me, excited. He sniffs the water, then bounds off. "Stay close," I shout to him.

Grant takes his time joining me, giving me space to get myself under control.

"Sorry I ran like that," I say once I feel I can talk without my voice shaking. "The sky was too much all of a sudden," I tell him the truth. He already knows I'm broken, but he's here with me. Maybe my truths won't chase him away.

"Stop apologizing." He reaches for my hand. I let him take it, his fingers firmly wrapped around mine. He leads me to a fallen log, "Let's sit."

I sink next to him, the length of his thigh pressed against mine. With the trees overhead and his body next to me, I feel grounded and safe.

"Why are you so patient with me?" I ask. "I mean, I'm pretty messed up."

"We're all messed up," he points out. I sense a story behind the simple words.

"Are you?"

He considers his words carefully before answering. "I'm a lot better now, but when my wife Sarah Jane died, I had a really bad spell too." He doesn't look at me as he talks, watches the creek's eternal rolling.

"What happened?" I regret the words instantly. His pain is none of my business, unless he wants to make it mine.

He does.

"She killed herself."

Three words full of untold sorrow.

"Jesus," I breathe.

"Sarah Jane battled with bi-polar disorder for years." He picks up a stick, slowly, methodically breaks it into pieces. "We tried pills, different doctors, even in-patient care."

I watch him throw broken pieces into the creek. Each one splashes into the water, then floats away down-stream.

240

"I couldn't save her." He throws the rest of the stick into the water.

"I don't think anyone can truly save someone else." I think how close I came to Sarah Jane's fate.

Bryson and the kids did save me, made me get up and get out of the cold. But Bryson and the kids weren't actually there.

No one picked me up off that ground, I got myself to my feet. No one carried me to the cabin, I forced myself to go.

Sarah Jane made a different choice.

"I tried. I really did." Grant picks up another stick, breaks it into pieces like the first.

"She was lucky to have you." I don't know what else to say. "Your boys were lucky to have you after."

"You know what the worst part of grief is?" he asks suddenly.

I'm intimately familiar with grief. I can't imagine what the worst part might be. "All of it."

He lets out a humorless chuckle. "Yeah, that. For me, the worst part was how no one ever wanted to talk about her after she was gone. It's like people think asking me about her would remind me of the pain of losing her. I never forgot she was gone, or how much it hurt. If someone slipped up and said her name, they'd instantly look ashamed."

No one had ever asked me about my family once they were gone. Of course, I've barely spoken to another human since. "I know what you mean. Nicole never mentions Bryson and the kids. If she doesn't bring them up, she thinks she won't hurt me. My mom never asks me anything. Her rare phone calls consist of details of the latest charity event she's the head of." I pick up my own stick and break it into pieces.

"It's lonely," Grant says. "You lose a part of your life, then you can't really talk about them."

"You want to tell me about her now?" I venture.

Grant turns his blue eyes to me. An electric shock jumps down my back. "I'd rather you tell me about your family." He squeezes my hand. "I know what happened to them, but I don't know anything about the people they were. I'd like to know them."

I can hardly breathe. Do I dare?

"Benny was my baby," I start. "He loved books and telling stories. I always imagined he'd grow up to be a writer someday." I expect my voice to break into tears. Instead, as I talk, my voice grows stronger, more sure.

Once I start talking, I can't stop. An avalanche of stories flows out of me. Grant holds my hand and listens. Asks questions where appropriate, laughs at the funny things my kids did. He adds his own stories of Sarah Jane and their life together. We even share pictures from our phones. For once, looking at the faces of my family doesn't shred me.

Indy tires of his explorations and lies down next to us, listening. With my dog at my feet and this man at my side, the tiny flicker of hope I felt earlier blossoms into something larger.

Here on this creek bank, far from my woods, I feel at home.

Chapter 27

Samuels

"The first thing you need to know, Detective, is I may have given birth to those boys, but I'm not responsible for what they did." Victoria says.

"Just a minute, Victoria. Before we get started, I need to let you know my partner Detective Alexander is with me, and you are on speakerphone. We will be recording this conversation."

"I understand."

Alexander takes out his phone and presses record.

"Let's start at the beginning," I tell her. "Paul Franklin is the father to the identical twins Jesse and Jacob, correct?"

"Paul was a mistake," she says. "When I met him, he was really something. Star athlete in high school, handsome and charming. He was a typical Aries, bold and driven. But he never could follow through on anything. Always doing things before he thought them out."

I look at Alexander and roll my eyes. "What happened

with Paul?" I ask, trying to keep her on track.

"We had a few good years, but we weren't compatible. Once the boys were born, things went downhill pretty fast. I tried, I really did, Detective, but those boys were bad. Born bad."

Not words I usually hear from a mother.

"They were just babies. How were they bad?"

"Once they could walk, they were always getting into trouble. Knocking things over on purpose, not listening, that type of thing. I'm not one of those women who think spanking your kid equals child abuse, but no matter how many times I spanked them, they did whatever they wanted. Geminis are full of energy and always doing something. Even as toddlers, I couldn't control them."

"The boys are Geminis?" The pieces start to fall into place.

"Of course. What did you think the marks were for?" She hisses with disgust. "Busy and persuasive and tending to have two facets to their lives. That's the traits of a Gemini. The boys are twins born under the Gemini sign. They were destined for trouble."

This time Alexander rolls his eyes at the astrology lesson.

"The boys didn't grow up together, so what happened?" I steer Victoria back to the information I need.

"When they were five, they went too far. The garage in our alley caught fire. Sure the boys said they didn't do it, but Paul and I knew they did. Jesse and Jacob were out of control, and I'd had it with Paul anyway. I tried, I tell you,

244

I did," she pleads. "I thought they'd be better if we separated them. I took Jacob with me back here to Chicago. Paul and Jesse moved to Fort Wayne. I never heard from Paul again. He lived his life, and I lived mine. I even gave Jacob my last name."

Alexander scribbles the details into his notebook. "Did the boys know about each other? Did they remember?"

"I hoped they didn't, but I never asked. I never told Jacob about Jesse, but who knows what went on in his head. He was a dark child, even without Jesse to help him get into trouble, he found plenty himself. I thought I could scare him straight, you know. Point out how bad he was, so he'd want to change."

Her idea of parenting is a far cry from mine, "You told him he was bad, so he'd be good?"

"I'm not a perfect person, but I did the best I could." Her defensiveness belies her words. I highly doubt Victoria Wilson was a picture-perfect mom, not after what her sons did.

"I'm sure you did," I lie. "Tell me more about Jacob, does he still live in Chicago with you?"

She takes a long time to answer such a simple question. "A few years ago, he started taking off for a few days at a time," she says hesitantly. Through the line, I hear her light another cigarette.

"Before Jesse started killing?"

"About that time, I suppose. We'd had a huge fight, and I threw Jacob out. He was twenty-two, for God's sake, time for him to be a man already."

"Do you know where Jacob went?"

"Not at the time. He was gone for two weeks the first time, then came slinking back. Said he'd been in Fort Wayne with friends."

"Didn't say which friends?" I ask.

"Might have, I'm not sure. You have to understand, by this time, I was afraid of my own son, Detective. You've seen him, nearly six feet tall and broad. Imagine being afraid of your own child. He was different when he came back that first time. I knew something had changed in him, but I learned not to ask questions. I just let him do what he wanted. He stayed mostly in his room anyway. Never did get a job or grow up. Every now and then, he'd take off for a few days, and I could sleep soundly knowing he was gone. But he always came back like a bad penny."

"You had no idea what he was doing when he was gone?" I'm starting to lose my patience.

"Not until he was killed."

I couldn't have heard her right. "What do you mean he was killed?" My case dissolves around me. I was sure Jacob Wilson was behind these latest crimes. If both the twins are dead …?

Victoria cuts into my musings. "I thought that's what you were calling about." Her tone turns sour, conniving. "I really thought you knew."

I grip my phone so hard, I'm afraid it will crack.

"You thought I knew what?" I bark.

"The man who died killing that detective's family was my son Jacob."

The stunned silence in my car rings in my ears. "Jesse

Franklin killed them," I manage to say.

"Only if you look at it like that. Jacob died that night. Jesse eventually found me, and I had my other son back. They really are identical, you know. Jesse's been here for the last two years, living as Jacob. Jacob never did anything with his life anyway, better if Jesse took it over. I had a second chance to save one of my boys. Jacob had found Jesse somehow, had poisoned his mind. Jesse said Jacob made him do all those horrible things."

My mind reels with this information. I don't buy the "Jacob made me do it" line.

"Where is Jesse now, Victoria?"

"How should I know?" she says innocently, enjoying the power she holds over us. "Turns out, I couldn't save him any more than could save Jacob. He was so upset that Jacob was killed. Of course, I didn't really know Jesse, but I could tell he wasn't right in the head after a while. I told you those boys were born bad."

I clench my teeth and ask her again. "Where is Jesse Franklin?"

"Haven't seen him for several days, at least. He loaded up his truck and took off."

I cling to this new detail, "What kind of truck does he drive?"

"One of those tiny pick-ups, you know the kind."

Alexander speaks up for the first time. "A white one?"

"That's right," she says.

The truck that rushed the crime tape earlier then sped off.

Jesse Franklin had been a few feet away from me, and

I didn't even know it.

Chapter 28

Jesse Franklin

Taking the boy had been a mistake. He'd been playing alone in his front yard. He looked so much like the bitch's son, I had to drive by three times just to look at him. I hadn't planned on taking him, but it was easy.

Jacob would be ashamed of my impulsive act. Taking the women and keeping them to care for us had been my idea, but Jacob was the planner. "The devil's in the details," he'd said a thousand times. We'd gotten the details right every time.

I messed up the details this time. I knew it the minute I had the boy in the truck. The bag over his head couldn't muffle his crying. I've heard the women cry plenty of times, but the boy's tears bothered me. When I was his age, Dad had made me cry nearly every day.

A broken bottle outside of his favorite bar had kept him from making me cry anymore. Paul Franklin died in a bar fight, according to the official report. Really wasn't much of a fight. He'd been too drunk to hit me in that parking lot.

He'd hit me enough in the past.

The boy didn't weigh very much. Was easier to carry downstairs than the women were. I'd tossed him on the couch, shouted at him to stop crying.

He just kept sniveling under the bag on his head.

"This is all her fault," I shouted at the walls of the basement. The fantasyland Jacob and I had created was covered in dust around me. A few places showed where the dark-haired girl had touched things. I told her not to touch anything, but she didn't listen.

"The bitch will finally pay," I told the huddled kid on the couch.

I needed a few things first. I had to get the details right. I locked the boy in the basement and went shopping, my blood tingling with excitement.

Coming back to find my house swarmed with police changes that excitement to rage. How the hell did they find the kid? I'd only had him a few hours.

The answer walks towards me down the street. Detective Samuels. If Jacob hadn't gotten himself killed, Samuels would be dead too.

The man saunters towards me, confident and sure of himself.

The rage boils, makes my ears ring.

I can take him down right now. I shove the truck into gear and barrel towards the man.

"Not now, they'll catch you," I hear Jacob in my mind.

At the last moment, I slam on the brakes. I turn my

head so Samuels can't see me and speed away.

His time will come.

Right now, I have unfinished business in the country.

Chapter 29

Maribeth

Grant's phone chirps with a text from his boys. "I'm sorry, I have to go pick them up."

"Absolutely." I stand up and brush bark off the rear of my jeans. "It's getting close to dark anyway." I want to tell him why the falling darkness matters, but I don't.

He takes both of my hands in his, stands so near I can feel the heat of his body. "I enjoyed this." The words are casual, the intensity in his eyes is not.

"Me too," I breathe. I know what's coming, but not sure how I feel about it.

His lips hover near mine, questioning, waiting.

I lean into him, brush my lips against his.

The contact sends tingles up the back of my neck. I push closer, inviting.

His hands slide around my waist, pulling me against him. A rush of emotions I didn't think I could feel anymore overpower me as the kiss deepens. I cling to his coat, needing his solid body against mine.

My body responds to the kiss instinctively.

My mind rebels. *Not Bryson, not Bryson.*

Bryson is gone.

My reaction scares me, and I tense.

Grant senses the change and breaks the kiss. He doesn't let me go, cradles me against him.

I don't think. I don't analyze. I just allow myself to feel.

He kisses the top of my head. "Let's get you back."

We step out of the trees.

With Grant's hand in mine and Indy by our side, the wide sky doesn't scare me.

Without the trees to block it out, the blaze of the setting sun intoxicates. The rays glare on the windshield, the intensity burning my eyes.

"Wow," I whisper.

Grant turns his head to me, concerned. "You okay?"

"Yeah," I breathe. "I haven't seen a full sunset like that for a long time. It's breathtaking."

His eyes turn sad as he admires the spectacle before him. "I hadn't noticed it. Strange how you get used to things and take them for granted."

The colors in the sky deepen to a dark red, flaming fingers stretch to the clouds above.

"You're right, it's amazing," he says after a moment.

Grant takes my hand and lifts it to his warm lips. His kiss flitters for the shortest moment, the flutters in my chest linger.

The sun disappears too quickly, and darkness fills the

field near my woods.

The flutter in my chest turns to thumping.

I need to get back.

Grant stops at the gate, and I jump out to open it before the truck comes to a complete stop.

The headlights shine on the keypad, and I punch in the code. The gate clicks open, a lonely sound in the darkness.

Just inside the woods, three forms shimmer into existence.

I look at them, then back to Grant, feeling like a child caught sneaking out.

I'm conscious of the headlights illuminating my every move. I feel like a deer caught unaware on a country road. I'm frozen with indecision.

Grant rolls his window down, "Maribeth?"

The soft word breaks the spell.

"I think Indy and I will walk from here." My body finally moves, and I approach his open window.

"I can drive you up. The boys can wait a little longer."

The boys. I latch onto the logical reason for needing Grant to go. "Don't make them wait. I can walk up by myself. I walk through the woods by myself all the time." I add a smile to put him at ease.

A smile I don't feel.

The three figures now stand on the lane, waiting for me.

I open the back door of the truck and let Indy out, giving Grant no chance to argue.

He's been so amazing today, I can't just scamper away

255

like a frightened animal without thanking him.

His bare hand sits on the open window of the truck. I take it in my own. "Thank you for today." I rub my thumb along the hairs on the back of his hand, conscious of my family watching me.

He leans closer to the open window, so close I can smell his cologne. "Thank you," he emphasizes. "I enjoyed talking with you."

The moment is preciously sweet, and tinged with awkwardness. I want it to last forever and to get over quickly.

I don't have words, so I just rub my cheek against his hand. I let his skin linger on mine, not caring that my family might be watching. They might not really be there.

Grant is solid and real.

"I drive by here nearly every day on my route," he says. "I can stop by for a quick lunch break tomorrow if you like."

"I'd like that," I answer immediately. "I really would."

Indy barks suddenly, intruding on our quiet moment.

"I better go," Grant says. He kisses the back of my hand again. "See you tomorrow."

I release him and hurry through the gate.

Once he sees me safely on the lane, he drives away.

Without his lights, the darkness threatens to smother me.

"That guy is hot," Lilly exclaims. "Way to go, Mom."

I shoot a guilty look at Bryson, his expression inscrutable.

"I guess so," I hedge.

256

"You left the woods," Benny says from near my hip. "I would have been too scared."

I yearn to rub his dark hair but hold my arm stiff at my side. "I was scared, Benny-buddy. Sometimes you have to do things that scare you."

I can feel Bryson watching me, but he still doesn't speak.

"Where did you go?" Benny asks.

"Just for a drive. We sat by a creek and talked. I told him all about you guys, even showed him pictures of you."

"Your first date, and you just sit by a creek and talk? I would have gone dancing or at least do something fun," Lilly says.

"I wouldn't call it a date." I look again at Bryson, anxious to know his thoughts.

The five of us walk in silence. I try to pretend we're just a normal family out for a walk in the woods with their dog.

I can't make it feel real.

My steps crunch on the gravel of the lane, loud in the silence.

Only my footsteps make a sound.

Bryson finally speaks. "I'm glad you had a good time." Sincerity, not a hint of sarcasm or accusation. "He seems like a good man."

A rush of relief fills me. "He's a lot like you," I say cautiously.

Bryson finally smiles, and my heart nearly melts. "I'd expect nothing less. You need someone, Maribeth."

"You're not mad?" I ignore the absurdity of the question.

Bryson doesn't.

"How could I be mad?" He looks down at his shimmery shape.

"I just…" I try to form the words. "It's just a weird situation, you know?"

"Is it?" he asks cryptically.

Indy barks, and I jump in surprise. The twists of the lane hide the gate from view, the trees forming an unbroken wall of darkness. Indy stares down the path towards the entrance anyway.

The hair on his neck stands at attention, and he lets out a low growl.

I look to Bryson for his reaction.

I'm alone on the lane.

Indy barks again. "Stop that, Indy!" I tell him, taking out my anger at the disappearance of my family on the dog.

He looks at me then down the lane again. His neck hair drops back into place, and the tension leaves his body.

"You're freaking me out," I tell him. "We don't have time for you to go chasing some raccoon. I just want to go inside."

Indy reluctantly follows me up the lane.

The porch light filters through the trees ahead, and I quicken my steps. The temperature dropped once the sun went down. I hadn't dressed for hours outside. The tips of my ears sting, my hands ache with cold.

I want my fireplace.

Indy bounds up the porch steps ahead of me and lets himself in through his dog door. I climb the three steps slowly. The emotional rollercoaster of the last few days has left me spent.

The warmth of the cabin surrounds me.

Tossing a few logs into the fireplace, I stir the dwindling flames back to life.

My phone chirps with a text from Nicole.

"Sooo???"

I told her I'd call after my time with Grant, but I don't have the energy to hash over the details right now.

I send her a quick text instead. "Went great! Don't feel like talking right now. Going to do the chores and go to bed." I add the heart eyes emoji to be sure she doesn't worry.

"Can't wait for all the details," she replies.

I need time to process the day. Bryson's strange, "is it?" bothers me.

I was surprised to see them at all after saying good-bye this afternoon. Bryson's cryptic comments don't help my confusion.

"I need to talk to you, Bryson," I say to the empty room.

Either Bryson can't hear me, or he has nothing else to say, because he doesn't appear.

I change out of my sneakers and clean coat and pull my chore scrubs over my decent jeans. I toss a work coat over my lovely blue sweater and slide rubber muck boots on my feet.

Chores, then bed. Sounds lovely.

Preoccupied with my swirling thoughts about Grant and Bryson and where I go from here with them both, I hurry through the double doors to the barn. The second door is unlatched, it's never unlatched. Curious, I push it.

The door swings open into the shadowy barn.

The barn is quiet, too quiet.

Chica and Rizo always jump up excited when I open the door. The chickens usually make their peaceful evening sounds this close to sundown.

The barn is silent.

My hand shakes with fear as I flip on the light.

Chapter 30

Maribeth

Feathers everywhere. Thick masses of feathers that coat the floor of the barn.

My mind strains to make sense of them. I take a cautious step into the barn, the feathers crunching below my boot.

I toe what appears to be a pile of fluff. The bloody corpse of a chicken rolls over on the concrete. The bird has been cut open and nearly plucked clean.

Other piles dot the barn, other slashed chickens.

Don't look, just run.

I can't run.

I turn slowly, steeling myself for what I know will be in the pig pen.

Carnage. Pure, bloody carnage.

They're all dead.

Rizo in his pen, Chica in hers.

I fall to my knees, my hands clinging to the fence bent where they fought back and lost. Even a protective mother is no match to a sharp knife.

Peering through the slats of the fence, I squint my eyes, my lashes fuzzing my vision. I need to see, to count them.

Five tiny bodies lie in the bloody straw near their mother.

Only five.

I open my eyes wider and count again. One piglet is missing.

Heedless of the bloody scene, I scramble over the fence into the pen. Frantic to find the last piglet, I dig through the straw, searching for the tiny body.

In one corner, a pile of straw shifts slightly. I desperately sink my hand into it, and something firm wriggles beneath my fingers.

I snatch the baby up and hold her against me. She squeals in protest at my rough handling. I rub my chin against her baby-down fur, the heat of her body warm against my chilled skin.

Tears of relief slide down my cheeks and drop on her squirming back, mixes with the three black spots on her spine. "You're safe now, little one. He didn't get you."

He.

My entire body goes cold. Someone did this.

The piglet wriggles against my chest as I slowly stand, every sense on high alert. The overhead fluorescents buzz quietly, an eerie soundtrack to the insanity surrounding me. I strain to hear footsteps, something, anything to let me know where he is.

The barn is as silent as the dead bodies surrounding my feet.

My eyes search the corners the barn for a hidden shape, but the shadows are all familiar, no one waiting to pounce.

The pungent smell of manure mixes with the metallic scent of blood. I lift my nose and sniff the air like the animal I've become.

A whiff of paint?

Behind me, something moves. I turn so fast, I nearly drop the piglet.

Jingles jumps from the top of a cabinet and lands on the tool bench next to the door. His green eyes bore into mine. He meows, a plaintive note of question and fear.

My eyes are drawn from the cat to the wall behind him. Bold red letters scrawled on the wall in spray paint followed by the Gemini sign.

Jesse Franklin left me a message.

"Come find me, Bitch."

My chest seizes, and chemicals flood my blood. The carefully constructed wall in my mind crumbles, leaving an empty void. The spider I've kept securely in its box climbs out, spins its web of truth.

The truth in front of me the whole time, every time I looked at the Gemini mark carved in my chest. The roman numeral two, the sign of the twins.

The video alibis suddenly make sense. One captured the women while the other made sure to be caught on tape far away.

The figure I saw under the tree last night was real.

Jesse Franklin isn't haunting me. There's two of them.

My earlier concerns about Grant and Bryson shrivel into inconsequence. Those men don't matter right now.

The only man my mind has room for is the one hiding in my woods. Half of the duo that destroyed my life and took the lives of eight other women.

My rage consumes me, focuses my actions to one overriding goal.

Destroy Jesse Franklin, again.

I should call for help, call 9-1-1. Sheriff Kinsley and his men can hunt Franklin for me. The old Maribeth would do just that, follow the rules. I'm no longer her. I take care of myself, fight my own battles. I place my phone on the workbench. Jingles watches with his intense eyes questioning. Staring the cat down, daring him to contradict, I hold the power button on my phone. I leave the now-dead phone with my now-dead animal family. The buzzing of the overhead fluorescents stops when I turn out the lights.

The barn is as silent as the tomb it's become.

With the piglet tucked in one arm, I search the cabin for something to keep her in. The plastic trash can in the corner of the kitchen might work. I dump the trash on the floor, heedless of the mess. I grab a handful of kitchen towels and place them in the bottom of the can, then sit it near the fire. I kiss each of the black spots on the piglet's back in turn, then place her gently in the bottom of the trash can. She's safe and warm for now.

I don't worry about Franklin seeing me, if he wanted to

264

kill me here in the cabin, I'd already be dead.

He wants to play, to prolong my torture. He needs me to hide in fear.

He won't get that satisfaction. I will play his game, but I'm changing the rules.

I peel off my chore clothes and the nice clothes I wore for Grant, tossing the useless garments in a pile on the floor. I replace them with warmer layers, pulling on camo pants and a matching camo coat over top. I leave my blaze orange safety vest behind.

Tonight I need to disappear.

With my service pistol locked away at Nicole's, my choice of weapons is slim, but I like my chances. I've honed my skills with my bow during endless hours on the practice range. The four-sided broadhead arrows glimmer razor sharp. I test the tip of one and pull my finger back in pain. I think of the pain they will inflict on Franklin and feel my face curl into a smile. "That will work," I mutter in a voice I barely recognize.

I strap my hunting knife in its leather sheath to my belt. Then wrap my release to my wrist. I try the small trigger to make sure it works, the movement giving me courage.

I only need to add two more things to my tools. I strain on tiptoes to reach the box hidden on the top shelf of my closet. The small leather square wears a fine layer of dust on the lid. I rub the dust with my fingertip, consider the objects hidden inside.

Just in case.

Before I can change my mind, I grab the items and

toss the empty box on the bed. I shove them into the inner pocket of my coat, where I know they'll stay safe.

Dressed head to toe in camo with my weapons ready, I'm prepared for battle.

I just have to take care of Indy. He's watched every move I've made with sharp blue eyes. He senses my intensity, pushes his head against my leg for comfort.

"You can't come, Indy," I say gently, dropping to one knee before my best friend. I rub his wide head, wrap my arms around him the way I do when we sleep. "I'll come back, I promise," I choke.

Don't make promises you can't keep.

I leave him in my bedroom, test the knob to make sure it's shut tight to keep him safely inside.

He scratches to be let out, his nails desperately digging at the wood.

"Not this time, Indy," I shout.

He whines, but stops scratching.

I imagine he's lying on the bed, his chin on his paws, watching the door for me to return.

"Back in a bit," I call with fake cheer. "Don't worry."

With my hand on the knob of the front door, I pause and look around the cabin. This space has been my home and my refuge for two lonely years. It suddenly looks smaller than it did earlier today, shabbier somehow. This space was mine and mine alone until Franklin defiled it.

Out of habit, I check the fire. It will last a while yet, but I add a few more logs anyway.

If I don't come back, someone will eventually come for Indy and the piglet, but I want them to stay warm for as long as possible.

It's ten paces from the fire to the door. I've counted them often. Tonight, I cross the space in only nine paces, my strides are so long and confident.

Without another backward glance, I push through the front door and onto the well-lit porch.

Chapter 31

Maribeth

The solar-powered porch light surrounds me in an island of light. I'm sure Franklin lurks in the shadows, watching, waiting. He prefers a blade to a gun. I'm counting on that detail, praying he won't just shoot me down like an animal.

The rage still boils in my mind, creating a strange clarity. I'm curiously unafraid. I'm conscious of the very essence of my life. I listen to my breathing, marvel at the blood pumping in my ears. Every day, every moment since my first breath has led to this night.

I welcome this challenge.

When no shot tears through me as I linger on the porch, I calmly light a cigarette. I know he's out there, somewhere, but I can't go running wild into the darkness. I have to be careful, precise. I have to get the details right.

I need to draw him out, make him follow me.

I lean casually against a post of the porch, pretending

I'm just out for an evening smoke, enjoying the night. He expected me to run screaming from the cabin once I found my slaughtered animals. I won't give him what he wants. I won't lose it.

I wait and listen to the night. I know every sound of the clearing. The coyotes yapping in the distance, I know that sound. It belongs. The scraping of two branches overhead, listened to it for hours. It belongs. The crunch of leaves off to the right.

That's Franklin. Game on.

Adrenaline floods my system, making my hand shake as I stub out my cigarette in the metal can by my rocker.

I pull my camo stocking hat lower over my ears, slide my bow over my shoulder and take the three steps off the porch to the ground. As calmly as going for a moonlight stroll, I cross the clearing and head down a path. I slip into the trees like a camo ghost into a fog.

To calm my nerves, I hum a tune I can't at first recognize. I keep humming, my feet falling into step with the melody.

Out of the corner of my eye, a shadow moves around the barn, crouches, waits. Franklin has taken my bait.

I recognize the tune I'm humming and start singing under my breath. The Farmer in the Dell. The song was a favorite of the kids. Lilly loved the "child takes the dog," part. Benny preferred the "cat takes the mouse" part. I never taught them the verse about taking a nurse. I'd taken care of my children.

I sing quietly. "The farmer in the dell. Hi-ho the dairy-o the farmer in the dell."

270

I may not have a dell, but I was a farmer before my pigs and chickens were slaughtered.

Once into the cover of the trees, I jog down the path. Even in the faint moonlight, I know each twist and turn ahead of me. Up ahead, run-off has created a small gully. Just past that, a low hanging branch might catch my head. This is my country, my land. I know it intimately.

Franklin only has the vaguest knowledge of it. Behind me, I hear him stumble over the hidden gully that I had expertly avoided.

As I planned, Franklin has followed me into the woods. My rational mind screams at the danger, warns me to run, to hide, to go back to the cabin and call the police.

My rational mind is useless tonight.

Dana Sanders was left at the far end of this path, just past the turn at the property line. I could draw him out there.

I sneak a look over my shoulder, see only shadows on the path. My eyes don't see him, but my instincts feel him following.

Now it's time to hide. I run faster.

"The farmer takes a wife, the farmer in the dell. The wife takes a child, the farmer in the dell." I repeat the song as I run, until the words become nonsense in the madness of my brain.

Panic sneaks past the words, starts asking questions.

Where are you going?

Not Dana's tree, that's too obvious.

In my mind, I can see the woods, follow where the

271

path leads. There's a pile of fallen logs just ahead. I could hide there. Not good enough.

I remember what else is on this path, and run faster towards it. "The farmer takes a wife," I sing under my breath.

This plan is nuts! The panic tells me.

I pound up a small hill and see the tree stand hanging nearby. I'd put it up the first spring I moved here. I only hunted from it once, didn't like how close it was to the path. Instead of moving it, I started using the other stands around my property. I'd forgotten it existed.

Until tonight.

I dart off the path and sneak to the base of the tree. I pull and twist the ladder to make sure it's still safe to climb.

You have a killer chasing you, who cares about the ladder?

This time, the panic makes sense, and I scramble up the ladder, repeating farmer in the dell in my mind.

I slip silently into the small seat of the stand. I nock an arrow on my bowstring and attach my release to the string. From this vantage point, I can see the path clearly in both directions. The range is a little short, the stand too close to where Franklin will pass by. It will have to work.

The blood thumping in my ears subsides, and I listen to the sounds of the night, strain to hear Franklin approach. I sing in my mind as I wait for my prey. "The cheese stands alone, the cheese stands alone."

Like a broken recording, "the cheese stands alone" repeats in my mind.

I'm alone like the cheese, waiting for the mouse to pounce.

A laugh suddenly threatens to escape my lips. I bite them hard to stop it. I can't tell if the laugh is from nerves or madness. "The cheese stands alone."

Madness, I decide.

My laugh echoes through the woods, high and wild. I bite my lips until I taste blood, but I can't stop laughing. From high in my tree, I'm a crazy bird of the night, cackling at the moon. I hope the sound scares him. I know it scares me.

Footsteps crunch on the path, following the sound.

In the shimmering moonlight, Jesse Franklin, or a man identical to him, steps into view.

I raise my bow and pull the string back. With my finger on the trigger, I touch the corner of my mouth with my knuckle and take careful aim.

Franklin knows I'm nearby, but hasn't spotted me yet. He searches each side of the path. My camo hides me in the air.

Take the shot. Do it before he finds you.

If I kill him now, it will be over too soon.

"Jesse Franklin!" I shout into the darkness, releasing the tension on my bow string.

His head snaps up, searches in my direction. His gaze slides past my stand. He can't see me.

"Haven't heard anyone call me by my real name in a long time," he says in my general direction. "Sure, it's in the news a lot, but they're talking about my brother."

My broken mind scrambles to make sense of that

273

information, decides it doesn't matter. One man or two, my family's still dead.

"Why are you here?" I ask.

"Why do you think, Bitch? What's the expression, revenge is a dish best served cold? I'd preferred mine hot, but it took me a long time to find where you'd hidden yourself here in the country. But I found you eventually." His eyes scan the trees again, linger on me for a split second, then move on.

"Why me? I'm not hurting anyone,"

"Because of you, my brother is dead," he shouts towards my tree.

"Your brother killed my family," I shout back. I raise my bow again, pull the string back, place my finger on the trigger. I could let go now and end it.

"Your meddling killed your family," he hisses.

The truth hits like a slap. I've spent countless nights telling myself the same thing. It was my fault they died. I lured a killer into our home.

"You and your brother killed all those women," I plead my case. "It was my job to stop you."

"Hiding behind your job won't change the facts. Why don't you come out of whichever tree you're in and face me?"

My arm shakes from holding my bow at the ready so long. My finger itches on the trigger. Cold sweat drips from my armpits and runs down my sides. Memories of my family flash through my mind. A colorful tumble of impressions of lives well-loved.

Benny's broad smile, disarming and innocent.

Lilly dancing at a recital, graceful, and impossibly beautiful.

Bryson over me in the darkness of our bedroom, our intimacy my entire world.

This man and his brother destroyed them.

Tears blur my sights, and I sniff at my running nose. "I could kill you right now," I say through threatening sobs.

"You won't," he taunts.

Every inch of my body goes cold, dead, and the spider squats in my mind. I blink away my tears and line up my shot.

"That's what your brother thought."

I trigger the release.

Click-thwack.

Chapter 32

Samuels

The sky grows dark as Alexander and I finish our conversation with Victoria Wilson. Once she started talking, she didn't want to stop. I appreciate the information, but I need to make a call, and I can't until I get her off the phone.

It's full dark when she finally frees up my line.

"Who are you in such a hurry to call?" Alexander asks. "Need to tell your wife you'll be home late tonight?" He laughs at what he thinks is a joke.

"I need to warn Johansen that Franklin is at large. He left Dana Sanders there, he might be heading there himself now that his Benny look-alike plan is ruined.

The call goes straight to voice-mail. "Shit. She didn't answer."

"I'm sure she's fine." Alexander looks over his notes

from our conversation with Victoria. "Try her again later."

I light a smoke and suck it thoughtfully. "Don't over-react," I tell myself and watch the smoke snake out the cracked window of my car.

Impatient, I try Johansen again. "Straight to voice-mail again," I gripe and hang up without leaving a message.

"You worry too much," Alexander says. "If you haven't gotten a hold of her in half an hour, then worry. She probably forgot to charge her phone. Does she even have power out at that place?"

I've never before wanted to smack Alexander, but my hand itches to do it now. "Yes, she has power," I say sarcastically. "She's made a nice home there. Nicer than yours."

"Jesus, sorry I said anything." Alexander holds up both his hands. "If you're that worried, call the sheriff up there."

I think that over. Kingsley and I got along fine on this case, but I'm hesitant to call him in on what might be a wild goose chase. I'm sensitive about Johansen, it could be clouding my judgment.

I toss my cigarette butt out the window and look at Alexander. Overreacting or not, I need to check on her. "Things are all wrapped up here. Can you finish without me?"

Alexander searches my face and asks, "Want me to come with you to check on her?"

I feel bad for wanting to slap him a minute ago. "No. I'm sure she's fine. I'd just feel better if I see her, you

278

know? At least tell her what's happened here. I owe her that much."

"Sure thing." Alexander climbs out of my car. "Let me know if you need me." The door slams behind him, caught by the wind.

Once on the road, my nerves play tricks on me. I drive faster than legal, even contemplate using my dash light. My gut tells me she's in danger. I push the gas just a little more. Any traffic cop past his first day on the job will recognize a detective's car with the light on the dash.

I trust my fellow officers not to pull me over and push even harder on the gas.

The drive from Fort Wayne to Maddison isn't that long, but even at my high speed, it seems to take forever. The farther I get into the country, the worse the pain in my belly grows.

Twice I picked up my phone and called her again. Voice-mail each time.

Twice I think about calling Kingsley, but dismiss that thought. "Let's just see what we've got once I get there," I say out loud, trying to calm myself.

Finally on Johansen's road, I remember the locked gate. I have the code listed as a note under her contact information in my phone. But when I park my car in front of the gate, I realize I don't need the code.

A wrapped chain locks the gate to the post.

Did she lock herself in, or did someone lock us out? In the glow from my headlights, I can see the original lock is engaged. Why add the chain?

My scalp tingles with fear.

I clamber out of my car and shake the gate, knowing it won't open that way. "Johansen?" I call into the dark.

I climb back into my car and speed down the road, not caring how fast I go. A few long minutes and some reckless turns later, I see the entrance to the access road where we went in to work the Dana Sander's case.

This road leads close to the back of Johansen's property.

It's my fastest chance to get to her.

I turn the car onto the bumpy dirt and gravel lane, the rough terrain bouncing me out of my seat until I slow down.

Her woods rise out of the darkness. My headlight cut a swath of light into the grass and brush at the side of the lane. The same white truck that tried to run the crime tape earlier sits half-buried in the tall grass.

Now that the threat to Johansen is real, I have no hesitation about calling Kingsley.

The sheriff tells me to sit tight and wait for them to arrive.

I sit for maybe sixty seconds, watching the woods for any movement.

"Fuck this!" I shout. I was unable to help Johansen before. I will not sit and wait now.

I turn off my engine and climb out of my car, my hand near my hip, ready for whatever waits beyond the trees.

In the shaded vastness of her woods, it doesn't take long to lose my bearings. I've never been much of an outdoorsman. Clinging brambles and slapping branches reaching out of the darkness stretch my already tight nerves. Give me a dark alley or city street any day.

Coyotes yap nearby, too near, causing a shiver to slide across my shoulders.

Alone in the woods at night feels like a nightmare. Add in a serial killer on the loose, and I feel like a character in a horror movie.

Maybe this time I'll be the hero of the movie.

Walking gets easier, and I realize I'm on one of her paths. The paths all lead to the cabin. Excited, I jog along, only occasionally missing a turn and starting again.

My breath grows ragged as I climb a hill on the path, then turn a corner, hoping to see something other than trees. How many trees are out here anyway?

My foot catches a hidden branch, and I slide down the far side of the hill on my belly.

More trees is the least of my worries.

The coyote crouches before my face, its yellow eyes and open jaws only a few feet away. It watches me with wary eyes. I shove onto my rear and scramble like a crab.

The coyote takes one step towards me. I paw at my hip and draw my gun on the animal, ready for it to attack.

It sits on its haunches, the yellow eyes level with mine.

A few yards to the left, I see more of the animals, feeding on what appears to be the remains of a deer.

The coyote in front of me makes a low grumble, and the others join it. Eight animals settle in a circle around me. Eight pairs of eyes, eight sets of jaws.

With my gun drawn, I watch them watch me, wonder if I'll be dessert to their meal of deer. There's eight of them. Even on my best day and with good light, I don't think I could shoot five before they got to me.

If they decide to rush.

They don't seem to be interested in attacking me, just watching me. I regain my feet and turn in a slow circle, looking at each wild animal in turn. I take a step down the path, and the coyotes growl in unison. They don't want me to move.

I'm no animal expert, but they have their reasons for holding me here.

Keeping my gun drawn and ready just in case, I give in to the coyotes and wait. As long as they don't attack me, I'll play their game.

The minutes tick by, the delay in getting to Maribeth agonizing. The faint sound of sirens carries on the wind. Kingsley and his team are miles away but coming.

The coyotes hear them too and shift their bodies in agitation. They wait.

Then, as if by secret sign, all eight of them raise their noses to the moon.

Their howls fill the night sky, one note, sung in unison. The song shakes through my body and into my bones. An overwhelming sorrow sinks into me as they howl.

The coyotes finish their mournful song. As quickly as they surrounded me, they lope away. Eight animals fade like ghosts into the darkness.

Chapter 33

Maribeth

From my deer stand, the click-thwack rings satisfyingly in my ears. I hold the bow in place, watch the arrow fly at the symbol of my sorrow.

The range was too short, and I overcorrected. Franklin grabs above his hip. The arrow passes through him and into the ground behind. I'd aimed for his heart, but gut shot him instead.

When I shoot a deer, I wait for him to die in the wilderness.

I don't wait tonight. I'm anxious to finish this animal off myself.

I swing my bow over my shoulder and scramble down the ladder. I'm shaking so hard, my boots slip on the rungs, landing with a crunch.

My feet sting from the impact with the ground, but I ignore the pain and crash through the brush to Franklin.

He's run off.

My arrow sticks out of the ground on the far side of the path, blood staining the bright pink fletching. I pull my arrow and scan for a blood trail. Even in the pale moonlight, the splatters are easy to spot. The red marks stain the ground, leading me farther down the path.

I follow the blood trail at a sprint, my bow bouncing against my back, the bloody arrow gripped in my chilled hand.

I don't have far to run before I find him.

Several yards ahead, Franklin sits against a tree, his feet stretched before him, his hands pressing his wound. He looks like a macabre doll, all loose neck and bent joints.

I don't trust him.

Hiding behind a tree, I watch the man, sure he's only playing dead.

I nock the blood-stained arrow and hold my bow ready to draw and shoot again. Exhilaration from shooting him the first time churns through me.

I want him to move, to give me a reason to shoot him again.

As silently as possible, I creep towards him, my senses on high alert. In the distance, I hear a car engine, the sound of technology foreign to this primal battle. The stank of my nervous sweat seeps out of the neck of my coat. I blow air through my nostrils to clear them of the foul smell. With my next breath, I catch the scent of his blood.

A mad grin spreads so wide across my face, my cheeks hurt.

I place my feet carefully as I creep closer to him. I ensure the sole of each foot is flat on the ground with nothing under it before I shift my weight and take another step.

My eyes never leave Franklin's still form. The distance to my prey dwindles.

A few scant feet from him, I see it, the barely perceptible movement of his chest.

He's only playing dead.

I let him play.

I step onto the path and draw my bow slowly, clearly visible to him. I touch the corner of my mad grin with my trigger finger and wait for him to make a move.

He doesn't take the bait, so I take a step closer. The movement of his chest continues, but he's otherwise still.

Another cautious step, and I can touch his outstretched foot with my boot. With my arrow still trained on his chest, I kick him.

He was waiting for it.

His still leg suddenly side-swipes me at me. I click the trigger.

No satisfying thwack follows. This close, the arrow barely has time to fly, but it still hits him. Bright pink fletching bounces at the end of the arrow sunk into his shoulder. A knife blade catches the moonlight as Franklin plows into me.

I hit the ground hard. My bow tumbles from my shocked hand, arrows scattering on the path. His bulk instantly flops on top of me. The arrow in his shoulder slides between my arm and my chest, and the nock catches on my coat, slowing his progress.

Taking advantage of the moment, I roll over, claw the

ground to escape. He grabs my legs, wriggles his way onto me.

I push onto my knees in a modified wrestling move as Franklin wraps himself around my waist. His chin jabs into my shoulder, and I can smell his stale breath.

"You shot me, Bitch," he hisses into my ear.

Disgusted, I slide one foot forward under me and feel his weight shift lower. My daily run has given me strong legs. I flex them now. My backward push throws him off balance and he lands on his back in the dirt.

I instantly pivot and throw myself at him. The arrow in his shoulder jiggles from his jarring landing. With both hands, I grasp the shaft and sink it deeper into him with all my weight. The tip of the arrow inside him grinds against his shoulder blade, the vibration of metal on bone slides up the shaft into my hands.

"Didn't think you had it in you," he says confidently, reaching to push me away.

The arrowhead slides down the bone, then pushes through his body and into the ground below. I shove all my weight on the arrow driving it deep, pinning his shoulder into the dirt.

He howls and kicks, flaps his hand at the arrow. When that doesn't work, he shoves his feet against the ground and tries to push away. The arrow holds him down, and his body rotates around the pivot point.

I snatch another arrow from the path. Standing over him, I hold the arrow over my head in two hands.

"You underestimated me," I growl.

I crash the second arrow it into his upper arm. The

arrow cuts through the flesh easily, then sinks into the ground.

Franklin screams when he realizes he can't escape. He kicks his legs and swings his arms. He's like a bug pinned to a board.

He's at my mercy. I let out a laugh that matches the wild cackling I made in the tree stand.

"Stop squirming, or I'll pin your legs down, too," I tell him, enjoying my power. I stand over him an arrow in each hand, ready.

He kicks in defiance.

"I warned you," I say.

In a flash, I sink another arrow into him, miss his calf and catch his pants. I'd hoped to hit flesh, but the arrow holds him anyway. He swings his only free leg in my direction, but I move out of reach easily.

"You just won't learn, will you?" I bark.

This time I don't miss, catch his calf muscle and pin his last leg down.

With my prey immobilized, I watch him wriggle. Blood seeps out of his wounds, the one in his belly flowing heavily.

I step over him, one leg on each side of his bleeding body, panting so hard that my side aches. I lock eyes with the face that's haunted me for years. Slowly, so he won't miss my intention, I unsnap the leather pouch on my belt and pull out my hunting knife.

"You like knives, don't you?" My voice calm and clear.

I drop to my knees and straddle his chest. He bucks to

get away, but the arrows hold him in place.

I touch the blade to his cheek. "You marked me, and you marked the others."

His eyes grow wide with terror. "Jacob did that to you, not me," he pleads pitifully.

The tip of my knife pricks his skin. He turns his head to escape. "You're the same person to me," I hiss.

Three quick flashes of my blade and he squeals. "One for each of my family," I say as three lines of blood appear on his cheek.

His chest rattles with fear as he pants below me. My mind fuzzes, and the past and present merge.

Another man who looked just like this one, another rattling breath.

I'd used Siri to call 9-1-1 the night my family had been butchered before my eyes. Who I thought was Jesse Franklin had gasped against the shards of glass from the broken coffee table stuck into his back.

It would take emergency response several minutes to arrive. I watched Franklin's chest rise and fall. My family's chests never moved.

Furious, I shoved with my feet until the chair tipped over. On my side, I wriggled my duct-taped hands over the back of the chair. Using a shard of glass from the floor, I sawed and pulled until the tape broke away.

I was free.

My family was dead, but Franklin still rattled with life.

I climbed on hands and knees and straddled the barely conscious man bleeding under me. He would probably die from his wounds. I refused to take the chance he might live.

Blood dripped from my crudely cut neck and down my arms. I pressed my hand against his mouth, blood dripping from my fingers onto his face. I clamped his nose closed with my thumb and squeezed. He wriggled below me with a last surge of life. Shoving my hand tighter against his mouth and nose, I struggled to say conscious long enough to finish him.

He didn't wriggle long.

Sure he'd never move again, I rolled onto the floor, shaking and cold from loss of blood. Indy curled next to my side, his warm body solid and alive.

Through the haze of shock, I heard sirens in the distance, my fellow officers racing to my rescue.

Footsteps ran through the silence of the house, and the kitchen door slammed shut. Indy growled, but chose to stay near me.

Did I really just hear someone else?

The thought skittered at the edge of my consciousness, joined the black blobs floating in the air above my eyes. The thought and a blob blended together and formed the shape of a spider.

The blobs and the spider grew blurry. With the last of my consciousness, I shoved the spider into a box in the far reaches of my mind. It was too hideous to look at.

I drifted away to the sound of sirens.

Chapter 34

Maribeth

In the cold woods, I have trouble determining if the sirens I hear are singing now, or only in my memory.

The moon reflects in this Franklin's terrified eyes. I don't have to cut the tape from my wrists this time.

I shove my hand hard against his mouth and pinch his nose closed with my thumb. He screams behind my hand and shakes his head.

I have no intention of letting go.

I raise onto my knees, place my other hand on top of the first and press down with the full weight of my body. His teeth push through the skin of his lips, grinds under my palm. The blood from the three slashes on his cheek warms my fingers.

"You stole my life from me," I hiss wildly. "You killed my beautiful family and destroyed me."

My head fuzzes, and my side stings. Franklin kicks and

squirms beneath me, but I press on. His kicking slows. I grind harder.

"Maribeth!" Bryson screams my name.

Shocked, I lift my head. My family watches me.

"Mom?" Benny questions. "What're you doing?" The fear in his precious voice breaks my heart.

I let up on the pressure against Franklin, but keep my hand closed over his airway. My vision fades to shadow then back again.

"Your pocket, Maribeth." Bryson urges. "What's in your pocket?"

I struggle to make sense of the question. "My pocket?"

"You put something in your pocket," Lilly chimes in. "Inside your coat."

"But he killed you guys," I plead, my hand loosening even more. Franklin gasps at the air seeping beneath my palm.

"You're not a murderer," Bryson says carefully. "This isn't you. Look in your pocket."

I mentally take a step away from the ledge I teeter on and remember what I'd stashed.

Just in case.

I let go of Franklin's face and unzip my coat. The lining is warm and wet as I fish out the two items.

My badge flashes in the moonlight.

My handcuffs jangle in the quiet.

I look at Bryson and the kids, questioning?

All three nod in unison.

Detective Johansen climbs from her grave. Her fingers claw at the dirt, throwing it off in large handfuls. My former self reaches for the grass above. Maribeth the recluse watches her struggle out, then walks away.

I shake my head to clear the vision and look at my badge in my bloody palm.

Franklin gasps air below me. I spring off him, the sudden movement making my head swim crazily.

I snap one cuff on his wrist then wrestle his other arm closer. With him pinned to the ground, I have to settle for cuffing him in front.

"Jesse Franklin, you're under arrest," I say, my voice so weak, I can barely hear it over the sound of the other cuff clicking closed. Blood drips from me and splatters on the metal of the handcuffs.

The pain in my side swells, too much to ignore. I finally look down to check it.

The knife flash from when Franklin rushed me suddenly makes sense. The handle protrudes from my side.

The woods swirl. I attempt a step, but my knees give out. I hit the gravel hard, roll onto my back.

"Bryson?" I ask, with waning strength. "Am I going to be with you soon?"

"Don't talk like that." He can't hide the panic. "You won't die, you can't die. You have to hang on."

My family kneels next to me, wearing matching expressions of terror. Bryson tries to touch me, to put pressure on the wound. He can't.

"We don't have much time now," Bryson says to the kids. "Be quick about it."

I don't understand what he means until Benny leans

closer.

"I love you, Mom," Benny whispers near my ear. "Be brave." Benny leans to my cheek and kisses me. For a moment, I imagine I can smell his hair, the precious scent of little boy sweat and sunshine. Panic surges hot and bright, knowing the words are coming before he chokes out, "Good-bye, Momma." My precious boy fades away. I claw the air to bring him back.

"No!" I try to scream, but it comes out as a croak. "Make him come back," I beg.

Lilly leans near me next. "Not you, too, Lilly. Please, please stay with me," I whisper to my beautiful daughter. Her chin quivers, but she raises it. "You're the best, Mom," she sniffles. "Keep fighting. You've got this. I love you forever." Lilly places a kiss on my cheek, and her silky hair slides against my skin. I'm not sure if it's really her hair or the wind I feel. I try to hold the hair in my hand to make her stay. My daughter fades away.

The pain of their loss sears me more than the knife. I turn my head to Bryson kneeling at my side. The movement causes black clouds to shift across my eyes.

"I'm so cold, Bryson," I whisper. "Stay with me till the end comes."

"The end isn't coming, Maribeth. You need to fight," he urges. "Too many people need you. Nicole, your mom, Grant, Samuels, they all need you. Even Indy needs you. Just hold on a little longer. It will all be okay, I promise. All of it will be okay."

Bryson leans close and kisses me, his lips warm on my cold ones.

294

Through my foggy mind, I hear coyotes howling. Bryson's lips stay on mine as the long note, deep with sorrow and pain, carries through the woods.

The howling ends. Bryson whispers, "I love you. Be strong," into my ear.

He jumps to his feet, and shouts into the woods.

"She's over here! Come save her. She's over here!" His voice echoes through the trees then fades away along with his shimmery form.

Alone and bleeding, I watch the branches sway overhead. The stars peek through the gaps, playing hide and seek.

Franklin hasn't moved since I cuffed him. His rattling breath tells me he's still alive, but only barely.

"You better live, you fucker." I think. "Living can be harder than dying. I want you to see the marks on your cheek every time you look in a mirror. I want you to know I won."

If I win.

I'm so cold, my teeth chatter. I fight like Bryson told me to. With every ounce of strength I have left, I will myself to survive.

Through my haze of loss, I hear footsteps crashing through the wilderness racing towards me.

"Maribeth? Oh my God."

Samuels hovers over me, his shape barely visible in the misty tunnel of my vision. He drops next to me and puts pressure on my wound. The sudden pain wakes me up.

"How did you get here?" I croak.

"Don't talk now. Help is on the way." My former

partner forces a smile that doesn't reach his worry etched eyes.

"Is he still alive?" I whisper. "I need him to live."

Samuels inspects Franklin's pinned body near mine. He stares at Franklin's blood-streaked mouth longer than necessary. "Again?" I'm not sure if he actually asks the question or if my guilty mind imagines it.

Samuels takes in the cuffs, lifts my badge from where I dropped it on Franklin's chest.

"You arrested him?" he asks with nervous laughter. "Shit, Johansen, only you."

He doesn't know how close I came. I'd planned to cut him up and feed him to the coyotes. Or maybe run him through the meat grinder and feed him to Indy. Or I could have burned him in the fire pit. I could have easily made it so no one found his body.

Samuels interrupts my mad train of thought, "Where's the other guy?" Samuels asks, scanning the woods. "The guy who called me over here?"

"Bryson." I breathe the one word.

The woods spring to life before Samuels can ask another question. Samuels shouts to them, and soon Sheriff Kingsley's bulk hovers over me.

"Shit, woman. What did you do to him?" Kingsley's deep voice rolls through the fog of my fading mind.

"Just get those EMTs over here," Samuels snaps.

More bodies crash through the underbrush as Samuels keeps constant pressure on my wound.

For once, I welcome the strangers on my land.

Chapter 35

Maribeth

Before I even open my eyes, I know I'm in the hospital. The smells of disinfectant and stale air fill my nostrils. I want the earthy scent of my fireplace. I want Indy to be next to me. I squeeze my eyes shut and will myself back to sleep. Maybe when I wake again, I'll be home.

Home is an illusion.

"I know you're awake," Nicole says softly near my bed. "You couldn't fool me as kids, and you can't fool me now."

I keep my eyes shut. "I don't want to be awake." Simple words full of sorrow.

Nicole slides her hand into mine and gives it a reassuring squeeze. "You'll get used to it."

"Is he dead?" Three terrifying words.

Did I kill him?

"He's alive. Chained to a bed here somewhere.

Samuels says he's under constant armed guard. He can't get to you."

I can't keep my eyes shut forever, so I open them.

Moving causes a sharp pain in my side, but I shove myself up on the pillow to a half-sitting position.

Nicole reads my intentions and pushes the button that lifts the bed so I can sit. I wince at the ache in my side.

"Four hours of surgery," Nicole answers my unasked question. "Luckily, it didn't hit your intestines, or you'd be...." Nicole looks away and swallows. Then lifts her chin and tries to smile.

For the first time in years, I realize the pain Nicole has gone through. Bryson and the kids were her family too. She's taken care of me all by herself, but no one's taken care of her. Even her husband left her alone to take care of Ella.

"I'm here now," I tell her. "I'm really here now."

Nicole squeezes my hand again. "You better be, because I've missed you."

The emotional moment makes me uncomfortable. "Man, I could use a cigarette," I say to break the mood.

Nicole chuckles, "Can't help you with that."

"Where's Indy?" I ask to keep the mood light. "And the piglet?"

"Grant went to get them. He paced around here for a long time, waiting for you to wake up. He needed something to do besides blame himself for dropping you off at the road with Franklin waiting for you."

"We had no way of knowing what was going to happen," I point out.

"He still feels guilty."

I understand guilt, so I let that go. "The piglet needs a mom. She's too young to be alone."

Nicole, as usual, has taken care of it. "I already talked to the vet in town, and she's going to look after her until you're ready. Indy can stay with Ella and me."

"Sounds like you took care of everything."

Nicole chuckles again. "Just the easy stuff. You're the one who took down Franklin alone. If you try something like that again, I'll kill you myself."

"Never again. I promise."

We sit in companionable silence for a while, the ache in my side growing deeper. "I'm getting tired," I tell my sister.

"Get some rest." Nicole kisses the back of my hand. "We'll all be here when you wake up."

After endless days in the hospital and later recuperating at Nicole's, the trees of my property welcome me home. "You don't have to come back here," Nicole tries again as we drive up the lane. "You can stay with Ella and me as long as you want."

I stare at the trees in wonder, the first buds of spring dot the branches, a haze of green fills my woods. "I know that, and I appreciate it." I think about my words carefully. "I can't run again."

The cabin seems tiny, the covered porch narrower than I remember. A few spring flowers add dots of color, but the air of melancholy surrounding the clearing persists. My heart sinks. I'd expected elation, or at least a tingle of happiness. Bryson and the kids won't be back to cheer up the place.

I feel empty.

"Home sweet home," I say sarcastically, throwing the car door open before I lose my nerve. This is the only home I have.

Indy bounds out of the car and runs around the clearing, sniffing the ground. "He seems happy," Nicole tries to be supportive.

I lug the pet carrier with the piglet tucked inside up the three steps to the porch. Nicole follows me to the door. I stop her before she can open it.

"I'd rather go in alone," I say, suddenly scared. "I need to do this," I explain.

Nicole doesn't like it, but she steps away. "I'm just a phone call away," she says reluctantly. "And so is Grant."

"I know." Tears sting my eyes suddenly. "You're still coming Saturday for the bonfire, right?" I sound like a desperate child and hate myself for it.

"Of course," she says carefully. "You still want to do it?"

The party was my idea, a thank you to all those I love. A symbolic gesture of my growth, I'd told my new therapist. She'd agreed it was a good idea.

"I'm doing it. I need that too." I tell her.

Nicole finally drives away. Indy finishes his sniffing tour of the outside and barrels through his dog door into the cabin.

I pick up the pet carrier and follow him inside.

I carefully set the carrier on the floor. "Come on out,

Hope," I say to the spotted baby. Hope pokes her flat nose out of the carrier, then waddles into the room. "This is home now."

The spring day promises warmth, but the cabin holds a chill that matches my mood. Even with the addition of Hope, the space feels lonely. I shove the thought away and busy myself building a fire. "Just keep yourself busy, and you'll feel okay again," I tell myself.

Once the fire blazes, Indy settles into his usual spot by the fire. Hope climbs onto the dog bed with him, tucks herself against his body. "You guys look happy," I muse.

While I was healing, Nicole and Ella had cleaned the cabin. The trash I dumped in the kitchen is long gone, the counters wiped and waiting. Even my bed is made. The clothes I'd left on the floor have been washed and put away. Everything is clean and in place.

I have nothing to do.

I'm drawn to the barn, searching for something to fill my hands. The barn is quiet just like last time, but the carnage is gone. I don't know who Nicole got to remove the mess, but I thank them. Every scrap of straw has been removed from the pens. The floor swept clean of feathers. Even Franklin's words have been painted over.

Inspecting them closely, I can see the faint message under the fresh paint.

I have something to do.

After changing into work clothes, I find more paint and an old brush. As I paint over the barely perceptible remnants of Franklin, I find myself humming, "The Farmer in the Dell."

I freeze once I recognize the song. I haven't thought of it since that night. I set my brush down carefully, then go find my ear buds. With my music blaring at full volume, I finish painting.

Grant tosses another log on the bonfire and sparks lift into the darkening sky. "You did a great job on this fire pit," he says as he settles next to me on the bale of straw.

"Needed something to do the last few days," I reply and lean against his shoulder.

"You're not over-doing it, I hope," Nicole says quickly.

"No, mother hen, I didn't over-do it," I quip back.

"Leave her alone," Ella tells her mom. "She's a bad-ass, she can do what she wants."

"Language," Nicole warns but breaks into a light laugh.

The evening shimmers wonderfully around me. Everyone I love, or am learning to love, surrounds me. Even Samuels and his wife Kay are here. After what he saw that I did in the woods, I'd feared he would run away from me again. I'd underestimated him. If anything, he'd become as protective of me as Nicole. He even brought his grill and some steaks to the bonfire party.

Charlie and Kyle, Grant's sons, approach the fire, bows and arrows in hand. "Getting too dark to shoot," Charlie says, taking his seat on a bale, noticeably close to Ella.

Kyle sits next to me and takes Hope into his arms. "Do you think she's hungry?" he asks. "I'll feed her the bottle."

"You fed her an hour ago," I chuckle. "She's going to get fat at this rate."

I look at the faces surrounding the fire, surprised at how content I feel with people surrounding me. As much as I enjoy the company, I'm exhausted, and my side aches. I lean against Grant's shoulder, struggle to keep my eyes open.

Nicole notices my changed mood. "I think maybe you did do too much today," she says. She stands up and starts cleaning, a strong hint to the others that it's time to go.

I offer a weak protest, but everyone pitches in to clean up and put things away. It only takes a few minutes until my little party ends and my guests prepare to leave. Samuels pats my arm awkwardly, saying, "It's nice to have you back," before climbing into his car. The small show of emotion from my former partner warms my heart.

Kay, his wife, unabashedly hugs me tight. "We really did miss you," she says near my ear. "It's just…."

I shush her before she can say the words. "I know what it was. That's the past. You both came today. It means a lot to me."

Kay squeezes my arm and joins Samuels in the car. Nicole and Ella follow Samuels with Nicole's customary, "Call me if you need anything," tossed over her shoulder.

"You know I will," I call to my sister across the clearing.

"You look pale," Grant says as he hugs me good-bye.

"I'm fine," I lie. "I just need to rest." I force a weak smile that he falls for. "Bye, boys," I call to the truck.

Kyle leans out the window, "Take care of Hope."

"I will," I shout back with a wave.

Grant kisses me gently on the lips. "Get some rest," he says, letting me go.

I watch his truck pull past the dwindling bonfire and down the lane. The sound of his engine grows fainter.

I light a cigarette, a habit I picked back up as soon as I returned to the woods. I sit in the second rocker Grant gave me as a gift. "Now we both have a place to sit," he'd said. Indy fills the other rocker, and I pat his head. I smoke and watch the night-filled clearing, the shape of the trees timeless against the starry sky.

Deep in the woods, three orbs of light flicker among the trees.

Might be early fireflies, might not.

Now that I'm alone, I can sign out loud the song that constantly plays in my mind. "The farmer in the dell," I sing. "Hi-ho the dairy-o, the farmer in the dell."

Indy doesn't like my singing and goes inside the cabin.

With no one watching, the strained smile I wore all day slips away. A mad grin creeps onto my face.

"The cheese stands alone," I sing into the clearing. "The cheese stands alone."

THE END

Want to read more by Dawn Merriman? All her books are available on Amazon and on DawnMerriman.com. You can also sign up for her newsletter and instantly receive a FREE creepy short story.

If you liked "I Killed You Once" please leave a review and tell a friend.

The next book in this series:
Inheriting Elyse
Maddison, Indiana – Book 2

Heart-breaking and heart-pounding supernatural thriller
After a crushing family tragedy, Melinda inherits her aunt's farm in Maddison, Indiana. The farm was once lovely, but her aunt was a hoarder and the house is packed with boxes, toys and dolls. Lots of dolls. Even hoarded, the farm should be the perfect place for her family to heal and rebuild. Melinda, her husband and teenage step-daughter soon realize they've inherited more than the farm. As they clear the house of boxes, their true inheritance is released. Can Melinda's mind survive the legacy left to her? Can her family?

Note from the Dawn Merriman:
Wow, writing "Marked by Darkness" was a wild ride! The premise for this book started out with a simple question: "What would I do if I lost my whole family?" Being a country girl that lives on a pig farm,

I imagined I would hide in the woods with my pigs. That simple answer grew into a crazy story of haunting and hunting.

I hope you enjoyed this book and that it touched you on some level. I'm not ashamed to tell you I cried quite a lot while writing Maribeth's story. I'm not sure how many times I told my beta team "this book might kill me". I was obsessed with this story. Maribeth became as real to me as an actual friend. I hated to put her through the traumatic events. The scene where her family was murdered took me several days to get through. I just couldn't do it to her, not after she kissed Benny good-night. I agonized over killing her pigs, kept looking for ways around it. They had to die in order for Maribeth to go over the edge, but I kept baby Hope alive. I just had to. The good-bye to the coffins scene almost broke me. Even now, I cry if I read it. I hope the emotions came through the words on the page.

When the book was done, I sulked. I missed my friend and didn't want to leave her. "You'll write another book," my husband kept telling me. I did start work on the next "Message of Murder" book and fell back in love with Gabby, but for the previous several months, Maribeth had filled my mind.

I hope I did her story justice. And I hope she affected you the way she affected me. I might visit Maribeth again, but for now, I leave her to Grant and Nicole, and wish her the best.

Special thanks and tons of love to my husband,

Kevin, for the hours of painstakingly listening to me talk about Maribeth and helping me through some tricky plot points. My heartfelt appreciation to my beta team of Liz, Lori, and Katie. Your insights and notes were invaluable. Discussing the book with women who truly care about the characters and about making the book as good as possible are highlights of a writer's life. Thank you most of all to God, who has blessed me with my writing gift. None of this is possible without Him.

God Bless,
Dawn Merriman
February, 2020

BONUS CONTENT

Book Club discussion guide with answers from the author.

As a special gift, please enjoy the following questions you might use during a book club. I've also included my own thoughts on the questions.

You can download a printable PDF on my website at DawnMerriman.com

Book Club/Discussion Guide of "I Killed You Once" by Dawn Merriman

Note from the author:

I'm so honored you've chosen my book as your Book Club selection! While writing this book, I often had imaginary conversations with readers about some of the symbolism and themes I wanted to include. (Yes, imaginary conversations are a thing I do. What can I tell you, writers are weird.) Below are some of the questions I pondered about as I wrote. I've also included my own comments on the questions. There are no right or wrong answers. Books are simply guides to help the reader "see" a story and create it themselves in their minds. Each individual has their own take on a story and what it means. That's why book clubs are so fun.

I'd love to hear from you after your discussions. You can e-mail me at DawnMerrimanNewsletter@gmail.com any time. Happy discussing! – *Dawn Merriman*

1. What would you do if you tragically lost your entire family? Would you want to be alone like Maribeth? Would you rather be surrounded by people? What would your plan be?

2. Are Bryson, Lilly and Benny actually ghosts or just hallucinations Maribeth creates?

3. How does unresolved guilt affect the characters and their decisions? How does Maribeth deal with her guilt over her family's murders? How does Samuels deal with his guilt? How does Grant's guilt over his wife's suicide affect his interactions with Maribeth? How can guilt affect your own lives?

4. Maribeth tells Grant at the creek, "No one can truly save someone else." In what ways is this true of not true?

5. In the same scene, Grant tells Maribeth the worst part of grief is that no one wants to ask about your lost loved one because it might upset you. How has this concept affected your own experiences with grief or the grief of someone close to you?

6. Speaking of Grant and Maribeth's relationship, Maribeth begins developing feelings for Grant while Bryson is still with her, sort of. Awkward! How might this situation be an issue for you and what are your thoughts on how Maribeth handled it?

7. There are several symbolic animal characters in the book. What do you think each one symbolizes and how did their inclusion shape Maribeth? - Indy – The hunted deer – Jingles the cat – Coyotes – Spider?

8. How do the different approaches to motherhood affect the characters? Maribeth and Nicole's mother is hundreds of miles away and not involved in their lives. How does this affect the sisters? Victoria gave Jesse away and then tried to "fix" Jacob by telling him he was bad. What ramifications did this have on the boys, if any? Maribeth was a busy working mom who loved her children fiercely. How was her relationship with her kids different than the one she has with her mom? What did that do to Maribeth? How do your own relationships with your mom or children affect you?

9. Victoria says her sons were "born bad," but they also had non-ideal childhoods. To what extent do you think they were born bad, or did their upbringing shape them? Do you think their twin bond being broken when they were so young contribute to their evil ways? If they are born sociopaths, do they have a choice of good or evil?

10. Maribeth is pushed over the edge after the loss of yet another family, her pigs and chickens. Is her subsequent brutality against Franklin justified? Are we all capable of brutality if pushed too far? If you were in Maribeth's place during the final battle, would you have let Franklin live or smother him? Would you have killed Jacob the night he killed the family, or let nature take its course for him?

11. The book opens with "Living can be worse than death." For Maribeth, how was living harder? By leaving Franklin alive and scarred, was that a fitting punishment? Is there a third choice of madness?

12. The last scenes of the book show two sides of Maribeth's new life. On the one hand, she's happier and had started letting family and friends into her life. On the other, she's alone on the porch, singing the song that represents her insanity of the night she battled Franklin. Will she choose the happy life or the madness? Can she have both? Can she truly be okay after all she went through? Is she actually okay or just pretending to be? Do we all pretend to be okay?

13. Would you stay living at the cabin after all that happens or move away? What are the drawbacks and benefits of either?

I hope this book not only entertained you, but gave you some things to think about. It's been fun answering these questions as well, kind of like being part of your discussion. Please let me know your thoughts, I love to hear from readers. DawnMerrimanNewsletter@gmail.com.

Book Club/Discussion Guide for "I Killed You Once" by Dawn Merriman

Dawn Merriman's responses

Note: There are no right answers. These are just my thoughts, in case you wanted to see them.

1. The premise for this book started with my pondering this exact question. As a country girl who raises pigs and loves the woods, I imagined I would leave the world behind and live off the land with my animals. I often joke that my family better come back to haunt me and keep me company.

2. Honestly, I don't know. I wrote it so the reader could draw their own conclusions. I did purposefully make each of them represent a different aspect of Maribeth's personality. Bryson is her rational, adult side. Lilly is her fun side. Benny is her childlike/primal side.

3. Ahh, guilt. A theme I know too well and visit often. ("How Murder Saved my Life" is really heavy with guilt and the destruction it can cause.) Guilt is a dangerous thing, and usually unwarranted. As women, we often burden ourselves with guilt over things we actually have no control over or are not our faults. I think we all struggle with this. I write about it a lot, because I struggle as well.

Maribeth takes guilt to an extreme. She didn't kill her family, but she feels responsible. She exacts the harshest penalty, and locks herself away in a self-made prison. Her guilt even drives her to the edge of suicide. Not a healthy way to deal.

Samuels more or less ignores his guilt over leaving Maribeth alone for so long. It isn't until she calls him that he even thinks about it. He works to redeem himself some by getting involved again.

Grant feels he should have done more to help his wife Sarah Jane. He's drawn to Maribeth in part because he couldn't help Sarah Jane, so maybe he can help Maribeth. He also hides in his work.

Bottom line is, guilt can destroy you, so you better deal with it.

4. Another tricky question. We can all help each other, but we have to do the work to save ourselves.

5. To get personal for a minute, our very close friends lost their son to a motorcycle accident a few years ago. We loved this young man like our own son. For a while, I was afraid to mention his name his parents in case it would hurt them. I then realized he was not a "tragedy" to avoid mentioning. He was a young man we loved who deserved to be remembered and discussed. The pain never goes away, but we remember his life instead of avoiding his death.

6. I struggled with this point a lot. On the one hand, Bryson is there, so having feelings for Grant seems disrespectful. In reality, of course, Bryson is dead. Can Maribeth really sustain a relationship with a dead man, even if he is a ghost/hallucination? I discussed this a lot with my husband and came to the conclusion that of course Maribeth needs to embrace a chance at a new happiness in her life. I skirted the issue, by having Bryson give his blessing to the new relationship. It was a fun and awkward issue to explore.

7. I love symbolism. There are so many I used in this book, but I'll focus on the animal ones. *Indy* represents Maribeth's loyal companion. He also is fiercely protective (he attacks Jacob in the house). He can't stop his true/instinctual nature when he eats the guts off the porch. All of these traits Maribeth shows at some point. *The hunted deer* is basically on giant symbolic image. When Maribeth hunts him, slits his throat, and dumps him in the woods, he represents the same things the twins did to their victims. Maribeth feels bad about it, though. The need to stock-pile the meat to feed herself symbolizes her planning to stay in the woods alone. When she no longer needs the deer and leaves him for the coyotes, she sub-consciously is leaving that meat for the "wild animals" because she is becoming more civilized. *Jingles the cat* shows up when there is a need for change for Maribeth. The first night she finds him, she realizes how lonely she is. When he breaks into the house, she decides to order cat food and thereby inviting Grant to the property. When he shows up after the pigs are killed, he more or less asks her "what are you going to do?" *The coyotes* are more subtle. Maribeth hears them when her wild side is waking up. At the end, the eight coyotes hold Samuels back until Maribeth can finish what she needs to do to change herself. There are eight coyotes and eight women killed by the twins. *The spider* is the dark secret that is too horrible to look at. By hiding the spider, she doesn't have to face that there are actually two killers involved and that she isn't safe. The spider is also the secret that she killed

Jacob that night and that she heard a second killer in her house.

8. Is there any relationship more tricky than mother/daughter? Maribeth and Nicole have to rely on each other, since their mom is distant both geographically and emotionally. She's not even a character in the book (on purpose). Presumably, their mother did a decent job raising them since they both turned out to be good citizens. Victoria, on the other hand, might have tried her best, but wow, did her boys turn out messed up! I also like that Maribeth creates new "children" for herself with her pigs and chickens. She is a mother at heart, even after losing her kids.

9. Nature or nurture? Another timeless question. I personally think it's both. If psychopathy is a mental illness you can be born with (I think it is), then the boys didn't have much chance, without a support system to help them. Yes, they are monsters, but they are also humans. The same way that "normal" people are humans, but a little bit of monster lives inside us all. Jesse and Jacob should have made better choices instead of murdering women, but did they even have the choice to make if they were born psychopaths? Psychology is fascinating.

10. We are all capable of being pushed too far, but just how far is too much is an interesting question. This is a work of fiction, so of course I took it to the extreme, but I think we can all flip to the dark side if pushed. For Maribeth, the brutality was justified. I'm glad she didn't kill him and hide the body at the end (she almost did, but I couldn't destroy her completely). As for killing Jacob that night, he was basically dead, she just had to make sure. Of course, that action destroyed her anyway. There are always consequences.

11. The major theme of the book. Death can be easier if you look at it from Maribeth's point of view of living without her family. The other major theme is "easier isn't better." It takes courage to live your best life, to embrace the good and leave the bad behind. Death is a permanent solution to a temporary situation. Maribeth journeys from not caring if she freezes to death to a life that's beginning to fill with love and people again. But her sanity took some hits in the process.

12. Broken or fixed? I left this ambiguous so the reader could ponder for themselves whether or not Maribeth is actually okay or just pretending to be. All of us have sides of ourselves we share with others and secret sides we hide. Happy or sad, sane or crazy? As humans we're a mix of all of it.

13. I had a hard time with this one. I mentally wrote several endings for the book. In one, she kills Franklin and grinds the body up, going completely insane in the process. In one version she burns down the cabin. Some versions, she moves in with Nicole and leaves the cabin to the ghosts. I tried to end it somewhere in the middle. My beta team had differing opinions as well. From "No way she'd leave all she worked so hard to build," to "Who would want to stay where all the bad stuff happened and she's so miserable." Reader's choice on this one.

Thank you and God Bless,
Dawn Merriman

www.DawnMerriman.com

Printed in Great Britain
by Amazon

26698928R00175